Picked and Mixed

Short Stories

U P Publications
2012

Picked and Mixed contains two previously unpublished collections of short stories. It is an eclectic mix of styles and genres, from funny to sad, from bizarre to strange, from weird to wonderful – in other words – something for everyone.

The Bay Radio Collection is a selection from the 2012 Bay Radio Short Story Competition, including the winning entry 'The Last Walk' by Andy Crabb.

The Picked and Mixed Collection includes stories from published authors from the U P Publications Label, other stories by Bay Radio Authors and two guest contributions, from the Editor and her late father.

All the authors are contributing the royalties from this book to Cancer Research UK. The publisher will match that donation.

You can find out more about the book, the authors and the charity on www.pickedandmixed.com

First published in Great Britain in 2012 by U P Publications Ltd
Head Office: 25 Bedford Street, Peterborough, UK. PE1 4DN

Cover design copyright © G. M. Griffin Peers 2012

A CIP Catalogue record of this book is available from The British Library

Paperback Edition – U P Publications ISBN 978-1908135254

9 7 3 5 0 8 1 6 4 2

Kindle Edition – U P Publications ISBN 978-1908135261

FIRST PAPERBACK EDITION

Published by U P Publications – Printed in England by The Lightning Source Group

www.uppublications.ltd.uk
www.pickedandmixed.com

Contents

'Picked & Mixed' Authors 237

Acknowledgements 244

Preface

U P Publications is delighted that after two years of planning our first collection of short stories is finally launched.

Soon after starting to collate the book, I was diagnosed with breast cancer. Aside from being an unwelcome distraction, as a third generation sufferer of this dreadful disease, I was forced to acknowledge how lucky I am to be alive now, rather than to have been born early in the last century. Both my grandmothers succumbed to their illness, my mother was intensely lucky in surviving hers. In contrast, I have benefited from the research drawn from all the cases before me. Whilst there are no certainties in life, the outlook for me and others in my position is so much better now than even twenty years ago. To the best of my knowledge, I am now clear, not everyone is so lucky.

This book is dedicated to all those researchers who have made life possible for so many of us.

All the authors who have contributed their stories to the book are also contributing their royalties to Cancer Research UK. U P Publications is proud to match that contribution and we are privileged to offer their stories to you.

If you would like to find out more about what our authors are doing next, or to find out more about what they have already published, the book's website is www.pickedandmixed.com

The Bay Radio Collection

This section comprises all but one of the stories broadcast in the 2012 Bay Radio Short Story Competition. The Winning Story, 'The Last Walk' by Andy Crabb, appears at the end of this section.

Flowers for the Lady - Sheila Skinner

"Yes Mr. Tyner, I'm doing flowers for Mrs. Tyner's birthday on my way home this evening, delivery Monday. I'll have your itinerary, tickets etc. all here for you Monday morning after your Wentworth weekend."

"Fine, thank you Miss Morrison and of course I'll be back for your leaving party Wednesday night, mustn't miss that must I?" His hollow laugh hung in the air. "Don't know what we'll do without you."

"I'm sure Miss Framley will be fine." She stopped herself adding 'sir', he hadn't earned that. "She does come highly recommended." She'd known Deborah Framley would be his choice, so shallow these young executives…

If Mr. Granton's ill-health hadn't forced his early retirement, Barbara would have happily worked on past sixty. Twenty eight years as his PA had established her at Denby Granton. He'd even called her Barbara, strictly business between them of course. This lucky young man, the nasty nephew as she'd nicknamed him, wasn't a patch on his uncle: all hair gel and handmade shoes. She'd known he'd want a younger, attractive PA to add to the trophies in his newly decorated office.

His wife, Claire, was delightful: a little older, and a lot classier. Her heart problem had struck soon after their society wedding. She handled it very well and played the dutiful wife but it wasn't long before Barbara picked up on the signs. Years as a PA had fine-tuned her instincts; this young man was "a wrong 'un", as Barbara's Mum would have said.

"Mr. Tyner, you won't forget, will you, to confirm what time

Donald needs to collect Mrs. Tyner on Monday. I've asked for the Bentley and it's a 3.40pm flight from City of London to Deauville. Reynaud will send the Chateau's car to collect you, of course."

"Ummm, well, yes," he stuttered, "leave all that with me will you? His voice sharpened. "I'll confirm it with him on Monday morning" Barbara hated loose ends, years of dotting i's and crossing t's had made her good at her job, she didn't intend to let her standards slip now.

It was Friday – gone six already, and she sensed his impatience to be away, with a big weekend ahead of him, hosting the Japanese agents at Wentworth; they loved their golf.

It had been Barbara's idea to include the London tour and theatre tickets for their wives. "Very well Mr. Tyner, would you like me to call in on Mrs. Tyner at the weekend and…"

"No, that won't be necessary Miss Morrison," his rude interruption cut across her offer. "No, no that's fine, just leave it, leave it all to me thank you. I'm off now, got to pick up our guests…erumm…thanks for getting those tee times sorted and the show tickets, great idea of yours Miss Morrison, well done."

Barbara wasn't impressed by the condescending tone … just as well I'm leaving she thought to herself, Mr. Granton would never have spoken to her like that. "That's what a good PA does, Mr. Tyner." She couldn't resist that. "Have a good weekend …any problems you have my home number, of course."

"Problems? No, no I think everything's arranged nicely, thank you. I'm off now then. Good night." He swept past her desk.

"Goodnight, Mr. Tyner." He was gone, leaving a whiff of cologne behind him.

Busying herself with his trip schedules, Barbara noticed he'd left the light on in his private bathroom and reluctantly went through to switch it off. Look at the mess. Tutting aloud, she straightened up the toiletries. That cologne's a bit obvious, a bit like Deborah Framley, you'll make a good pair, she chuckled to herself. Bending down, she picked up a paper covered in his now familiar doodles. Can't even use a waste bin! She noticed Claire Tyner's name circled and the note he'd scribbled next to it stopped her dead. In capital letters it read, RING CLAIRE MONDAY EVENING HAPPY BIRTHDAY DARLING.

There were various signs and squiggles next to it. Barbara repeated it out loud; it didn't make sense, unless she'd got it all wrong. Going quickly back to her own desk she grabbed the Diary, no, here it was, all written down:

Mr. T, Wentworth w/end with Jap.

Remind him I'm at Dentist, in later.

Mr. Mrs. T, Airport City–Deauville

Monday aft. Chateau 2 nights. Laurence cooking privately for them. Donald there and back?? Confirm times??

Barbara still felt disturbed. Unusually Mr. Tyner had insisted on doing the bookings himself, so she didn't have a copy to check. Not a problem though, Reynaud at the Chateau would soon confirm everything was in order. She dialled the number from memory; he'd always complimented her on her French and her professionalism. The confirmation booking form was emailed over instantly, but did nothing to calm Barbara's fears.

The Chateau catered for every whim and Mr. Tyner had made a mess of the options. Mrs. Tyner always insisted on a non-smoking twin room. This form showed a double-smoker had been booked and only when Barbara checked the reference did she begin to understand. The booking had been made from Mr. Tyner's personal laptop, using his private code; the name on the form was Miss D. Framley. She thanked Reynaud.

The next call, to Wentworth Golf Club, cleared up any doubts Barbara had. Again a double smoking room booked in the name of Miss D. Framley.

So that's the game, is it? Barbara was angry and upset. So Deborah's going to Wentworth and Deauville, is she? My God, Reynaud will think I'm part of this sordid little set-up and Mrs. Tyner too if she ever finds out. The thought horrified her. Twenty-eight years loyalty and discretion and you think you're going to blemish my reputation just as I leave. I don't think so!

Mr Tyner, she wrote, do not forget that my dental appointment (Mon. a.m.) means I'll be later than usual. I'm sure Mrs. Tyner will want a bit of notice to pack for her birthday trip, so I'm putting the tickets in with her flowers tonight. She will get them first thing Monday. I trust that's what you would have wished and that Wentworth lived up to expectations.

Initialling the note 'BM', she picked up the tickets and turned the lights off on her way out.

The Maze - Jennifer Nesteroff

Today is a good day. Today I know where I am and what I am doing. This is a good feeling, but I know it will not last. The maze that my mind is beginning to become will catch me unawares, will desert me and throw me into confusion and fearfulness at any moment.

Yesterday, if it *were* yesterday, I lost my way. I went out to visit the shops, setting off along the street in which I have lived for thirty years, turning left at the end towards the shopping centre and then stopping. Where was I? What was I doing, standing there in a street I did not recognise, and where was I going, anyway? I looked around me in total bewilderment and felt my heart racing and tears beginning to fill my eyes as fear clutched at my throat.

Then I saw a strange man coming toward me. He asked me if I was all right and all I could say was that I wanted to go home. He addressed me by name, took my arm and led me to my house. Having taken my front door key from my bag, he let me in, settled me in my chair in the sitting room and left.

Looking out of the window, I saw him enter the house next door.

I saw him again this morning when I was watering my garden. Today I know who he is.

Now I sit looking at photos – reading old letters from people who were my family and friends – and remembering. I want to recall every detail of my life whenever I am able to do so, to begin to say goodbye to the person who is me, but who is gradually leaving and will one day be a complete stranger to me.

In From the Cold - Sue Frost

Head down, eyes squeezed tight against the slamming rain, Annie hadn't yet seen the warm glow of the house lights. The remaining wheel of the battered trolley that contained her life, bumped and twisted against her frozen heels as she walked through the pitch black of night: on and on.

Stopping abruptly, she bent her knees and waited for the hot urine to trickle down her legs. Come on, come on, she muttered. She'd abandoned underwear years ago. With numb hands she pulled down the rim of her dripping hat over her ears and tugged at the string around her middle. Even with five layers of other people's cast offs, the cold had seeped into her bones and she cursed aloud as she groped behind for the handle of her trolley before setting off again.

Had it been daylight, Annie would have seen that the houses lining the lane belonged to the very rich: huge and arrogant, with their in-and-out drives and fancy names. Trudging on she was only aware of her urgent need for food and shelter. There was bound to be a place nearby where she could stop and eat the remains of her sandwich.

She saw it then, the house, just a short way ahead with its upstairs rooms lit up against the night. Although there was no-one to see her, she wedged her body back against the bushes and peered round into an open gravelled drive. The porch light illuminated a sleek dark car with its boot open and engine humming. She watched as its windscreen wipers worked like manic metronomes. Edging sideways, she dragged the bulky trolley behind her and crossed the front of the house towards the wide-open door. Three suitcases sat in the porch waiting to be loaded. In a moment she was inside.

As she stepped into an enormous hall the heat hit her like a furnace. There were doors leading off left and right. In the middle, an elegant staircase swept down to where she was standing. She heard the angry voice of a man upstairs. "Look, Jane, if we don't leave now we'll get stuck on the bloody motorway. It's the first flight out so it won't be delayed. Just hurry up!" He was at the top of the stairs now and about to come down with their last suitcase. "Christ Jane, what have you got in here? We're only going for three weeks not three months!"

Annie bolted left and along the corridor until she came to a door at the end. She let herself into the room's darkness. Jane reached the bottom stair and wrinkled her nose – "Whatever's that dreadful smell?" but Colin was already in the driver's seat impatient to leave. She shut the door with a heavy bang dropping the keys into her handbag.

Annie lay on the floor hidden by a bed, her breath rasping in her throat. Exhausted, she staggered up, pulled back the thick duvet and climbed in. Daylight began to light up the room. Her son's room had been blue like this. Immediately she was there again. Robbie, her precious child: even after so many years she saw the walls and ceiling awash with his blood: his battered severed head lying grotesquely on his pillow.

She thought of the psychiatrists who, over the years, had tried to help her. The section orders after she'd tried to do away with herself, and the brutal Victorian hospital with its locked doors and smell of stewed food. A just punishment, she reminded herself. She'd left him alone in the house to go across to Sally and within an hour that maniac had got in and destroyed both their lives.

So now she was walking her life away. One more day, one day nearer Robbie. Yesterday, some boys had come across her sheltering in a doorway. They'd called her a stinking vagrant and tried to take her trolley. She'd kicked out with her hard boots and screamed like a banshee until they'd run away. No-one was going to take her trolley with all that remained of Robbie inside. Now here she was in a strange house in a strange bed. She'd heard the man say they'd be away for three weeks. She would be quiet and keep the lights off.

The coffee pot in the kitchen was still warm and the black liquid ran down the back of her throat and made her splutter. The cupboards were full with enough food in the freezer for a year. She pulled out a chicken and set it on the counter. Then, with shaking hands, she tore open a packet of biscuits and crammed them in her mouth two at a time.

There were fifteen rooms in the house and Annie went into each one just to see. In the magnificent master bedroom upstairs she sat on the edge of their bed and stroked the silky cushions. This is where she would sleep, she decided. A door led into an enormous clothes closet. She would be wearing a few of those fancy dresses too! After pouring three bottles of oil into the steaming water in their roll-top bath, she slowly discarded her wet filthy clothes layer by layer. Standing in just her old boots, she walked over to the full-length mirror and blanched; her emaciated, dirt-streaked body was covered with terrible sores and blisters, her sparse grey hair flattened to her head. What have you done to yourself, woman, she asked, how much punishment is enough?

Hours later, smelling of musk, Annie lay warm and snug on the plush sofa in Jane's drawing room, wearing Jane's best Dior satin gown, a second bottle of champagne at her feet. With the smell of roasting chicken wafting in from the kitchen she picked up the photo of Robbie and held it to her heart. Allowing herself a little smile, she told him – we'll stop running soon, son, I promise.

Green Gunge - Irene Hogg

Edith gazed into the bathroom mirror and scrutinised the imperfections of her skin. She still couldn't tell if those were age spots or tarnishing on the mirror. She accepted that she and her home were ageing. Looking at her body encased in the wonders of modern control garments, she knew that, like her house, she was crumbling, decaying, sagging and losing the battle with nature.

With a weary sigh, she studied the ceramic jar: '100% natural ingredients. Regenerating, renewing, revitalising'. The words seemed to leap from the label. Another load of advertising bunkum? I'm becoming a soft touch, she told her reflection.

Visitors to her cliff-top home were a rarity nowadays, obeying the 'Danger: Cliff Erosion' warning signs. So when a young girl clad in the gentle flower-power garb of the Seventies appeared, Edith was only too willing to buy one of her jars of natural remedies in order to prolong the conversation.

Dubiously, she unscrewed the lid and scooped out some green gunge, slapping it on her face. She peered at her mirrored reflection and thought, If I'm burgled tonight, the poor guy will die of fright ...and off she went to bed.

Throwing open the bedroom curtains, Edith stroked the old tom cat rubbing against her ankles, "You know, Sylvester, I do believe the sea looks much calmer today. I must be losing my marbles. I thought most of those rose bushes went over the cliff in the last erosion. Time for breakfast, old boy."

Creaking floorboards marked their progress to the kitchen.

Sylvester launched himself into his Kit-e-Kat while Edith put two eggs on the stove to hard boil.

Halfway along the hall en route to the bathroom, Edith heard the most awful kerfuffle in the kitchen. She charged back to investigate. Two speckled hens flapped and squawked as they tried to perch on chairs and worktops. A young kitten was doing its best to capture the errant poultry.

"What the…" Edith grabbed a broom and eventually shooed all the creatures out into the garden. She turned round to admonish Sylvester. "You should know better, you lazy…" Her voice tailed off. No sign of Sylvester and the pan boiling merrily on the stove was bereft of eggs. Weird, thought Edith.

Warm water cascaded over her in the shower. The soap glided smoothly on her body and when it fell from her hands she easily picked it up.

Joints are better this morning. Not so stiff, she thought.

Automatically wrapping a towel round her hair, Edith vigorously rubbed herself dry then turned and, using the towel, removed condensation from the bathroom mirror. I need new glasses, she thought. Before her stood a slim, trim woman, face smooth. She raised her arms …no bingo wings, no cellulite; thick, waist-length auburn hair tumbled free as she removed the towel.

All round the house everything she had touched gleamed and shone like new. Dressing, she grabbed a belt and pulled it tight to emphasise her new waistline. Her brain whirled …the potion? It had to be the potion. She had the secret of eternal youth, of life's existence.

For days Edith patrolled her house and garden; she touched everything with tiny globules of the green gunge. Within a week flowers bloomed, the cliff edge backed away from her house and all around regeneration slowly advanced.

On the eighth day of applying the potion, she woke up, swinging her legs gracefully out of bed. Horrified, she squealed with shock. Her toes were webbed. Slipperless, she rose from the bed and yelped when her feet were pricked by tiny twigs that pushed up from the floorboards. Suddenly the glass began to crumble to sand in her windows. Rushing to the bathroom mirror, Edith could see, just before it disintegrated, a green gloopy face. Not hers, surely. She felt her neck where fine gill-like openings were developing. Her skin was smooth but shiny and she had a desperate need for mud or cool flowing water.

Deserting the land, she waddled then floundered her way to the cliff edge. There she launched herself through the air and marvelled that all her memories stayed with her; yet as she splashed into the sea she felt truly regenerated.

The Final Whistle - Linda McGillycuddy

He wasn't even looking at her; he was so engrossed in the Football Match on TV, as usual. It was his great passion, his religion, and he must pay homage to the 50-inch plasma-screen that dominated the room like a grotesque monster.

"I've done the ironing and here's your dinner, ok?" A grunt was all she got for answer; was he even listening?

It hadn't always been like this, she remembered the heady days of their early relationship, when they were eager to be together, to do things together. She was realistic enough to know that such excitement couldn't last and had hoped for something deeper, more caring, as the years passed. As far as she was concerned, love is a decision, and she had decided that she loved Gary and would be faithful to him and would care about him and their life path together.

Now, it seemed, she was reduced to carer and their life path was a one way street. Football, bloody Football! They used to go places and try new things, now their lives revolved around the premier league fixtures and the transfer window. She couldn't care less about overpaid, over-hyped prima donnas who could barely string a few words together. She had met Golden Retrievers with better communication skills, but her darling Gary was copying his heroes, beginning or ending his sentences with, "At the end of the day," for God's sake...

She wouldn't mind so much if he looked like Beckham, but a personal fitness regime consisting of sitting in front of the plasma monster, drinking and eating all evening, did not make for sleek thighs and six-pack abs. The only six-packs she saw were the ones she had to pick up trying not to block the view – but it was hard not to get in the way of a 50-inch, even if all you were blocking was a hard-faced manager chewing gum and saying exactly the same thing he had said the week before.

Nevertheless she was determined to bring their lives back to something more fulfilling. He worked hard and was a good person. Perhaps if she had made more effort to be interesting he wouldn't have to turn to his plasma buddy for entertainment. He was perfectly happy with their life together; she had to let him know that she was not, to give him a chance to do something about it; it was the right thing to do...

Because something had happened, she now had a secret.

She panicked a bit when she first realised; she had checked the facts over and over again. She knew that this would change everything. Once she told Gary, the decision would no longer be hers.

She timed it carefully: an evening with no important Derbys between the reds and blues, no big qualifying matches: only the two of them, unusually sitting down together at the dinner table. He still had no idea of the secret she was carrying. Gary was enjoying the meal, which she had prepared with great care: all his favourites. They still had so many things they could share; they hadn't grown too far apart, had they? They could have good times ahead, once she had confided her secret.

They had been chatting for a while, full and comfortable after the meal and wine, it was now or never. "Gary ...do you think it might be time that we got married? I know we talked about it before, but now perhaps we should just go ahead and do it!"

"What's all this about pet? We're fine as we are." It was a predictable answer but still she pursued the subject, even suggesting a trip abroad to combine the ceremony and the honeymoon but could see that he was not interested.

One last effort and she ventured, "You've always wanted to visit Italy; we could go to Rome..."

His eyes sparkled. "Rome, that could work, funny you should say that. The lads at work were talking about some cracking deals for the European Cup next year, yes... I can check it out with them and see what the deal is." He became quite animated and rushed from the table to the computer to chat online to get the latest news.

She continued to sit at the table. He wasn't going to change, she knew that now, but at least she had tried; she would never have forgiven herself if she hadn't at least given him a chance. He could have shared everything with her, the joy, the responsibility, and the changes that would inevitably come. Instead he would be just as happy with his la-zee-boy armchair and his plasma buddy, as he would be with her.

What would he say when discovered what she had hidden from him, would he plead with her to return and swear his undying love? Probably not, she thought as she felt the Lotto ticket in her pocket, where she had kept it for days. She had looked at it many times and it had never left her side. It was as if she were carrying a ticking time bomb. Well, it would go off only when she was ready for the explosion.

She quietly gathered up her things and brought down her bag from the bedroom. Looking at him from the hallway, she watched him checking out the football travel packages enthusiastically, online ...and blew him a kiss as she left.

She could afford to be generous.

The Wall - Tony Henderson

The wall groaned. He was strongly built and didn't really mind people sitting on him, especially children. However, he recognised the large man coming up the path towards him.

Big Humphrey was enormous and passed by on the way home when he'd been to the alehouse. He was usually drunk and would sit on the wall talking to himself, cursing, and kicking his heels, which gave the wall a splitting headache all night.

The man reeled towards him. He was obviously very drunk tonight and had a lot of difficulty climbing up. However, he seemed in a better mood than normal and, when he was perched on the top of the wall, he started to sing. The wall groaned. He'd been looking forward to an early night.

After a while, Big Humphrey decided he could give a better rendition from a greater height. He clambered clumsily onto the top of the wall, where he swayed precariously and added wild arm movements to his singing.

The wall began to get very nervous. A number of loose stones were dislodged and, then, the inevitable; with an anguished shout, Big Humphrey fell headlong off the wall and landed heavily on the path. There he lay, groaning. The wall looked at him dispassionately. Serve him right the boorish oaf.

At that moment he heard the sound of a horse coming down the road towards him. It was one of the soldiers from the King's castle nearby, who stopped his horse, dismounted, and walked towards the wall.

Oh no! The wall knew what was coming. Why did men need to urinate against walls and trees? He was right. A warm steady stream started to roll down him, and he groaned. The revolting smell would last for days and he already had a headache from Big Humphrey's antics.

As he was getting back onto his horse, the soldier heard Big Humphrey's moans and turned towards him. He recognised him as one of the village nuisances. The horse also realised who it was, and remembered clearly last week when Big Humphrey had jabbed the end of a sword into his side to make him rear.

Before the soldier could stop him, the horse took great delight in kicking Big Humphrey in the head. The soldier shrugged and rode off into the night.

The wall had watched this exchange impassively and then, even with a headache and smelling like a urinal, went to sleep.

When he got back to the castle the soldier reported seeing Big Humphrey. Some soldiers went and carried him back to the castle, but he died during the night – it was assumed from a broken neck.

The next day, the wall saw a strange fellow skipping towards him. Tall and thin, he was dressed in a weird mixture of extravagantly coloured clothes, carrying a large exercise book and a pencil case.

'This is where it must have happened,' the odd character said to himself, as he clambered onto the wall.

The wall suddenly realised who this man was. The previous day, George, a large blackbird who often came for a chat, had told him of a strange event. Apparently some woman had caught twenty-four of his mates and put them all alive into a pie. She'd then heated the pie, and delivered it to the palace. When the pie was opened by the King, the blackbirds all flew out screeching, not surprisingly, as they were all scorched and pretty annoyed.

Apparently a man called Claude was wandering around the countryside writing up strange events as a series of short stories. He had this peculiar idea that these stories would become so famous that they would be passed down from generation to generation. Hardly likely, thought the wall, from what the blackbird had told him the other day.

Apart from blackbirds in a pie, the other ridiculous stories

George told him about were an owl and a pussycat in a pea green boat, a cow jumping over the moon and a woman living in a shoe. How on earth did this idiot Claude, think that such a set of improbable and inane stories would ever have a chance of lasting for hundreds of years? And now, how was he going to write a story about a drunk falling off a wall and being kicked by a horse?

Claude selected a sharp pencil and opened his exercise book at a clean page. "Well Big Humphrey doesn't sound right. What shall we say? How about Big Humpty? No that's not catchy enough. What rhymes with Humpty? I know – Humpty Dumpty."

The wall couldn't believe he was hearing this.

"Umm! A soldier and his horse? Perhaps if I said, 'All the King's horses and all the King's men', it would sound more impressive? Now, how about, 'They tried to revive him'? So, what have we got? Humpty Dumpty sat on a wall. Humpty Dumpty had a great fall. All the King's ..."

He started to mumble to himself.

A few days later George, the blackbird, landed on the wall and said, "Hi. What news?"

"Not much," said the wall. "Big Humphrey fell off me, a soldier's horse kicked him to death, then that fellow Claude came round and made a silly rhyme about it all. Other than that it's been quite boring, although I've just had a nice chat with those kids Jack and Jill. They said they were going up the hill over there to look for water. I tried to tell them you don't find water at the top of a hill but you know what kids are like these days, they know it all."

The Dead Dog - Vonnie Giles

"You killed my dog, Marcus! You killed my dog!"

"For God's sake, shut up about the damned dog and close the bloody windows –there's a force nine gale blowing outside!"

"You killed my dog, Marcus, and if you want the windows closed, you do it!"

"Why the hell do you always insist on eating by candlelight? Supposed to be romantic, is it? Though how someone built like an all-in wrestler thinks she can possibly exude romance defies belief!"

Shadows fluttered on the wall as the candle shimmered, then faded to nothing. The room was now lit only by a tentative moon peeping out nervously from behind the clouds. As Marcus stood up, swearing and muttering under his breath, his chair scraped against the tiled floor like chalk on a blackboard and fell with a clatter behind him. He grabbed hold of the table to steady himself, knocking over the wine bottle and soon felt the wetness of the very expensive Burgundy over the front of his very expensive trousers.

The curtains continued to swirl and dance frantically as the wind outside increased in strength, and now it sounded as if some spectral entity of ill-will were whistling down the chimney, clambering for admittance.

"Forgotten where the table lamp is, have you, Martha? No? Well, in that case, turn the sodding thing on!"

"You're a foul-mouthed little swine, aren't you, Marcus? But I suppose it's a bit late now for your mother or anyone else to make you wash that sewer of a mouth out with soap and water!"

God, how she hated him: the pompous, ill-tempered bastard! Suddenly he was there, illuminated, as he switched on the wall lights: small and dapper, his mean little eyes glaring at her angrily through his rimless glasses. Quite frail looking, he was, nevertheless, strong enough to have kicked poor little Monty like a football, from one side of the kitchen to the other, breaking the dog's slender, elegant neck in the process. That was four weeks ago, but the hurt and the shock remained as acute as when it first happened. She would never forget and she would never forgive!

She remained sitting at the table, while Marcus went over to the windows and closed them. Glancing at the grandfather clock she realised that it was almost midnight. In five minutes it would be her forty-second birthday, and what would be the lovingly chosen gift this year: another cheque, another Premium Bond, another wad of notes left romantically on the kitchen work surface? If he remembered at all, that is – and it certainly wouldn't be the first time he had forgotten altogether!

"Well, Martha! Almost twelve o'clock! Almost birthday time ...again!" he said mockingly. "I wonder what my little love would like for a birthday present this year."

"I want nothing from you. I'm more than surprised you even remembered."

"Oh, this year everything's different. I've thought long and hard about it." He smiled at her, showing his small, sharp teeth. "Let's have a glass of champers to celebrate, shall we?"

"I've nothing to celebrate," she replied, tasting the salt tears on her lips. "You made sure of that, didn't you? When you killed Monty!"

"Tut, tut! You're no fun anymore, are you, Martha?" he sneered. "But I'm going to put a smile back on your face. Just sit where you are and be patient. There's a good girl!"

With those words, out went Marcus, with his little scuttling steps, into the hall from where he returned carrying in his arms a large gift-wrapped parcel decorated with red ribbons and a red bow which he placed on the table in front of her.

"Now, just pull the bow and all will be revealed... Ooh, and I nearly forgot ...happy birthday, Martha!"

Martha's screams filled every corner of the house and the whistling ghost in the chimney, shocked into silence, made a hasty retreat.

"You lucky girl, Martha! 'The trumpet shall sound and the dead shall be raised incorruptible'…just for you! Your Monty has truly come back to you from the grave!"

The hideous glass eyes stared at her and the dog's beautiful neck was still bent at the same strange, twisted angle that it had had when she last saw him, his mouth still smiling in agony.

"So much more realistic, don't you think? A more faithful representation of his unfortunate demise! The taxidermist, I think, was quite taken with the novel idea."

Martha fell onto her knees, her arms wrapped around her, banging her head on the tiled floor. Blood oozed from her nose and her screams continued unabated.

"That'll teach you to keep your damned dog under control and not let it dig up the flower beds!"

Marcus righted his fallen chair and placed it where he could have a better view of the entertainment. Lighting a cigarette, he then poured himself a glass of champagne and raised it in a toast.

"To the miracle of resurrection! To the proof of life after death! To Monty!"

He watched with an amused expression on his face as Martha, now wailing, placed her hands on the edge of the table and staggered to her feet. He laughed out loud as she rose to her full height, her face covered in blood and tears.

"Sometimes, you bastard, it pays to be built like an all-in wrestler!" she yelled – and with that she rushed at him, swinging her chair in the air and bringing it down with all her strength upon his head. The top of his spine cracked as she hit him again and he slithered onto the floor where she then gave him a vicious kick in the neck though, by then, he was past feeling any pain.

Slipping and sliding on the red wine that had spilled onto the tiles, she dragged the body out into the hall; he was really hardly any weight at all! Then she quickly made a mental note of all the things that she needed and systematically went through the house collecting them.

The spectre in the chimney had, by this time, returned and was once again making its presence known, whining and whistling for all it was worth. If it had stopped to listen, however, it would have heard a car engine starting up and the house gates opening and closing...

Much later that night, the windows in the dining room were once again wide open, the curtains once again gently moving in the wind. All around the room were placed lighted candles casting a dreamlike glow over the scene. At the table sat Martha, a half-finished bottle of champagne in front of her, her face still covered with dried blood. In Marcus's chair sat Monty, his neck now erect as it had been in life, a thick woollen muffler kept it upright and he was still smiling at her broadly.

Out in a field somewhere, under a cold silvery moon, stood a scarecrow, a man of straw, protecting the growing plants. His scarf waved about furiously in the blustery night air ...pebbles super-glued onto his dead eyes, a carrot super-glued onto his nose, his mouth, drawn back in a rictus of death, the small, sharp teeth now exposed eternally to the wind and the weather.

Hands in Gloves - Margaret Cornwell

The room was dark, and bare except for a low table in the middle. On it there was a pair of gloves, an ordinary pair of workman's gloves: working gloves that you might see on any building site or garage, except for one thing. Joining them was a long string ...a long string that would be useful for a child: up one sleeve, across the back of the neck and down the other sleeve so the gloves would not get lost. These gloves, however, were far too big for a child. They were adults' gloves, working gloves and the long string was thin and dark.

Jumilla and Mahmoud stood silently in the background, pressed against the back wall, slowly realising that this was the biggest mistake they had ever made in their short happy lives.

"Go! Mahmoud, GO!" whispered Jumilla. "I am a woman. They won't want me."

"It's too late," sighed Mahmoud, "they've seen me. We just have to hope and pray." Jumilla shuddered with fear.

"Oh, Allah, the almighty, most merciful, please, please help us," she prayed. She thought back to how it had all begun – in the sunlight, in the square, with hopes high and careless freedom. She could picture it clearly.

The hot sun beat down on the white-washed square, on the row of dusty shops, on the broken-down cars and on the seething mass of angry, restless youth. The air cracked with anger, frustration and bitterness. The smell of dust and sweat rose as the crowd pressed forward, jostling each other, trying to hear the speaker on the makeshift stand. He was well known, feared by some, and knew how to rouse the deepest feelings of his listeners. His message was clear, as clear as all the other messages being organised on this national day... 'Oppose the tyrannical government and its hated Western allies'.

A bell tolled. The speaker disappeared, melting into the crowd. The stand was quickly dismantled and the only people left to face the charging riot police were the innocent listeners, students and those who had stopped on their way back from market to see what was going on.

Jumilla pressed herself into a narrow doorway, which miraculously opened and swallowed her up into the dark interior of a vegetable shop. Mustiness, rotting vegetables and the smell of a sick old man stung her nostrils.

"Quick... Through that door: run."

She ran.

As Jumilla arrived panting, in the main road, a man brushed up against her. She recoiled and then recognised him from the speaker's platform. He was too old for a student, too scarred. As he rushed past her he thrust a piece of paper into her hand. "Tomorrow, 9pm," he said, and was gone.

She stood in shock. The touch of his hand was disgusting, slimy and sweaty. She looked at the scrap of paper torn from an advertisement, a baker's shop on the edge of town, a quarter she would not normally go to, but she was intrigued. Another meeting? Maybe. She might be able to meet the charismatic speaker, learn from him, might even be able to help the cause, as a lookout or an eavesdropper. She felt a thrill go through her and her cheeks flushed.

As Mahmoud came round the corner he saw Jumilla, saw her cheeks flush and decided that that was because of him. Rules were lax these days. No one would condemn Jumilla for standing talking to him as long, of course, as there was daylight to be seen between them. "Hey! Jumilla," he shouted. "What are you doing here? Be careful, the riot police are out in the square back there."

So Jumilla told him about the meeting, her escape and the note.

"No!" Mahmoud shouted, "No, no, no, no. You are not to go." He was angry and afraid. He'd heard what that group was up to, but Jumilla thought of herself as a liberated, modern, young woman. She was not going to be dictated to by a MAN. The argument turned into a row and, in despair, Mahmoud decided to accompany her to the baker's shop the next night.

As they neared the baker's shop there was a hushed whistle and the scarred man led them into the bare, dark room with the low table on which there was a pair gloves with a thin, dark string joining them.

The speaker was ranting against the government, the West, the stupidity and sheer selfishness of the majority of the people... They should be ashamed of their timidity... They were not true believers and would not be transported to heaven at their death. Then there was silence.

Slowly the speaker moved to the table in the centre. He pointed at the gloves. "Here is the gateway to paradise," he said quietly – and then they knew. They knew that one of them would be chosen. Willingly or unwillingly they would have to perform the duty the speaker put upon them. There was no release.

"You," he shouted, pointing at Jumilla. "Come."

"No." Mahmoud's cry of despair was cut off as two burly men pinioned him and covered his mouth.

The speaker smiled at Jumilla. "I saw you yesterday," he said. "I saw the glory surrounding you. You will be our most famous martyr."

"No," she whimpered. "Please, no. I am to be married."

A burst of laughter greeted this statement.

"You will be the bride of Allah," shouted the speaker.

They held her tightly, grabbed her hair and forced her head back while they poured liquid into her mouth. They strapped the explosives round her body and carefully, very carefully, threaded one glove through the sleeves of her coat and put the gloves on her hands.

"Do not clap your hands here," said one, "or we will all be with you in paradise." Mahmoud struggled free.

"I will go. Free her. Take me," he screamed.

The speaker smiled. "AH! A true patriot. Yes, you can go. Your family will be proud of you. You will go with her and make sure she does what she is told. They will not suspect such a loving couple. Truly, God is Great!" ...and he laughed.

Mahmoud realised there was no escape; he needed time to think. "God is Great!" he shouted. "To meet HIM I must be clean. I must make my ablutions."

This was a request, he knew, that could not be denied. A man brought clean water in a basin and Mahmoud slowly poured some of it over his head, looking hard at Jumilla. The drugs were taking effect but Jumilla knew that Mahmoud was trying to say something. He stepped into the basin and smiled at her and then Jumilla knew. Memories of her science lessons came back to her. They would meet Allah hand in hand. With her last bit of strength she lunged forward as Mahmoud's hands came out and clasped hers.

Murder Most Horrid - Jennifer Nesteroff

I love sitting out here in this little courtyard. They bring me here nearly every day when the weather is fine. I can watch the small birds that come hopping around among the bushes growing along this high wall that surrounds the courtyard. The thing I like most though, about being out here, is the peace and quiet: no-one grumbling or shouting or nagging at me to do something for them and then complaining that I haven't done it right. Oh look, there's a robin perched on top of the wall. Isn't he sweet?

I like all animals. I liked my mother's cat and felt sorry about having to kill it. I had to do it though, to pay her back. Mother had been beastly to me because I'd accidentally broken a bowl. She took away my portable radio to teach me not to be clumsy, so I decided to take away her beloved cat to teach her how it felt, having things taken from you. I took a big kitchen knife and went to find the cat. It was sitting outside in the sunshine, just like I'm doing now. I stroked it for a bit and then plunged the knife straight though its back. The blade stuck out through the cat's chest and it died immediately, so I must have stabbed it through the heart. Then I tied it into a plastic bag along with a big stone and threw the bag out into the river that ran by the back of our house. I was careful to wash my hands well and make sure that I had no blood on me. All pretty neat for a kid of ten, I think. Of course, the cat was never found and my mother was upset for weeks.

I guess my mother never really liked me. I didn't have a father that I knew of. Whenever I asked her about him, she would always say, "He was a bastard and that's all you have to know."

Anyway, we always lived on our own, Mother and I. We never went anywhere. I attended the local school for a few years and then, when I was sixteen, Mother said I should stay home and help look after the house – and her. Whenever I said I'd like to go out sometimes, maybe join a Club and meet some young people, maybe even find a boyfriend, my mother would just look at me sourly and tell me that I was boy mad, that I was too plain to attract a boy anyway, and that I would be better off staying at home and attending to the housework. So we stayed at home – Mother and I.

All those years! All that time spent dusting and sweeping, cooking and cleaning, trying to keep the house in a state that would satisfy Mother and all the while watching her growing older and gradually deteriorating into an arthritic cripple.

I tried to ignore her bitterness. I would play music and sing the latest popular songs to myself: 'Love me tender, love me true' and 'We are going on a summer holiday'. Mother would yell at me, telling me not to be so stupid, telling me that I couldn't sing anyway, and should keep quiet. I would try to antagonise her further by singing louder, 'She loves you, yah, yah, yah!' I'd dance, too. Watching Top of the Pops on TV, I'd whirl around the room pretending I was dancing with some good-looking boy. Then Mother would stamp over and turn off the TV.

There was this one day when everything suddenly became different. I was cooking my mother's lunch. I fried steak for her, making sure it was done just the way she liked it. I could hear her grumbling that she was hungry and for me to hurry up. When I brought the steak in to her, she eyed it suspiciously and said it didn't look well done. This quite upset me. I had cooked it so carefully. I went to walk back to the kitchen, but Mother shouted that I'd forgotten to cut the steak up for her. "You stupid girl! You know I can't use my hands properly anymore." I came back and picking up the steak knife and fork, began to cut the meat up into little pieces, just the way she liked it ...but all at once, there was blood everywhere! It was all over Mother, all over the table, all over me.

I couldn't understand it, but I kept on cutting the steak, cutting the steak, cutting the steak. Mother screamed and screamed and then she was quiet. I saw her lying on the floor covered in all that awful blood. I knew I had to get help, so I ran outside to the street. I saw an old woman, rather like Mother, just standing there, staring at me. Then I noticed that I still had the knife in my hand and realised that it might be scaring her. I walked up to her to explain that I'd been cutting up my mother's meat, but she started screaming just as Mother had done. Then there was more blood spurting everywhere: on the old woman, on the pavement and all over me.

I like staying here. I have ladies looking after me, the way I looked after Mother, only they talk quietly to me and they smile. I like that. Sometimes some people come and look at me. They all wear white coats and speak softly to one another. The other day I managed to hear one of them say, "Such a pretty woman and she looks so nice and calm ...hard to believe that she's capable of murder, and murder most horrid." I wonder why someone would say that about me. I sometimes wish that Mother would come to see me so I could show her how nice it is here. Still, knowing her, I don't suppose she would come and it's probably just as well. She might start shouting at me again and I wouldn't like that.

Perhaps I shall sing 'Love me tender' to my ladies tonight. It's the latest song on Top of the Pops, you know.

The Great Unknown - Linda McGillycuddy

How did I get here? I don't remember driving here, yet here I am, at the lookout point by the sea. It has always been one of my favourite spots over the years, but I haven't visited for ages. I leaned on the railing and watched the water swirling far below and the seagulls swooping and circling in the wind. The letter is still in my pocket, I can feel it as I keep my hands warm. I don't have to look at it again to know what it says, Notice of Redundancy at the top, with many regrets etc expressed. How can 35 years count for nothing? I had hoped I would be bypassed, but mine had come with the final batch of letters. It was just a short letter in a thin cheap envelope, not very important looking, and yet it held the power to turn my life upside down.

I felt numb. I sat down on the bench and thought, how was I going to tell Gina? She was getting so excited about Katie's wedding and her days were filled with flowers, dressmakers, and lists for everything. I was really going to burst her bubble wasn't I, and how could I tell Katie that there wouldn't be the money for the honeymoon we had promised them? My head felt as if it were going to burst and I closed my eyes. Their rock, their strong man was starting to crumble. I longed for some oblivion from this black feeling, just a release from this awful void that seemed to engulf me.

I heard footsteps and hoped that whoever it was would keep on going. I was in no mood for company and small talk. Someone sat down heavily beside me and I had to open my eyes.

"Hello Robert, haven't seen you for a while."

"Oh, hello Mr. Buckley, no I haven't had time for these walks recently..." I drifted off, hoping he would take the hint and move on. Normally I would be up for a chat with my old school teacher; he was a nice old guy and had always treated us well when we were kids, but I couldn't manage it today, not on this blackest of days.

"I walk here most days now. I had stopped for a while when I lost my Betsy; you remember her don't you Robert?"

The old black Labrador was a familiar sight for many years, always trotting along beside her master, "Yes, of course I do, sorry to hear she's gone now." I tried to sound sympathetic – I knew how much the dog meant to him, living alone after his wife had died, but I couldn't truly focus on him, only on my own blackness which consumed me.

"She broke my heart, did old Betsy when she went, but you know life must go on eh? I couldn't face these walks on my own for a long time, but now look..."

I hadn't even noticed but he had a young pup on a lead beside him, a golden Labrador this time, who was tying himself up in knots around the legs of the bench and the lead. Mr. Buckley laughed as he bent down to rescue the pup from his efforts. "I thought I would never feel the same way about another dog, but nothing ever stays the same thought does it? Sometimes, something vital to us is taken and we feel we can't cope, but we do, and there are good times ahead."

I saw him glancing down at my car far below with the door still open and the side lights on. The little pup jumped around my legs with excitement and I instinctively put my hand down to pet him, and felt the warm silky softness of his head. What was I thinking? I was worth more than the sum of my job. I would get over this new change in my life, I had a lot to live for, I loved my family and they loved me, no matter what. My throat felt constricted with emotion and I started to speak but could not. I saw the concern in the old man's kind eyes and felt the blackness loosen its grip on me just a little.

"You know the future is the great unknown Robert, with every day bringing the chance of something new, sometimes it isn't always what we want, but there can be good times ahead, you just have to hang on for them." I cleared my throat and petted the pup one last time. Already I felt more in control.

I smiled at him and said that I had to be going, my family would be waiting for me and I didn't want them to worry. I felt his eyes on me as I walked back down to the car. Before getting in, I looked up at him continuing his walk with his companion along the cliff top and waved, I was going home.

The Last Walk - Andy Crabb

For the last six months, Concepción and Elena had spent time together on Tuesdays and Fridays in the IVO, the Oncology Institute of València, that prestigious hospital of skill and advanced medical knowledge that brings hope to sufferers of cancer and their families. Teams of radiographers, specialists and surgeons work night and day, consulting, diagnosing, listening, reassuring, and offering sympathy when diagnoses are adverse.

Eighty-one years lay heavily on Concepción, and she was constrained by the limitations of her wheelchair. Her mind was clear, her eyes were bright, but underneath the exterior lay the sadness of what she knew was about to happen.

Her eight-year-old grand-daughter laid her finger-tips lightly on the veined hands of her grandmother. "Why are your veins sticking out so much? Why are they so big? Mine are only small and you can't really see them." Elena was the queen of childlike questions, innocent ones that demanded frank replies.

The old lady managed a smile. "When you get old, all that nice young flesh that covers your bones starts to get less and less, but your veins and your arteries have to keep on going, to carry blood around your body. They tend to stand out a little. Do they tell you about veins and arteries at school?"

"Yes, but Señorita Monte made it very complicated. She showed us the picture in the book and then we had to answer the questions." Elena looked up at the lined face of the old lady. "Gran, what exactly *is* cancer?"

Concepción paused before answering. "Has Señorita Monte told you about the cells that make up your body?"

"No. They do all that stuff next year or even the year after that. But I saw a programme on the television."

"And what do you remember about what they said?"

"It was a bit confusing. They said that our bodies are made up of millions and millions of little cells that you can only see with one of those microscope things. There's an uncountable number of cells in our bodies. I got bored when she started talking about it, so I thought about something else."

The old lady shifted uncomfortably. "Cells are like very, very small bits of material that make up our bodies. And you are right, they are so small that you can't see them without a special machine. They make up the whole body; they are everywhere. When everything goes well, those little cells stay normal, but if something goes wrong then they start to do strange things. They can get bigger very quickly and grow into giant cells, or they can change or they can even split into little bits and move to another part of the body and start causing problems there."

"Daddy says they can't operate."

"Sadly, your daddy is right, darling. Some of the places where the cancers grow are in really difficult positions and, no matter how clever the doctors are, they can't operate. They can't do anything."

"So the person dies?"

"Yes."

Elena gripped her granny's hand tightly. "And how do people die?" The old lady tried hard to smile.

"I've thought about that a lot during the last few months, and I think it's like sliding slowly down a nice warm tunnel into a comfy bed."

"And is the bed full of bunnies, and baby lambs and chicks? I like chicks." Elena looked up at the faded grey eyes. "And does it hurt?"

Concepción turned the question over in her mind for a short moment before answering. "I don't think so. The doctors can give you something to make everything really, really peaceful."

Elena said, "Does it help if somebody holds your hand?"

"Yes dear, very much. Nobody should take their Last Walk alone. We should always have someone to talk to as we slip away down that nice, warm tunnel." Her eyes moistened faintly.

The next question was Elena's. "So when the time comes, we can hold hands and talk a lot."

"That would be wonderful."

Elena took her Last Walk three weeks later. Her mum and dad were there, doing their best, as the cancer finally took the little girl in its fatal grip. Her granny was there too, and talked to her for hours about her childhood, rabbits, lambs and what lies behind the clouds, and what language rainbows speak and why fish are not so bright.

As the little girl's breathing became fainter and fainter, Concepción told her about princes, and valiant knights with golden swords, and the factory where they make sunbeams, and places where ducks and mallards swam, and far-away places where the num-tree grows its silver fruit.

...When she finished telling the stories, the little girl had indeed taken her Last Walk, but certainly, most certainly, not alone.

The Picked and Mixed Collection

The short stories that follow come from both new and established authors.

They are an eclectic mix, picked because we enjoyed reading them and jumbled together to make it more fun to read!

Only a few have ever been offered to the public before (for these please see the Acknowledgements) and none has ever been published outside of blogs and magazines.

Shots - Gail Tucker

They shot the white woman first, just as the first rays of sunlight oozed above the horizon to throw the mountains into sharp relief against the dawn sky. Flashes of other light caught the pearlescence of the naked body as it turned to reach up the rock face. Flickers of flesh – smooth buttocks, downy nape beneath damp tendrils of auburn hair – caught the attention of the boy watching from behind the truck. He dared not breathe for fear of being discovered.

Away to his right, a cluster of women stirred. In the blooming light, individuals could be picked out amongst the figures huddled against the cold of pre-dawn. The movements closest to the rock face became prosaic as three or four men armed with swatches of grass swept away all trace of the white woman whose perfectly paced footprints had led to the final stir of sand as she had thrown off the loops and coils of metal and cloth, in dramatic prelude to that first shot. Other men turned away to busy themselves with black boxes; metallic clicks punctuated the silence; a murmur of voices drifted over the encampment; the earlier, silent tension broken now as female figures tested themselves against the coming day. Arms stretched, hands flexed, heads rolled on night-stiff necks.

He could run it all even now, a film sequence forever embedded in his memory. With more light had come the colours: deep ochres of sand, whites of eyes and teeth. He had looked down then to see a purple scorpion scuttle into the softness beside the wheel of the truck. Driven by the need for company, he had threaded his way through the assorted items that littered the camp until he was within the compass of the main body of women. His nostrils flared as the pungent stench of stale bodies reached him. He wondered if all women stank like that in the morning. He could not recall a time before. He knew only this now – tagging along with the men, mindful of his father's injunction to keep out of the way.

For a boy-child in a man's world, especially a world ruled by his father, life was full of threats and forebodings. There were no others of his age to neutralise the overwhelming sense of constant hazard. There had been earlier overtures by some of the younger men which had promised companionship, even friendship of a kind, but all had ended abruptly. He sensed it was something to do with his father, that The Great Man had forbidden any intimacy with his son, but he could not be certain or begin to understand and any thought of raising the subject rapidly perished when he came to his father for the allotted half-hour at the end of each day.

Instead, he sought to belong by keeping a tangential existence near to the women. He loved their giggling and whispered words, which he could not really fathom: words which, although in his mother tongue, carried endless hidden meanings. When any of the women addressed the boy directly the tone had such a teasing quality that it took away certainty and left him stupefied, unable to develop any meaningful dialogue. He would have liked to say how much he admired their faces, that their smiles gave him a warm feeling inside, but he was tongue-tied.

In ones and twos the women began leaving the safety of their night pack; they disappeared behind rocky outcrops where he knew he could not follow. When they came back, each carried herself with even greater grace than before: a transformation had occurred, the tentative movements of early rising had become serene composure: a composure broken only 'on demand' as it were, the giggling left behind with their blankets.

The morning had worn on. Smells of cooking replaced the sleep-stale sweat in the air. He was hungry as usual and knew that he must eat carefully now, before the intense heat of the day, and all that it would contain, turned his stomach sour. During his first few days here he had been violently and embarrassingly sick each afternoon, retching with feverishness and fear lest his father see his inadequacy. He had to be brave, to stand alone. He finished his porridge and drank, trying not to gulp the sweet tea, watching the adults slipping in and out of the makeshift canteen.

For the most part the women were still casually dressed but elaborately braided hair and the painted eyes of some showed that yesterday's ritual would be played out again today. He had not seen his father since that glimpse at dawn but he could feel his presence in every step made around the camp, nothing would be left to chance as the sun rolled inexorably across the open sky. All too soon, just as it reached its zenith, would come the moment: the scintilla of time when all their futures hung in the balance, at the whim of The Great Man.

Already, the familiar, strong young men had moved into position beneath a carefully erected awning and the long shadow cast by the rock had shrunk to a narrow fringe at its base.

Now he saw his father, leading the apparently random assortment of women across the ground; they halted as the scrub gave way to bare, pristine sand. One by one they stepped forward until held by command in suspended animation. Each appeared to gesture forward, upwards or across to the rock face. He could see the tension in their taut calves, the only visibly naked part of their bodies. Eventually, his father stood alone before making his deliberate way to join the other men beneath the awning.

The sun burned.

The boy held his breath. The cry echoed and bounced against the rock face. The women spun round – a flourish of bright cloths, glittering jewels and the gleaming tones of naked black bodies caught forever in the lens.

"It's not a bad Rioja," she said, handing him the glass. He shifted the catalogue under his left elbow to take the wine, barely glancing away from the photo-diptych on the wall. Following his gaze she said, "I wonder how he managed to get such movement, amazing how the monochrome works both with and against the vibrancy of colour."

"They shot the white woman first," he said.

"How can you tell?"

"I know."

"Oh. Did you know the great man?"

"No," he said, "I never knew him."

Split Revelation - Margaret Cornwell

My feet hurt, but I must keep going, only another fifty yards to the bench and then I can stop and rest. The park is so beautiful at this time of the morning with the mist over the pond and the ducks all dabbling.

Thank goodness, that's better. Now I can take the weight off my feet and sit and watch the youngsters beating the flab. Oh! There's a new one today, attractive girl, nice coffee colour. That scarlet tracksuit does suit her.

Anna had chosen the scarlet tracksuit purposely so that she would stand out from the rest. She'd been watching the park for a few weeks now, dressed inconspicuously, wheeling a pram and watching her quarry, watching where she went and how long she stayed. This was, at last, going to be the culmination of her long and arduous search.

Thank God for the internet. She'd never have found the old witch without its help. Foul, old, murdering witch: she had it coming to her and get it she would. All the other times she had failed, but not now. The hate had been smouldering inside Anna for over twenty years. Twenty years of missing her twin sister. Twenty years of feeling as if half of her had been torn away. THEY said it was necessary. THEY said it would be best for both of them, but Anna knew it would never be the same.

She jogged carefully along the track putting off the moment she would act. She thought about Eva. Little Eva who loved Anna unconditionally, went everywhere she went, helped her if she could. When Anna felt frightened at night Eva would laugh and sing to the angels to protect them. Then Anna could sleep. Anna had not slept peacefully for over twenty years, but tonight she would. Once she had avenged her Eva, she would sleep and sleep and dream of the lovely days at home when Eva was still with her.

The sun is lovely now shining through the trees reminding me of home. No, not home any longer. My home is now here, my tiny 'sheltered' flat. No trees to shelter it like my old house in the village with the huge cedars and the bananas and mangoes. All gone now, but I was the fortunate one. I was working in the hospital when the army came, hyped up with drugs and local gin. I'm lucky. I got out. I came west. Gosh! That girl in red is running faster and faster. "Careful! Oh no! You poor dear, let me help you to the bench. That was a nasty fall. Here I have a bottle of water. Please, help yourself. No, no I don't need it. It's only for emergencies. Careful, put your head between your knees, just rest, and drink a little more. Look, my name's Matilda and my flat is just near here. Why don't you come and have a cup of tea and then I can phone for a taxi to take you home."

Anna hobbled along beside Matilda letting out the occasional groan as she played out the scenario she'd planned. It couldn't have been easier, but she hadn't meant to fall quite so hard and her head was buzzing. She needed all her strength to do what she'd planned.

When they reached the flat she went straight into the bathroom and plunged her face again and again into cold water, but she still felt dizzy. Matilda was asking too many questions, prattling on like an old woman. She mustn't find out. This had to be quick and clean and no clues left. She sat staring at the cup of tea in front of her. This is what she had been waiting for. She felt for the razor in her pocket. She was in charge. She lunged across the table and pressed the point into Matilda's neck. "Sit still and listen," she hissed. "If you move I'll slit your throat."

"Oh my God. Please, please don't hurt me. I have money.

Take it. Take anything you want. I haven't much but you can have it all. Why are you laughing? O.K., O.K., I'm listening. Yes, I am from Buganda. Yes, I was a doctor at the hospital. How did you know? No, I don't remember operating on any girl called Eva. What was it? Tonsils? Appendicitis? It's so long ago I really can't remember. She died? Oh, that's dreadful. I'm so very sorry. Honestly I always did my best but you know what it was like, lack of equipment, no electricity and often the patients came in too late. Ouch! That hurt. Please don't. No, I don't remember. You can see I'm old. Yes, I'm listening. Oh…oh: Anna and Eva: yes, of course I remember now. I had to operate. We didn't know Eva would die. We discussed it fully, all of us, and did what we felt was best for both of you."

Anna's headache was getting worse. Her eyes felt swollen and her legs and arms heavy. Her grip loosened and the razor clattered to the floor. She looked at Matilda, but Matilda didn't move. Why didn't she run? What was going on? It was then that Anna realised her mistake.

"Oh, dear, Anna. You shouldn't have tried it again. I was ready for you but this time, I'm sorry, I can't let you get away with it. No, I'm not calling the police. No, this isn't my flat, just rented for a few months. I knew you'd come and I want security for my old age. So, I made sure I could be seen in the same place at the same time each morning. Yes, the internet is very useful. Remember I'm a doctor and I was very careful never to drink the water I carried with me …I don't intend to die before my time.

I'm sorry Eva died.

I did my best to save her, but you only had one liver between you. We thought we could divide it, but it didn't work so I gave you life and freedom …twenty-five years of health and strength. Siamese twins don't have much chance in life but you had yours Anna."

Family Portraits - Vonnie Giles

They watched as the blue ball bounced down the rough stone steps, glaring at me in disapproval, lips pursed, eyebrows knitted. Yet again I was the object of their disapprobation. It sometimes seemed to me that whatever I did, I could never ever get it right in their eyes. Indeed, that afternoon, it seemed as if even the very trees were displeased with me, their heavy branches lowering over me, stopping the sun from smiling at me.

"Please, please, someone say something nice to me! Anything!" I silently pleaded. This was my loving family sending their darts of displeasure in my direction, so I was therefore more than mortified to see the ball hit the bottom step, then continue its way relentlessly across the beaten earth of the terrace until it came to a stop at my grandmother's feet. She slightly lifted her blue skirts and, with her right foot, distastefully nudged the ball back in my direction. Sniffing disapprovingly and gathering her black lace shawl more tightly around her shoulders, she raised her cup of camomile tea to her lips and glanced around at the rest of the family.

What a miserable, judgemental bunch they were, or so it seemed to me at the time! There they were, in this favoured, temperate spot overlooking the lush vineyards that surrounded Montpellier, yet looking as though they expected the world to come tumbling around their ears, glum and completely silent. It looked to me as though grandfather, in fact, had fallen asleep: his eyes closed, his grey side-whiskers touching the top of his starched white stand-up collar, his face red from too much sun, his lips thin and taut.

If only he had held out his arms to me and given me a hug! It would have made everything so much better.

My twin sisters both looked at me accusingly for having spoiled the atmosphere of the moment with my silly, childish, blue ball. They too were in blue. Silvie, seated at the small table, was on a spindly gilt chair that seemed barely strong enough to support her weight, and Francine moped on the low wall that surrounded the terrace, her chin resting on one hand. Why they always insisted on dressing identically I could never understand. Had they so completely merged as to become one person in two separate bodies? I sometimes thought so, for they certainly looked alike, sounded alike and often I would become so confused that I was unable to remember which of them had ordered me to do something! One thing was certain, however – I did not like them and they did not like me!

I just wished that someone would smile at me! Please! It wasn't much to ask, was it?

As I stood, uncomfortable and embarrassed, the blue ball stationary at my feet, I glanced across at my mother and father; she, seated next to Francine, wearing her favourite gown with its broad black and white vertical stripes and he, behind her, his right foot on the low wall. If looks could have killed I would surely have fallen dead on the spot!

Why didn't somebody, at least, speak to me? I felt so sad, so unhappy!

I can never forget that it all this happened on a Sunday because that was always the day upon which the coachman was sent to Montpellier to fetch Cousin Marie-Louise from the Institution where she lived: a place for people who were not quite right in the head. What a sweet little person she was, in her tartan dress and her funny green garlanded straw hat. She was always the happiest, most smiling member of my family, but today even she had a lost, bemused look on her gentle face.

Please, Marie-Louise, I thought, make one of your funny faces at me and make me laugh! I so want things to be back to normal!

What on earth had I done wrong! Surely bouncing a ball down the steps did not warrant this amount of censure. Was it maybe because I had refused to eat my cabbage at luncheon? Or perhaps it was because Francine, the sneak, had seen me pulling the black cat's tail! Or, even worse, had my governess Mlle Julie complained that I seemed completely unable to master the art of subtracting one number from another? I just didn't know. Whatever it was, I most certainly was not going to do it again – not if this was the result!

Can't you all see that I want to say something, but daren't?

This, like all my silent pleas, went unheeded.

However, I soon forgot these unpleasant deliberations when the blue ball suddenly became the sole focus of my attention as a yellow butterfly landed on its surface. Fascinated, I watched the butterfly standing on its thin spidery legs, its yellow wings closed and I wondered at the fragility of it, wondering even more at the mind that had created it; a strange thought, you might think, for a child of my tender years, but I distinctly remember this passing through my mind, as indeed I remember every other detail of that day! Monsieur le Curé's teachings had obviously not fallen completely on deaf ears while I fidgeted and fretted during his homilies!

I was roused from my reverie by the sound of soft voices and, when I looked up, there standing in front of the tree was my eldest sister Claudette, arm-in-arm with her husband. Claudette, in her Parisian white-organza gown, was giving me the evil eye and obviously whispering about me.

Sidling up to them, newly arrived, was M. Corneille from the neighbouring vineyard, never a welcome visitor to our house, always slightly under the weather from tasting too much of his own vintage. Why had he turned up, I wondered.

"Speak to me, someone speak to me, please," I begged silently, but again there was no response; even the birds had ceased to sing and the black cat had deliberately turned its back on me!

There they all were, frozen in time, motionless as in a painting, completely removed from me!

I could feel the tears beginning to spring to my eyes and was just about to break into sobs, when I happened to glance over M. Corneille's shoulder and saw, amid the foliage of the tree, a friendly face smiling at me, the one I'd first seen that afternoon. I'd thought then that I must be mistaken because he was not supposed to be home until next month, but it was him! It was Jean-Luc, my best friend in the whole world, my brother! There he stood in his fine military uniform. I opened my mouth to shout out his name, but he immediately put his finger to his lips to silence me.

Pushing the branches aside, he moved forward and walked around the edge of the terrace until he was standing immediately in front of me, then he stooped down and picked up the blue ball which he handed to me.

"Here you are, Jérôme, keep this in a safe place, won't you!"

Then he placed his hands on my shoulders and kissed the top of my head. With that, looking down into my eyes, he gave me one final smile, turned, and went back the way he had come, disappearing among the branches. What I could not understand was why no one else seemed to have seen him; no one spoke to him, no one's eyes followed him, no one gave him a hug and a kiss to welcome him home.

Then everything changed in an instant and the world came to life again. I could hear my mother and my sisters sobbing quietly and I could see tears escaping from beneath my grandfather's closed eyelids, but what I remember most from that moment was poor Cousin Marie-Louise, her cheeks wet, her mouth wide open, sitting there as still and white as a marble statue.

I was suddenly terror-struck because I realised then that this terrible grief was nothing to do with me, it was nothing that I had done. How self-centred of me to have thought that my small misdemeanours were worthy of all this seeming reproach. What great tragedy had fallen upon our family to cause such unhappiness?

My father, his eyes red-rimmed, wearily came over to me, bent down in front of me and took me in his arms. My gallant brother, my best friend, Jean Luc, was missing in battle, perhaps taken prisoner by the Prussians ...perhaps not. If we were very, very lucky he could come back to us one day, but, whatever had happened, we must pray for him.

A flash of insight, however, suddenly told me that Jean-Luc would never return to us, that he was gone forever, but I also knew that he was all right and that there really was no need for us to worry about him. It was on the tip of my tongue to say all this to my father and to tell him what I had seen, but some childish instinct told me that it was far better to keep my thoughts to myself and remain silent.

However, even now, forty years after that strange afternoon, I still, in moments of stress, catch glimpses of Jean-Luc smiling encouragingly at me ...and the blue ball? Well, it sits on my mantelpiece in pride of place, next to Jean-Luc's posthumous military medal awarded for valour.

Growing Pains - Mac Black

It should be something to look forward to, shouldn't it?

Being told that you are going on a little holiday, and that you will be staying on your own with an aunt in another town, can surely only be good. All perfectly acceptable of course, if the intended visit is to be with an aunt you know well, one you like a lot and okay too if a long journey, on a smelly bus, is not part of the arrangement; travel sickness is very unpleasant to suffer at my age, you know...

Not having a say in the matter is bad too, but democracy, in our house, simply means me doing as I'm told. That's one of the biggest troubles of being five years old – everyone treats you like a child and not knowing this aunt very well, the one who happens to be my Gran's sister, who has a lot of prickly hair on her upper lip, does not make me feel at all comfortable about the visit. This is a maiden aunt who always insists on kisses. I don't think it means that she waits on people like a kitchen maid. If what I overheard is correct, she nearly had a husband once who walked out on her... That's the sort of woman she is – and never mind me hardly knowing her – I am expected to go and stay with her!

Anyway, we've arrived at our destination.

Mum was left at home. I haven't said it to anyone, and certainly not to her but I think, recently, she has become decidedly plump. "I will miss my little boy," she said. "Now please be good while you are away – for Mummy..." My head was given a pat and I could see she was trying hard not to cry. Dad and I waved back to her as she stood at the window, looking sad. I was brave and didn't cry either...

It rained all the way from Glasgow to Falkirk. What a long bus journey, and all I could do was to try looking out of steamed-up windows, and saw nothing but other buses, and lorries, and cars, all going *much* faster than we were. Don't know why we had to get on the slow bus...

And, I told you ...I knew it would happen ...I was sick on the bus – but only once. It was just before we reached the bus stop in Falkirk, so we didn't have to suffer the unpleasant smell for long. I was very glad we weren't going farther – it might have happened again.

My dad kept giving me one of his looks that made me feel really guilty, but what could I have done? As we left, going along the passageway between the seats, I behaved like a little gentleman to make amends. Smiling and saying sorry to everyone who was still on the bus seemed the right thing to do. No-one smiled back. They weren't very friendly; just gave me strange looks.

Aunt Mary was standing at the bus stop, waiting, with a walking stick in her hand, but, as it turned out, she didn't seem to need it to hold her steady as she tottered along. It looked very suspicious to me, the way she carried it, more like a weapon. I was very careful, because I guessed it might be used to fend off stray dogs that annoyed her, or she could maybe even use it on small boys who did the same thing...

"Ten days," Auntie Mary tells me that I've been here and, today, my dad is coming to collect me, to take me home, but I don't want to leave her. We have had a super time. I never have to eat my dinner if I don't want it; sweeties every day, and visits to the park, walks along the canal bank, and she can really kick a ball, you know – better than my dad can.

One afternoon we went to the cinema. It was a funny film, but she fell asleep. When we got home, she put me to bed, and then wanted to know all about the film she missed. It was a bedtime story for her – but I fell asleep before the end...

She is the greatest auntie ever.

Auntie Mary says that my dad will have something especially exciting to tell me when he arrives. I can't guess what it might be, and she's not giving me any clues, but it is something worth waiting for, she says.

He'll be here any moment!

If he is going to give me a big surprise, I think I will give him an even bigger one. If I hide somewhere in the garden, when he comes out to look for me, I'll jump out and frighten him, and see what he says to that...

"The bus must have been on time today," shouted Auntie Mary, "your daddy is coming in the front gate." So, I jumped into the big box that was in the garden at the back of the house, and waited for him to come looking. It was dark inside the box, but I wasn't scared – well, just a little bit – but when I heard his voice I pushed up the lid and cried "Boo!"

Why did he start shouting at me? How was I to know I would get covered in coal dust in Auntie Mary's coal bunker? I am only five, remember...

Back home again, in Glasgow, and this time, I wasn't sick on the bus; Daddy was very happy about that. Mum was really pleased to see me. She's not as fat now. I think she must have been missing me an awful lot and didn't eat any food on any of the days I was away – mum's are like that.

And what was the exciting news that my dad told me...? Nothing much; it was just about me having a new baby brother – huh – what is so exciting about that? Babies can't even talk. I can, and I can read real words.

Oh dear me, babies are not much fun and they are not very clever either, and do you know what? He doesn't even have a name! Mummy says she'll need my help because we have to decide what his name should be. They bought him in the local shop – cheap – and that is why he has no name, she said.

I can understand her buying the cheap one, because daddy never has any money, and it is good to get a bargain, but I wish they had spent more and bought a quieter one. What a lot of noise he makes – am I glad there wasn't a special two-for-one offer – one is noisy enough.

Mummy says that I will have to remember, now that I have a little brother, to help her more; and smile – even though the baby's nappies smell terrible. "It is a very responsible job being a big brother, you know," she said. "You will have to help him as he gets bigger, help him to grow up."

I would like to say, but I can't, because it would make her very unhappy, I didn't want to have a little brother, nobody asked me. He keeps making loud noises in the middle of the night, and I need my sleep, and anyway, it's just attention seeking...

Life can be so cruel. I used to be king of the castle, but now ...this baby. It is so obvious that no-one cares about me anymore.

Where did it all go wrong?

A *has-been* – at five...

Accident or Design - Margaret Cornwell

"Brian, Brian. Wake up. Wake up. What's the matter?"

"Jenny, is that you?"

"Yes, of course it's me, stupid. Who else would it be? Your phantom lover?"

"No, honestly, I'm all confused. I thought I was dead." Brian shivered in the cold of the early morning. He felt frozen in his bones. Jenny held him tightly.

"It's O.K. Brian, I'm here. You're having a nightmare." Jenny was worried. This was not like Brian at all. He usually slept solidly all through the night. "Brian?"

"I could see his face. He was screaming and the car was flying through the air, coming at me and there was nothing I could do. It was a little red car and it landed on top of me and there was an enormous bang, and then, silence. I felt nothing. And then I was looking down on the scene. I could see myself dead at the wheel. For a moment it was terrible. Terrible ...and then I thought, Funny. I'm alright. Who's that then?"

Jenny was silent for a moment.

"Oh, Brian, it's all my fault. I shouldn't have given you all that cooked cheese last night, you know how indigestible it is – and we watched that car chase on TV. I know; a cup of chamomile will help both of us. I won't be a minute."

Sitting up in bed, sipping his tea, Brian felt a little better, a bit more relaxed. "Jenny, I don't want to die but, if I'm going to, I want to make sure that you and the kids will be O.K."

"Shush, Brian, you're not going to die. Dreaming of death does not mean death. It means the end of something leading to a new beginning. Like finishing your job and starting a new more exciting one. In fact one book says that if you are married it foretells young children. That'll be fun, more kids. Shall we?"

The next morning Brian's mind kept going back to the scene of the dream.

"Brian. Hey, wakey, WAKEY."

Ted was surprised. Brian was usually slap, bang on the ball, but today, obviously, something was wrong. "Come on, Brian. Spit it out. Had a spat with the missus?"

"No, Ted, I had this dreadful dream and I can't stop thinking about it."

Ted listened carefully because he could see the beads of sweat glistening on Brian's forehead and realised that he was deeply disturbed.

"Look Brian, my missus knows this woman who reads the cards. She is very good. She's read them for friends of ours and has really helped them. Let me make an appointment for you."

"Don't be so absurd, Ted. Fortune telling? That's all rubbish. You're joking, of course?"

A few days later Brian found himself outside an insignificant, suburban house. He hesitated, but then decided to ring the bell. A middle-aged, cosy-looking woman opened the door. "Oh, I'm sorry. I was looking for Magda."

"And you've found her. Come in, come in. You must be Brian. Oh, dear. You must have been expecting a gipsy wearing a black shawl and hoop earrings ...Sorry."

Magda led Brian into a small study and sat him down at a card table covered in a green velvet cloth. On it there was a pack of cards. The lighting was subdued. She sat opposite him. "Now, Brian, I want you to know that reading the cards is not an exact science. All I can do is to interpret the meaning of the cards as they fall. If at any time you are not happy you must say so and I shall stop. Do you want to continue? Right. Take the cards. Hold them. Think of the questions you want to ask. Now shuffle the cards. Now cut them.

Magda took the cards and laid them out.

"I see you are content with your life, but are very worried. Now, this card, number ten, known as the Wheel of Fortune, is a very significant card. The Mystic Wheel symbolizes reincarnation. It could mean a change in your home circumstances, or your work. Now this last card, number thirteen, is called Death, the Grim Reaper. No, no, it does not, or need not, mean physical death. In the end is the beginning. Its real meaning is a complete change of circumstances, the end of one cycle and the beginning of a new one. Are you thinking of changing your job? Or re-locating to a new country?"

Brian left Magda with more questions buzzing round his head than when he arrived. What if card thirteen really did mean death? What should he do? He decided to have a word with Father James after church on Sunday.

Settled in Father James' study, with a good slug of whisky in his hand, Brian poured out his worries.

"Well, Brian, I think what you need is a good holiday. You've had a lot of stress over your mother's death and I know you work long hours. Could you and Jenny get away for a bit, do you think? As for your dream, it's not often, in fact it's unheard of, that our Good Lord lets us know when he is calling us to him, but if you are really worried why don't you insure your life so, if anything happens, which I'm sure it won't, you'll be happy to know that you've done your best for Jenny and the kids."

After some thought Brian went to visit his insurers. The insurers were hesitant. "You say you had this dream, Sir?"

"Yes, I was driving home down this motorway, and this car, a little red one, came flying over the central reservation, crashed on top of me and killed me."

Too much dinner and too many bedclothes thought the insurer. "Yes, I see Sir. And you wish to insure your life for a million pounds, Sir? You do understand, Sir, don't you, that your wife will only receive the money IF, and I must make this quite clear, Sir, IF you die in this exact manner. Well, Sir, if you are absolutely sure, please sign here."

Brian went home very relieved. The next day at work he handed Ted the policy. "Ted, I've decided to take my holidays early. I've settled it with the boss. I'm taking Jenny and the kids to Florida."

"Good idea. I'll just lock this in my safe. Have a good time."

Brian and Jenny had a wonderful week in the sun. Brian seemed to be back to his normal cheerful self. "Jenny, should we think about a job here? There are lots of openings and opportunities in America." Privately he thought, the cards suggested re-location.

Ted was very pleased to see Brian back at work. "Hey! I thought you might decide to move to the good ole US of A."

"Well, I did think about it, but how could I manage without you in the office?"

Jenny was looking forward to a quiet dinner at home. She popped the boeuf bourguignon into the oven. It had been a lovely holiday but she was tired and decided to put her feet up in front of the Tele. She quietly drifted off to the Florida beaches and the hot, hot sun.

Suddenly she woke. The TV News was blaring out. The News Reader was sounding excited. "We have some breaking news just coming in. There has been a freak accident on the motorway. A red car travelling north burst a tyre. The car's excessive speed caused it to cartwheel over the central reservation and land on top of car travelling South. Our 'spy in the sky' is just picking up the pictures now. You can see the little red car crashed on top of the black one."

After months of enquiries the Insurers accepted their fate and paid out the full amount.

Leaving la Madeleine - Vonnie Giles

The very last time! The end of a life! The beginning of another! The gilt tipped railings that surrounded the great church of la Madeleine sparkled in the moist air as the worshippers descended the steps: their sins washed away, their souls cleansed for another week.

For Monsieur Perrault, however, there would be no forgiveness, no absolution! He felt that his guilt must surely be so clearly etched on his aging, white-bearded face, that it was fully visible for all to see. Even the priest had seemed to look at him in a particularly searching way, as though he could read his soul. He stood at the gates and looked around trying to imprint the scene on his memory so that later, far away in his new home in America, he would be able to conjure up the people, the buildings, the smells, the noises of Paris as they were on this final Sunday morning.

His wife preceded him with their daughter and, in front of them, walked the nursemaid with their little grandson. He could feel the tears stinging his eyes, a lump forming in his throat: an unexpected sign of weakness, of sentimentality! The sacrifice, however, would be worth it. It would have its own reward!

There she was – his prize, his darling, his own sweet Natalie, trim and slim in her black dress, holding her missal, a white petticoat showing as she lifted her skirts to protect them from the wet pavement. She was far too young for him, of course: an aging man's fancy, but why not? After all, you only live once and life was hurtling past him at an amazing speed.

Madame Perrault suddenly stopped in her tracks and signalled for her daughter to go on ahead to where the coachman was waiting for them. She then turned around to face her husband and, grabbing him by the elbow, forced him out of his reverie, forced his old man's eyes away from Natalie!

"Are you all packed, Gustave? Are you all ready for your great journey?" This harsh, sardonic voice was not one that he recognised; this was the voice of a stranger! Where was the gentle, considerate, conciliatory tone that she always used to him? This was how she spoke to the servants. What was she talking about anyway? Packing? Great journey? Surely she couldn't ...no, that was not possible. He had been so careful!

"I'm neither blind nor stupid, Gustave and I'm telling you, here and now, that there will be no more of this silliness! This is my first and my final acknowledgement of your unseemly behaviour!"

He looked at her face closely, saw her eyes following Natalie's retreating steps as she walked towards the Rue Royale. Yes, she knew! She knew very well what he was planning to do, but no one in the whole world had the power to prevent it! Love, infatuation, madness – whatever it was, it was truly unstoppable!

It had been years since M. Perrault had studied his wife's face so intently, and he saw her for the first time as she really was – an old woman with white hair, with wrinkled skin criss-crossed with red veins. Plump and stooping, she smelled stale and there was the faintest odour of sweat about her. Either she or her dress needed a wash in something fragrant. At that moment he knew he hated her, for she was trying to prevent him from following his desires and M. Perrault was someone who was not used to being thwarted – whatever he wanted, he would surely have.

However, she had shocked him, for he could feel his heart pounding and a pain at the base of his skull warned him that he would very soon have a splitting headache. He needed food and a bottle of Burgundy to revive him; he needed one of the fine restaurants in the Bois de Boulogne to calm his nerves.

"Remember my words, Gustave, because believe me, at ten

o'clock tomorrow night you will not be boarding a ship bound for America; you will be at home – with me!"

M. Perrault said not one single word in reply. He simply stood in silence, amazed that she should have discovered his secret. He watched her turn and make her way towards the waiting carriage which, after a few moments, moved off into the distance.

So there he was, alone, stranded outside la Madeleine! He then smiled inwardly and his thoughts turned inevitably to Natalie. He imagined her at that moment approaching the apartment which she shared with her mother; her expensive leather suitcases filled with beautiful velvet and silk gowns, her striped hatboxes filled with frothy creations of tulle and lace and her heart filled with excitement and love! All provided by him!

It was just such a shame, he thought – in fact, the only blot on the landscape that her mother did not wish to travel with them across the ocean, for she was such a good-looking woman: red-haired, buxom, exuding unspoken promises of sexual delights. Delights that he had, on several occasions, savoured and found very much to his taste! However, it was Natalie's warm, smooth, scented, and above all, young skin that he most desired! To have had her mother as well would have truly been the icing on top of the cake…!

…As he lay dying on the steps of la Madeleine, the rain now falling upon him, a priest standing conveniently by, M. Perrault's threatened headache had turned into such a blinding, excruciating pain that death, when it came, was a welcome release but, even in extremis, his last words and thoughts were for Natalie.

"Forgive me, Natalie! Our dreams are over! Our happiness gone! Say a prayer for me when I am dead so that my soul will fly up to paradise. I love you, Natalie…!"

By the time these last, touching words had left M. Perrault's lips, most of the remaining members of the congregation were gathered around his recumbent form. The ladies among them were, on the one hand, snuffling into their handkerchiefs and, on the other, thinking what a splendid story this would make at dinner parties. Who was this Natalie? Surely not Natalie from the patisserie! The one with the red-haired mother! Well, well, it very much looked as though the upright M. Perrault had been a rather naughty boy...!

By ten o'clock the next night M. Perrault, as his wife had predicted, was indeed at home, in an ornate and extremely expensive coffin! The scent of incense still filled the air and clung to the heavy damask curtains, but the insistent clicking of rosary beads and the discreet murmuring of prayers had finally ceased as the steady flow of visitors trickled away, leaving the tearful widow alone with her grief.

As darkness fell, however, the maid wearily ushered one final visitor into the sumptuous drawing room, a lady, heavily veiled, who was sobbing into a pristine white lace handkerchief.

On seeing her, Madame Perrault immediately rose from her chair and held out her hand ...laughing as she did so! Her husband's propensity for pretty young women was finally at an end!

"Congratulations, Natalie! Well done! You wore him out, you naughty girl! You really made the whole exercise so very simple, and there was no need, after all, for your poisons, or your potions, or anything unpleasant of that sort, was there? I'm so grateful to the nursemaid for recommending you! A very profitable little side-line in murder you have there, Natalie!"

Later that evening, M. Perrault's widow and M. Perrault's mistress imbibed several well-deserved glasses of celebratory champagne over the body of the dear departed.

Even later that evening, anyone caring to watch would have seen Natalie, the sweet little girl from the patisserie, leaving the house of mourning with her large handbag positively bulging with bank notes!

Teddy's World - Vonnie Giles

Captain Teddy Brown sat in the half-dark, cocooned in the hub of the universe, the gentle humming of the space ship's engines the only sound to be heard. He, and he alone, was in command of the thousand men and women who travelled with him through the immensity of space. He was their captain who walked tall, walked straight, talked firmly, talked kindly, whom they all loved and respected for they had gone through so many wondrous exploits with him, survived so many hazardous missions with him and because of this they knew exactly the sort of man who led them, someone whose judgement they trusted implicitly and into whose hands they had entrusted their lives.

The blue glow from the instrument panels meant that all was well, so now Captain Teddy was able to relax his watch. He slipped a quantum disc into his personal instrument panel so that he could listen to his favourite music, watching the kaleidoscopic patterns that moved over the monitor.

Suddenly a light shone over Captain Teddy as the cabin door opened abruptly, shattering the blissful peace. It was Star Lieutenant Brown who entered, bringing with her his bedtime chocolate drink and biscuits.

"Come on, Captain Teddy," she said firmly, "time for bed, or you'll never be in a fit state for school tomorrow."

Poor Captain Teddy, back to reality, back to a universe where he would never walk tall, never walk straight, never talk firmly, never command anyone! "Come on Captain Teddy. Time to log off! And anyway there's thunder in the air, so you really should switch the computer off."

So Teddy manoeuvred his wheel chair away from his desk, and allowed his mother to help him undress and put on his pyjamas. She placed his duvet gently over his useless legs, his favourite duvet, covered with scenes from Star Trek, and in the distance the thunder rolled and reverberated in the night sky. Teddy's mother kissed him and turned out the light and Captain Teddy, as best he could, thanked Star Lieutenant Brown and told her that he loved her, but only she would have been able to make out his words.

It's very hard when you're nine and a half years old and it seems that almost everyone else except you is able to walk and speak normally, but as he lay there he tried to imagine a different scenario, a world in peril, a world saved by the combined talents of a disabled Captain Teddy and his faithful side-kick, Star Lieutenant Stephen Hawking: the caped crusaders in their wheelchairs hurling themselves through the ether towards victory. Surely it was possible to have heroes who didn't walk tall, didn't walk straight, didn't talk firmly. Wasn't it?

With these comforting thoughts, Teddy, in his nice snug bed, could feel his eyes closing. Outside the rain was throwing itself against the window panes and the thunder continued to vent its anger. By now the lightning flashes were almost continuous, but Teddy was once again roaming around the universe in his dreams.

Suddenly, there was a thunder clap so overwhelmingly loud that it forced its way even into Teddy's starry dream and he opened his eyes. He had been disturbed in the middle of a galactic battle and was sorry that he would never now discover its outcome. So he lay awake, unable to get back to sleep, and his thoughts turned inevitably towards his computer. He began to think about holographic universes, participatory universes, simulated universes, parallel universes and knew, now that sleep had eluded him, that there was no way he could wait until morning to surf the net in his search for even more knowledge. He wasn't in a school for gifted children for nothing – his body might have failed him, but his mind certainly had not.

He desperately needed access to his computer, but to do so

would mean having to cross the room by himself because it was now three o'clock in the morning and the fine Star Lieutenant needed her rest. She already did so much for him that it would be unfair to ask for her help. So he leaned over the side of his bed and managed to grab hold of his wheelchair and pull it towards him. With great difficulty and breathing heavily he slithered from the bed into the chair and propelled himself over to his desk.

Overhead the thunder was rolling noisily around the heavens, the lightning flashing its forked patterns onto the darkness and Teddy knew that he really shouldn't plug in the computer, but all the information that he had carefully programmed into it had been saved onto a memory stick, so there was really no need to worry, was there? He bent down, inserted the plug into the socket and switched on the computer.

The noise was amazing, frightening, all consuming – the room seemed to be filled with the firing of a hundred gunshots, with the rumbling of a hundred trains passing through the house. Suddenly the monitor cracked from side to side into a hundred pieces and the slivers of glass seemed to rush towards him. He was then dragged by an irresistible force out of his wheelchair and found himself spiralling, whirling down a glittering, sparkling tunnel whose walls moved strangely in and out of focus as he passed by them.

Now, at least, the fearful sounds had ceased and all was silent, except that somewhere, a long way away, in the distance, far, far behind him, he could hear his mother's voice, terrified, tearful. "Oh, Teddy, Teddy! What's happened. Where are you, Teddy! Please don't leave me! Please come back!" Unknown to him, she then held out her arms towards the vortex, which pulled her, helpless, unresisting, towards it…

Teddy sat in his pyjamas, leaning against a large, orange, jagged boulder, on the hard gritty orange sand, the pink sea in front of him, looking up in amazement at the two orange suns hanging in the greenish sky. He felt helpless, bewildered. Where and what was this place? How had he got here? …and the strange tunnel – what had that been all about? Was this just another one of his dreams or was it reality?

Suddenly behind him he heard the sound of feet crunching over the sand and into his line of vision appeared the first Glerg of the many that he was going to meet. Standing there in all his orange glory, his tall, hairy, orange body clothed in a bright blue robe, his long snout twitching and sniffing the air, the Glerg looked at Teddy through his shining green eyes.

"Hello, Captain Teddy! said the Glerg, bowing towards him. "On behalf of all Glergs I welcome you to our home, the fifth planet in the fifth solar system to the left, looking from Earth that is, in the galaxy of Andromeda."

Teddy then heard the most surprising sound he'd ever heard in his life: his own voice, speaking strongly and firmly. "But Andromeda is a hundred million light years from Earth – that just isn't possible. It only took me two minutes to get here."

"The wormhole, Teddy, through the wormhole!"

Of course, how silly of him! The tunnel had been a wormhole and he knew all about wormholes, those strange creations that could connect different parts of the universe or even one universe with another.

"Your computer became one end of a wormhole when you plugged it in and here you are at the other end! But we must hurry, Teddy – there's not a nanosecond to lose. We desperately need your help, which is why we sent for you. Quickly, Teddy, follow me!"

"But I can't w…"

Teddy was just about to say that he couldn't walk – but he could …and he did! He stopped leaning against the orange boulder and slowly raised himself until he was standing upright, his feet planted firmly on the orange sand. What a strange and wonderful world this was where he was able to walk and talk, like everyone else! "But my mother! What about my mother? She's worried about me! I must go back and tell her that I'm all right."

The Glerg made no reply but, with a long bony orange finger, pointed towards the top of one of the sand dunes and there, smiling down at him, was Star Lieutenant Brown, dressed in her pale blue fluffy dressing gown! She ran towards him, her arms outstretched.

"Oh, Captain Teddy! I can't believe it! Here you are, safe and sound …and walking and talking! I'd no idea that at the end of that strange tunnel I should find such wonders!"

Quickly urged on by the Glerg, they made their way up the tallest of the sand dunes and at the summit looked down, open-mouthed, at rank upon rank of Glergs lined up in what could only be battle formation, strange silver spears held aloft in salute. In front of this impressive army was a silver chariot, surely power-driven, gleaming brightly under the twin suns, in which stood a huge Glerg clothed in what Teddy could only think of as chain mail on whose head rested a plumed helmet – surely their leader. Indeed it was – the great Glerg general, Gorgo!

"We salute you, Teddy! And we salute your mother!" he said. "We want your brave spirits and your pure hearts to help us in our fight against the dreaded Frets, our only enemy, but a formidable one."

He handed spears to both Teddy and his mother.

"I'm very sorry," replied Teddy, his stomach churning, his eyes filling with tears as he held out his trembling hand to receive the tall spear, "but I'm not brave, because I don't want to kill anyone. I'm of no use to you!"

"Take heart, Teddy. We never kill; it is strictly forbidden. These spears cause numbness and they cause pain, but they never ever cause death! Come, ride with me in my chariot, Teddy – you will honour me with your presence."

So this was how the great General Gorgo and the brave Captain Teddy came to be at the head of the Glerg army on the day of the Glergs' greatest victory, a victory that would be talked about in every corner of the galaxy of Andromeda for thousands of years to come.

Suddenly, the ground beneath them began to shake, heralding the approach of the Frets. In response, the Glergs lifted their spears high and began to stamp their feet, shouting out their battle cry, "Glergs to Victory, Glergs to Victory."

In the distance, Teddy could just make out dark shapes moving over the sand. Gradually a squeaking sound filled the air and swiftly the awful sight of the hideous Frets was upon them, their huge spidery legs quickly covering the distance between the two opposing armies. Their horrendous beaks snapped open and snapped closed, each time releasing a very long, very vicious and very lethal green tongue which, once wrapped around its hapless victim, spelt death and so the battle was now upon them.

Hardly had it begun when tragedy struck. All of a sudden Teddy was aware of a huge green tendril, like that of some mutant tropical vine, winding itself around General Gorgo and lifting him from the silver chariot. As the Glerg disappeared from view, Teddy heard him shouting out, "Fight, Teddy! Fight, Commander Teddy! Fight to the end."

Teddy therefore raised his spear, urged his army forward and shouted out the battle cry of the Glerg in his loud, firm voice. His clear, logical mind saw the battle like the game of chess he so loved to play and he placed his troops at every moment in the most advantageous positions possible, so eventually, after several hours of hard fighting, victory was theirs. The defeated Frets, overwhelmed with shame, dragged their exhausted bodies away over the sand dunes and into the sea where they drowned themselves as was their tradition after such humiliation.

The first thing that Teddy wanted to do after the battle was find his mother and make sure that she had not been hurt. Soon he found her, kneeling among the sand dunes, comforting the great General Gorgo as he lay dying, his orange face now grey and his bright green eyes dull and full of pain. Teddy was still stroking his head and holding his hand as he died, the General's heroic soul floating off into a parallel universe, just a breath away from where they were.

As Teddy sat on the sand crying, he felt a hand on his shoulder and heard the voice of Lorha, the dead general's second-in-command and now the new leader of the Glergs.

"You must leave us now, Teddy," he said, "You and your mother must go back through the wormhole to your own part of the universe and to your own time. If you don't go now, the space-time continuum will be irretrievably damaged and we can't let that happen, even for you."

"But when I arrive home will I still be able to walk tall, and walk straight and talk firmly?" asked Teddy anxiously.

"I'm so sorry, Teddy," he replied, shaking his head sadly, "but that can't happen because that's not how things work. But we'll always need you – for your brave spirit, for your clear mind – so we will come for you, again and again and again. And each time you will walk with us, and run with us and shout out our battle cries for us! Commander Teddy!"

They did indeed come back for him, many, many times and with that he was content.

The Ups & Downs of Life & Death - Tony Henderson

As he lay in bed asleep, a cockroach ran up his bare arm and onto his shoulder. With a shudder he awoke, scooped the filthy creature off, and heard it scuttle away on the wooden floor.

He pushed himself up, and his eyes swept the room: mildewed walls, stained curtains and a naked light bulb, its shade long since broken and abandoned. From his bed he stared out through the dirt speckled window over Hong Kong's roof-tops. Instinctively he reached down and picked up the bottle of whisky, his only companion when he woke up each morning. He poured a little into the cracked glass by his bed, and quickly swallowed it. Clatter from cooked-food stalls in the street below came through the open window. He could hear animated chatter from families having their breakfast, perched on tiny wooden stools on the pavement.

Early heat, coupled with the hubbub from below, aggravated his headache. He realised, not for the first time, that alcohol so soon in the morning was stupid, especially before going into work. He'd let his cleaner go some weeks earlier to try saving on costs, and now the state of his apartment reflected how his life was deteriorating. The whisky had left a sour taste in his mouth, so he stood up and slouched towards the kitchen.

As he glanced back into his bedroom he flinched as he saw the filthy sheets on his bed. What time had he got home last night? Good grief, he was still wearing his suit! He grabbed a bottle of milk from the refrigerator; other than a can of beer and a few mouldy-looking vegetables, it was empty. He found a box of cereals in a cupboard, took an unwashed dirty bowl out of the sink, and dribbled some breakfast flakes into it. As he tilted the bottle over the bowl, a glob of congealed sour milk fell out. In fury, he threw the bottle against the kitchen wall where it shattered, sending shards scattering over the floor.

There was silence for a moment, until a shrill, complaining, Chinese voice from the adjoining flat, penetrated with ease the flimsy walls. Screaming obscenities at her relieved his tension and a shouting match erupted. It continued until honour was appeased. The fact that he understood little Cantonese and she no English, seemed irrelevant. Shrugging, he returned to his bedroom, undressed, then staggered into the bathroom. After a cursory toilet he donned his only other suit, which did not look as if it had been slept in, and some scuffed, worn shoes.

After slamming the front door behind him, he waited for the lift. When it came he entered and stared at himself in the mirror. God, he looked a mess. His headache still hammered behind his temples as he fought his daily battle with the ancient lift – never serviced in the two years he had lived there – which eventually stuttered its way down to the ground floor. He snarled an acknowledgement at the Chinese watchman who was managing to scoop a vulgar mixture of rice and what looked like animal innards into his mouth, picking his teeth, at the same time, with a grubby toothpick.

When he emerged into the Wanchai side-street the oppressive heat hit him like a wet blanket. After an inquisitive stare, some nearby children resumed their morning chore of skilfully shovelling their breakfast rice into their mouths. Their parents continued eating and talking to each other, while giving orders and advice to the local food stall proprietor, and shouting greetings at neighbours and passers-by.

Squinting into the morning sun, he waved away the taxis parked nearby on the street, knowing he needed a walk to clear his head before appearing in the office. Ragged child-beggars were everywhere and he passed a blind man who sat holding on a length of string a jabbering monkey, which was running up and down the pavement waving a small pewter cup towards every passer-by.

He stepped under a shop awning to try drying his face a little with a sodden handkerchief. He was nearing Central, the business area of Hong Kong, and wealthy Westerners in safari suits sauntered leisurely down the road, while wide-eyed peasants from the country circled them, staring curiously. Drunken sailors, of all nationalities, after a heavy night in Wanchai, staggered along the street or sat retching in the gutters. Chinese pedestrians glared at them in disdain.

Hearing a grunt behind him he turned, and saw a coolie lean against the weight of his cart. The large wheels wobbled as the man set off at a run, and he skipped out of the way when the coolie shouted something unintelligible at the top of his voice, his straw sandals slapping the concrete as he careered down the pavement. His ragged blue trousers, held up by a thin length of string, flapped at his skinny knees like sails in the breeze.

He followed and, despite himself, grinned at the havoc as pedestrians ahead jumped for cover. Then his shoulders drooped as his spirits fell. He had never felt so lonely. How things had changed. When he arrived he was full of enthusiasm, and had soon begun to fall in love with this wonderful city. With plenty of money, life as a bachelor was carefree, exciting and fun. He'd known he had to be careful about drinking, which had always been his weakness in London. However, in that city he'd had sensible friends; here in Hong Kong life was different; there were no restraints.

Initially he had kept to bars and nightclubs. Life had been exhilarating, with a succession of young willing Chinese women eager to go to bed with him, albeit only for money. Then a Chinese whore had introduced him to a gambling club and soft drugs, and later heroin. It transpired she worked for gangsters and he soon found himself massively in debt to a triad organisation.

Sacked from his high-paying stockbroker's firm, his British public school accent had eventually found him a poorly-paid job in a shipping company, where his employers reckoned an educated expatriate accepting a Chinese clerk's salary was a rare bargain. With no relatives in the UK to fall back on, he'd sold nearly all his possessions to repay the triads, and his life had quickly spiralled out of control as his savings vanished.

He spent his day pushing papers around his desk and retired, as usual after work, to a succession of seedy bars where he normally drank alone. He'd long since lost the few friends he used to have in the heady days when money, being no problem, he'd spent his evenings in expensive restaurants and smart clubs.

After eight pints of beer, barely soaked up by a revolting cheese sandwich, he staggered back towards Wanchai. A number of whores had propositioned him but had rejected them all. Now, alone and depressed, he regretted not taking up one of their offers.

He lurched drunkenly into his apartment and threw himself into the only chair. During the day he'd remembered this was his twenty-first birthday yet here he was, drunk and friendless. He gazed around the squalid room in despair, sank his head into his hands, and wept.

His doctor had prescribed sleeping pills and tranquillisers to get him through his depression, so deciding he needed a good night's sleep he retrieved them from the bathroom cabinet ...then picked up the whisky bottle and glass from his bedside.

Clutching the pills in his sweating hands he staggered into his kitchen. Looking down at the tablets he closed his eyes and considered the unthinkable. His neighbour started a shrill tirade at her husband, choosing that moment to play her part, as if aware of the nearby drama. A cockroach suddenly ran out of the sink onto the draining board beside his elbow.

With a shudder he filled the glass with whisky and took a handful of pills. He brought them to his mouth, and then hesitated. Angered by his weakness, he threw the glass at the cockroach, dropping the pills on the floor, before rushing out of the apartment to the streets. He must get away for a moment from the place that reminded him of the temptation of drink, drugs and gambling, which had almost destroyed him. He needed to see the beggars out there, the drunken sailors, and even the man with the monkey: people with far less than he, but who had the courage to face their miserable lives – a courage he was determined to find.

The lift was still on his floor, and he threw himself in. With a crash, his fourteen stone smashed into the back panels, the last straw for the frayed cable above, which snapped.

A first fleeting revelation of something wrong was as the lift started to fall with its internal door still open. His brain, befuddled by drink and confused by his mental trauma, was slow to absorb the shocking truth.

His coffin plummeted eight floors to a rendezvous with death and the toothpick-chewing watchman on the ground floor, foolishly balancing his chair against the lift wall.

The Garden Rake - Vonnie Giles

As the November dusk fell, the garden rake was leaning against the tree trunk, alone, unattended, unwanted, until Sarah, knowing that she was unobserved, went over to it and started to stroke its wooden handle and, with her foot, to rub its metal tines. A light shining from the sitting room window suddenly illuminated it and made her heart quicken. David must have put on the table lamps so that he could see to make up the fire.

So she continued with a sly, satisfied smile on her face: stroking, rubbing, stroking, rubbing! Suddenly the front door opened and out David stepped.

Quickly, she stopped caressing the rake and stared fixedly at him, wondering about him, trying to read his thoughts, but, as usual, he was a closed book to her!

"Do you ever think about your old girl friends, David? And where they are now? Or perhaps you know that anyway!"

"Why should I want to remember? What does it matter? It was all such a long time ago! I've got you now, haven't I?"

"Have you? Have you really got me? I sometimes wonder. Half the time I don't think you even like me."

"I don't have to like you, but I'm here, aren't I! That must tell you something!"

"And love! What about love?"

"Love?" He smiled wryly, grabbed the rake and walked into the middle of the lawn. It was a strange sort of conversation to be having; out there in the twilight, gathering the autumn leaves, dressed in woollen hats and thick leather gloves against the cold. Especially a conversation about the nature of love, which for her was a totally alien emotion! Though no one, of course, would ever have guessed. She'd always been a good actress, able to put on a good show!

She cringed as she watched David suddenly direct an angry kick at the rake over which he'd just tripped. She so hoped that he hadn't hurt it! She would go over later and comfort it! She then felt drizzle beginning to fall on her face and began to shiver. A nice warm brandy was what they both needed and a nice big log fire in front of which to drink it! Sounded so cosy, didn't it? To nestle up to each other on the deep sofa! To sit there together with the table lights casting a homely glow. A sham, of course!

Recently she had begun to think about those she had sent away. Especially about Ralph, the one who had said that his heart would break into a thousand pieces if she ever left him – poor Ralph, she'd wiped him from her life with no more thought than wiping a fallen crumb off her sleeve.

It had always been about control, of course, the fear of rejection. Dump them, before they have a chance to dump you! That way you always keep the upper hand...

She stood pouring their drinks while David closed the curtains, shutting out the world, when, out of the blue, he asked, "What happened to Ralph, by the way, the one who used to follow you about like a lost sheep?" How strange! She sincerely hoped he hadn't suddenly acquired the ability to read her thoughts – what an inconvenience that would be!

"I'm afraid, I've absolutely no idea what happened to him – and I care even less! What a strange question ...but while we're on the subject, what happened to that woman you used to hang around with! What was her name – Mary, Marion?"

There was a three second pause.

"Marion", replied David sharply. Sarah, of course, knew very well that the woman's name had been Marion; she never forgot details like that! Then another three second pause. "Yes, Marion!" David repeated.

Sarah waited as she slowly removed the top of the soda bottle. She could sense that more was to follow and so she took her time letting the liquid fall into the glasses ...almost drop by drop. In fact, it seemed that time had stopped in its track, until, suddenly, David said what he had to say. "I love her, Sarah, and I think I'll die if I don't see her every day of my life!"

Sarah gave him a quick sideways glance and then screwed up her eyes as she considered his words. Not what she'd expected to hear; especially not such a brazen confession, not such an easily spoken revelation – dear me, no – but it didn't really matter, did it?

It wasn't after all the first time that this metaphorical slap in the face had happened to her. Anyway, the solution was near at hand: in fact, half an arm's length away in a little bottle at the back of the drink cabinet. Little did he realise the mistake he'd just made. "That sounds to me, David, as though you've been just a tad deceitful!"

As she surreptitiously poured a good measure from the little bottle into his brandy the anger welled up inside her! A serious misdemeanour, a very serious misdemeanour indeed, had been committed; one for which he would truly pay, as the others had done! Peter, Gavin and Tony: they were the ones whose rejection she hadn't seen coming and who were now helping to keep the garden nicely fertilised.

She'd always remembered an episode from 'One Foot in the Grave' where Mr Meldrew had accidently burned a tortoise to death in the garden waste: a situation that she'd found hilariously funny, but not as funny as what she was going to do to David. Let him join the others who had thought that she was expendable!

At any moment the narcotic in his brandy would have done its work – so convenient working in a pharmacy – then she would unceremoniously trundle him down to the garden shed in a wheel barrow. There she'd scrape his body with the ever faithful rake until scraps of flesh hung from him like deep pink ribbons and blood ran in rivulets onto the wooden floor. It was a ritual which was really quite unnecessary, since he would be so deeply drugged that he'd be completely incapable of fighting her as she consigned him to the autumnal bonfire, but it was …well, it was just a little something that she enjoyed doing!

After the event she would, of course, do what she always did – deny to herself that it had ever happened, shut it out, cut it out of her awareness and keep it firmly locked away in her subconscious never to surface. Until the next time!

Once again dressed up warmly against the bitter chill and carrying a can of petrol, she went to the bottom of the garden to make sure that the bonfire was still alive and was shocked to notice the poor rake lying haphazardly under a bush where David had obviously flung it. Tears came to her eyes as she gently lifted it and promised that very soon, in the gloomy darkness of the shed, it would have its revenge.

As she undid the petrol can, she was suddenly aware of someone moving behind her …and a voice speaking softly into her ear. "Surely, Sarah, you didn't expect to get away with such an obvious ruse, did you? Believe me, you little bitch, you're going to pay for what you did."

"What did I do, David!"

"You killed him!"

"Who did I kill?"

"My brother!"

"Your brother?"

"Ralph, Sarah, Ralph!"

"Ralph was your brother! But I didn't kill him! I swear to God I didn't!"

"You didn't shoot him, or stab him or poison him, but you might as well have done! He loved you, Sarah, and you discarded him, breaking his heart in the process. He killed himself because of you and you're going to pay for it." With that, quickly sprinkling the petrol onto the smouldering heap of garden waste, he grabbed her beloved rake, her particular fetish, and hurled it into the bonfire.

Sarah's screams filled the air as she flung herself after it …but whatever mischief David had intended was denied him, for she suddenly rose up in front of him: the blackened rake in one hand and a flaming brand of wood in the other. His hair immediately caught fire and soon he was moaning in agony, his face a blistering mass of burnt flesh.

Her cheeks now wet with tears and from the falling drizzle, she knelt down on the damp grass, took off her coat and wrapped it tenderly around the charred rake. Keening and wailing over its suffering, she rocked it in her arms and crooned soft words of comfort.

"David's almost ready for us, my angel! And when he is, then we will avenge your hurt and you will be healed!"

Big Brown Eyes - Irene Hogg

Big brown eyes looked pleadingly out through the glass in the patio door. Two pairs of adult eyes looked in with despair and dismay.

"Nice one, Sula! That stupid dog has managed to lock us out." Panic in the ranks. "What can we do? There's no way in!" squawked my husband like a headless chicken, totally over-reacting before collapsing on a garden chair.

"Don't panic. Don't panic till I tell you," I placated. A childhood spent in the tenements of Clydebank is very handy on these occasions. So, as my husband flopped, head in hands, deflated like a punctured balloon, I went into action.

One of the bedroom windows on the ground floor was open, albeit behind a locked mosquito screen. Nothing to it! Two broken finger nails (newly manicured), a couple of wire-serrated wrists and I was helping shove my husband's heaving backside through the window.

"I was ready to put my shoulder to the door!" he exclaimed as the computer chair rolled away from under him, suspending the same backside between window and floor. Crash!

"Yes, dear," I said and moved to the patio door to await the grand opening. I stood with Sula beside me. Gordon opened the door and the penny dropped. What was Sula doing here at my side? She had been trapped in the house as we were trapped outside. Ah! While we struggled to gain entry, the dog had used the same paw/handle technique to open wide the front door and was watching our antics, obviously wondering, "Why don't they use the front door?"

Yes, nice one, Sula.

We now have a key hidden outside the house.

Broken manicured nails and raw wrists. What a contrast to my last spell of forced entries when scraped knees, elbows, knuckles and palms were all part of a day's play. Every summer the doors and windows of the two, three and four storey tenements would be flung open, and every summer a quarter of the occupants would find themselves locked out.

No need for locksmiths. The distraught woman (it was always a woman) would scan the street. A child would be selected, depending on the mode of entry. Small, skinny ones were picked for the through-the-letterbox option. A lot of soap usually accompanied this, and a wire coat hanger.

Wiry athletic boys were chosen for first and second storey entry through the bathroom window. There was always a large, rickety, rusty iron waste pipe with a good foothold. Basic equipment for this manoeuvre was a strong pair of sannies (sandshoes) with rubber toes and soles to shimmy up the pipe. Raw knuckles, scraped knees and elbows were badges of heroism guaranteed with this mode.

The 'big yins' were for the ground floor where some forcing of window catches with a knife might be required, or to provide a solid platform for another conscript.

Whereas most of the children could be grabbed from the street, occasionally a mother had to be involved. Far from forbidding the use of their wean, they usually came along in a supervisory capacity.

"Maw, ah've skint ma knee," would draw the response,

"Well, don't rip yer troosers. Get them aff."

So the child would fly onto the desired window ledge. "Ah'm stuck!"

"If you dinna get in that windae I'll unstick you aw right, and dinna break Mrs Morgan's teapot. She left it in the sink."

Being tall and lanky when young, I was a much-in-demand housebreaker. How nice to think that half a century later I haven't lost my touch.

PS: Sula locked me out again on Sunday. Gordon was in the house but as Status Quo were 'Rocking All Over The World' he failed to hear my cries for entry.

The Luncheon - Vonnie Giles

"You little bastard!" she thought, helping herself to a second portion of the delicious chicken offered to her by the butler. "Yes, I'm watching you. Can't stuff the food into your greedy mouth fast enough, can you? Pity it doesn't bloody well choke you!"

"You old bitch!" he thought, viciously cutting the last piece of meat on his plate. "I can feel your beady eyes upon me and I know damn well what you're thinking."

What happy thoughts between a mother and her son, weren't they, but what else could you have expected? After all they both had murder in mind. He wanted her money and she wanted her revenge and the unfortunate butler caught in the crossfire of hate and resentment ...what did he think? What did he want? Well, his thoughts and wants would have surprised both of them but that will keep until later.

The sombre, airless room was now silent, except for the unpleasant sucking sound that Philippe made as he gnawed the final morsel of chicken between his sharp, little teeth. The watery sun that was shining half-heartedly through the window suddenly gave up the effort to illuminate the room, discouraged by the dark furniture and the heavy velvet curtains. Rain began to splash against the glass as Madame Béraud, pale and flabby-faced, put down her knife and fork and sat, straight-backed in her black bombazine dress, staring at Philippe. The butler, smiling to himself and sensing that trouble was about to break out yet again, beat a hasty retreat across the thick red carpet and out into the hall.

Glancing across the table at the place laid for her dead daughter, as it was every mealtime, Madame Béraud managed to prise her pursed, disapproving lips apart and let the usual torrent of recrimination spew forth.

"Have some more wine, Philippe. I would so hate to think that you were stinting yourself. We mustn't let you feel neglected, must we? I'm sure your poor sister would have loved a little glass of something, but, unfortunately, when you're lying six feet under in the cold, damp earth feeding the worms, that's just not possible, is it?"

Philippe, for once obeying his mother's exhortation, poured himself another glass of red wine and in a single motion gulped it down, the red liquid dripping down his chin and onto the table like blood. Pity it wasn't blood, her blood, his bloody mother's blood!

"It's not my fault she's dead, Mother! You were the one who insisted she should come riding with me. I didn't make her horse rear up and trample her to death, did I?"

"But it wasn't her horse, was it? It was your horse and you should have been the one mounted on its back. Yours should have been the body lying lifeless on the edge of the forest – not hers. Not my darling daughter's! You're just like your useless father – the luck of the Devil's always with you – as it was with him until finally, thank God, he took one glass of port too many and fell dead at my feet. So what I say to you, Philippe, is drink deeply, so deeply that you end up just like he did – but don't take so long over it, that's all!"

Backwards and forwards, forwards and backwards across the table went the sniping and the sneering, while the glassware and the silverware gleamed and glittered happily on its surface. Then a brooding silence fell once more upon the scene and the protagonists were left alone with their thoughts.

Gustave, Jean-Luc, Jean-Pierre, Didier – they could all go to smart restaurants and to the theatre without having to count every last centime, they all had allowances that meant that their gambling debts could always be met, they didn't have to walk around Paris looking like paupers – but, of course, they didn't have a tight-fisted, dried-up, old witch for a mother! He wanted her dead, dead and buried and the sooner the better, because he was frightened, he feared for his life, he really did – the sort of people from whom he had been forced to borrow money would have no mercy on him if he defaulted.

Yes, dead, that's how he wanted her! The sheer pleasure it would give him if only at that precise moment she were suddenly to fall forward, and, with a plop, bury her face in the sauce-covered pieces of chicken that remained on her plate: how relieved he would be!

Madame Béraud was having an equally pleasant daydream. She was conjuring up a vision of a very sharp piece of glass finding its way into his portion of the raspberry meringue that was to be the next course. That would serve the miserable, spineless creature right for causing his sister's demise.

So, thus continued the deliberations of Madame Béraud and her son! The festering that went on in those two hearts would have amazed their acquaintances. Poisoning, stabbing, shooting, an unexplained tumble down a flight of stairs – or something a little more subtle?   What method would best satisfy their murderous intent?

Suddenly Philippe stood up, pushing his chair away.

"For God's sake, Mother, can't we have some fresh air in this mausoleum. It's stifling!" Across the room he went. He opened the French windows and stepped out onto the balcony where the rain had now stopped. What a relief to see the green trees that lined the boulevard, to hear the carriage wheels and the clip-clopping of the horses' hooves on the cobbles, to watch the vendors and the smartly dressed citizens of Paris going about their business. This was life, this was freedom, so different from being incarcerated in the claustrophobic apartment.

As he looked down upon the scene below, Philippe was suddenly aware that his mother had come out onto the balcony to join him, her scent of camphor and lavender filling his nostrils. She stood with her shoulder against his and then turning her head began to whisper into his ear. This was her moment of triumph!

"Poor Philippe! How pathetic you are!" she hissed, her saliva falling onto his cheek. "I know all about your little financial difficulties, but, believe me, there's no money coming your way. Even by killing me, there will be no money, because it's gone – all of it! And at precisely four o'clock tomorrow afternoon, this apartment and everything pertaining to it will no longer be mine, and I shall be on my way down to Villefranche-sur-Mer to live with your Aunt Clothilde on whose charity I now have to depend. And as for you, well, you can do what you damned well like. I would think that suicide would probably be your best option, don't you? A much easier death, no doubt, than the one your creditors will provide for you."

The anger and frustration that had eaten into Philippe for so long suddenly erupted, as he grabbed his mother by the hair, turned her around and rammed her head so hard against the window that the glass shattered. The shards that remained in the wooden frame, he used as a blade across which he moved her neck backwards and forwards, so that there could be no doubt whatsoever that she was well and truly dead.

Then, for the second time that afternoon, Philippe decided to take his mother's advice and, covered in her blood, he climbed onto the balustrade and propelled himself into space. The last thing of which he was conscious in this life, as he plummeted downwards towards the street, was the sound of the chestnut seller's voice screaming in horror and, as he lay on the cobbles, his final breath was well and truly squeezed out of his body when the hooves of a horse clip-clopped over him. Madame Béraud would have considered this poetic justice!

As for the butler – no, he hasn't been forgotten, for it was he, bearing aloft the luscious raspberry meringue, who discovered the somewhat gruesome scene. He'd long been considering leaving Madame Béraud's service and, as insurance against not finding a better paid situation, had for some time been pilfering small items of value. His late, by now virtually decapitated, mistress had, of course, noticed their absence and had erroneously blamed her errant, by now virtually unrecognisable, son. The pieces of silverware he had placed on the table earlier that day, in preparation for the luncheon, had especially caught his fancy and, before you could say 'raspberry meringue', there they were nestling in his capacious pockets!

That evening, in a back street somewhere in Paris, surrounded by their small hoard of valuables, he and his buxom mistress consumed an especially delicious pudding. No prizes for guessing what it was! Well, you know what they always say – waste not, want not!

The Face - Linda McGillycuddy

When the woman known as "Mary Mac" first approached, Kate was more than a little suspicious. She had learned the hard way not to be taken in by a smile and a kind word but over time, and with plenty of patience from the older woman, Kate had begun to trust her as she could few other people and she started to unwind a little during their conversations.

Kate lived in a bedsit that she kept strictly private. There was little enough privacy in her world and she treasured the small space with her few books and pictures; she didn't want grubby hands fondling her stuff as they did her body on a nightly basis. She had learned to move to a different mental state when she was working and could distance herself from what was going on but, at home alone, she could be herself.

A few chats over coffee though, with Mary Mac, weren't enough to open up her past, her thoughts, but she liked the woman well enough to tolerate her well meaning intentions. She was actually Sister Mary Immaculata if you please, now in trousers and sweatshirts, but had laughed when she said she drew the line at makeup.

She lived amongst the Soho community and was a familiar figure with the working crew. Kate would alert her to any new young blood on the block, not just out of good intentions but also because she didn't want to be moved farther down the pecking order. The way Karl ran the show, one minute you were premier division, the next you were the human version of Charlton Athletic.

Mary Mac knew Kate was her real name and that she was from the West of Ireland but that was all, so Kate was surprised when Mary told her that her family wanted to contact her and there was a letter. She had left the small rural town many lifetimes ago believing her face would be her fortune and that her good looks would guarantee her entry into a glamorous life.

As a child, in a family of strong men and stronger women, she had stood out like a delicate flower in a field of wheat. They marvelled at her fine features and fairy-like curls that framed her face. Everywhere she went, they said she had the face of an angel.

Once in England, the few dodgy photo-shoots and occasional bar work soon took a downward turn and when she could no longer continue to write home with stories of agents thrilled to take her on, and how she was on the road to discovery, she had stopped writing altogether. Karl had taken her on all right but she was on a road now that she couldn't get off.

The letter stood unopened for a few days, silently waiting while Kate worked up enough courage to open it. A few drinks and a little hit just to take the edge off was the plan, but then she would wake hours later and would have to wait until after work.

At last she was sober enough to be able to open the letter. It was from her Mother. It wasn't a very long letter but spoke of the love they had for her still and how they missed her. Her Father was now long gone, but had always spoken of his wish for his golden child's return. The letter said that they suspected life had not worked out for her as they had all wished and after many years of searching for her there would be no judgments, no questions, only a loving, warm welcome for her in her home.

It contained a plane ticket to get her there.

She pictured the kitchen of her old home, the warmth from the large range in the heart of the room, the constant mugs of strong tea and, in the mornings, the smell of freshly baked bread, apple tarts and sizzling rashers frying. She could almost smell the food and felt her stomach contract with the want of it all.

She looked down at the ticket in her hand and quickly threw

some clothes into a small bag. Her excitement rising now, she imagined her brothers and how they had grown into fine men with healthy children around them. Her Mother would look older now no doubt, maybe a little smaller with age but she knew that her clear blue eyes would light up when she would see her beloved daughter, her golden child.

She dressed carefully in her civvies, plain dark trousers, buttoned-up blouse and jacket, definitely no high heels, she was heading back home: no place for stilettos there ...just a little bit of gloss for her lips perhaps? She applied the lipstick in the mirror and turned to walk out.

Just before putting her hand on the door, she paused and walked back to the mirror to look at her reflection. She stared at the brassy blonde hair, which had long lost its lustre and then slowly appraised the hard lines and scars that told of a thousand encounters. She searched in her eyes for the sparkle of her youth, the girl her family once knew. There was nothing there and the girl was nowhere to be seen.

Kate slowly took off her plain trousers and jacket, put away her bag, changed again into her working clothes and zipped up her long black boots. The plane ticket fell to the ground unnoticed. Closing the door behind her she went out, into the street.

The freezing cold air stung her wet cheeks but she just kept on walking.

Season of Mists & Mellow Fruitfulness - I. Hogg

Soft and gentle, my husband's voice lilted round the room. As I gazed out of the window, the soft orange glow from the sodium streetlights in the village were dimming and vanishing beneath the enveloping fog, which crept up the valley towards our farm.

Curtains closed, I turned on Gwen's nightlight. John finished the story and kissed his daughter on the forehead. "Sweet dreams," he murmured as he left.

"Mummy, do I have to go to school tomorrow? Can't I go up the hills with Dad and David?"

"No, Gwen. You're going to school. Dad and David can manage the sheep on their own."

"David doesn't have to go to school and it's the last day before the mid-term holiday." Gwen's eyes pleaded. "Please, Mummy, don't make me go. I don't feel well."

"Given I teach at the secondary school, how would it look? Now put on your mittens and we'll wrap you up against that nasty fog. I don't want to go to school either but we both have to. Now, give me a hug."

Only as I said the words did I realise that I really did not want to be in the valley tomorrow. Like Gwen I wanted to be in the mountains with David and John, where the sun would be shining and the air clear and fresh.

Snuggling into bed I wrapped my arms round John, warming my freezing feet on his. "John?" A short grunt acknowledged me. "What time are you leaving in the morning?"

"About seven. Sun up."

"You will be careful, won't you? The ground will be sodden

after all this rain. Don't let David go near any of those bogs, even if there is a sheep stuck."

"No. Now go to sleep, woman, I'm tired." He turned to cuddle me, his breathing growing soft and slow.

I lay for hours, unable to sleep. Sometimes, in the darkened room, the wind would carry the lowing of a cow or the rush of overflowing streams on the hillside, but the fog muffled the sound. Insidiously phantom fingers of cold entered the farmhouse. Finally I slept, my breath forming puffs of damp warmth despite the gnawing chill I felt in my heart.

An ominous crash followed by a cry of terror from Gwen had me dashing out of bed. The room still blacked out, I bumped into furniture. The hall light came on as I entered Gwen's room.

"Sorry, love. Accident in the kitchen. No harm done!" bellowed John's voice from below. I rocked her fears away, assuring her that lump of a fifteen-year-old brother would pay for whatever he'd broken. Eventually she laughed and we headed for the kitchen just in time to see the two miscreants heading out the door.

"John, David. Come here!"

The bashful pair turned and smiled. "Sorry, Mum. I done it. Don't be too mad. You never liked that plate anyway."

"Come on, my pretties. Give us a kiss and tell us we're forgiven."

After kisses all round the menfolk headed for the hills. Gwen and I readied ourselves for school.

Outside the fog grew increasingly thick like smog.

"I don't like this, Mummy."

"Hold my hand. We'll soon be there. And then it's the holidays. You can run in the sun every day."

Appearing through the fog, the school's lights channelled mothers and children to the entrance. I left Gwen chatting her way inside but blowing me a kiss as I headed for the Senior School.

From my classroom I could hear the children at Assembly. 'All things bright and beautiful' is a hymn I always associate with spring and summer but not autumn. Strange, I thought, as

Class 4A settled to work.

Thunder crashed and roared, reverberating around the classroom. Anxious teenage faces looked to me for assurance. I thought of John and David out on the hills. The thunder grew to a continuous deafening roaring, and the building trembled and shook. Black water was gushing around the school, a tide of black was rising, children were screaming. Outside in the street some were trying to run, others were rigid, looking towards the school: then darkness.

Cloying mud was rising over us, climbing the walls, enveloping the windows, which shattered under the weight of rock and slurry. I felt myself consumed in blackness, fighting towards one tiny ray of light ...and then nothing.

My eyes opened to the light and silence.

In that silence you couldn't hear a bird or a child in Aberfan.

The Suitcase - Vonnie Giles

Dmitri, shabby and sick with fatigue, stood on the bleak, windswept station platform; his battered suitcase, reinforced with string, comfortingly touched his foot. As long as he knew it was there he felt safe, because it contained everything that mattered to him: photographs – of his ageing parents in Moscow – of his wife and son, Galina and Maxim, both long-buried somewhere in the frozen wastes of Siberia: his little notebooks with the smudged charcoal drawings of them that he had made during their last holiday together all those years ago and, especially, his music manuscripts into which he had poured all the love he felt for his friends and family, each vibrating note a memory of how they looked and spoke.

"Comrade, move yourself if you don't want to get killed," said the railway official. "We cannot shift the crates if you stand there."

Dmitri, oblivious to the man's voice, was still lost in thought, his mind focussed on the contents of his suitcase.

"Comrade, move yourself," said the railway official once more. "I won't tell you again."

Suddenly Dmitri became aware of the man's voice and the touch of a hand on his arm as he was pushed gently away from the edge of the platform. "You were dreaming, Comrade. It pays to keep awake or you will find yourself train-fodder. The train won't stop for you or anyone else, only perhaps for Stalin himself, and maybe not even for him if he falls into its path."

Dmitri clutched his coat closer around his thin body, realising that it was now snowing lightly, flakes beginning to fall on him and his fellow travellers. From his pocket he took out a cigarette and lit it, taking comfort from the momentary warmth of the flickering match.

Feeling himself drawn into the blue haze on the edges of the flame he could see tiny pulsating points of light that sparkled and twinkled and, as he climbed up and down the long white stairways, some going somewhere, some going nowhere, he sensed that in some strange way his existence had shrunk to an infinitesimal size. It was as though he had slipped into an alien world where everything seemed unpredictable yet possible, everything nothing more than a probability. Nevertheless, he was able to take comfort from the familiar feel of the suitcase handle clasped snugly in his hand, but when he glanced down at the suitcase itself, it was shape-shifting, strange, different and, as he loosened his hold, off it floated – up this stairway, down that – until he finally lost sight of it.

"I did warn you, Comrade," said the railway official, as Dmitri found himself lying on his back, having been struck by a large wooden crate that was being trundled to the front of the platform. "But where were you? It is as though you have just appeared from nowhere, you and your suitcase!" Readjusting his wire framed spectacles, Dmitri put his hand out to reassure himself that the suitcase was still in one piece and then, slowly and painfully, picked himself up amid the sniggers of the other passengers who had been grateful for anything that would break the monotony of their long, cold wait. He was trembling with tiredness and an aching sadness had entered into his soul. What he most desperately craved for, at that moment, was what was contained in the suitcase: his old life full of love and laughter: a life dedicated to his wife and son and to playing his music in the great concert halls of Russia.

As he looked through the thickening curtain of snow, he suddenly glimpsed her in the distance: Galina in her favourite gauzy, pink dress, her bare arms lightly tanned and, behind her, Maxim, laughing, as he chased a yellow butterfly. The trees were full of shimmering blossom and there were bluebells at their feet. Unexpectedly they both looked at him, and waved before fading away into nothingness.

"Why the smile, Comrade?" asked the railway official, peering at him curiously. "You must know something we don't. Share it with us, Comrade!"

Behind them, the station clock ceased to stretch, bend and twist and its hands, which had been furiously going backwards, resumed their normal pace and direction.

Everyone on the platform gradually became aware of the distant rumbling of the approaching train. Suddenly, however, a group of young men excitedly surged forward, and one of them, in his eagerness, knocked against the suitcase and sent it slithering across the slushy paving towards the edge of the platform. Dmitri, horror-struck, cried out in panic, then, feeling a sudden, agonising pain in his chest, he fell onto his knees, his arms outstretched in despair as he watched the suitcase fall beneath the wheels of the train.

The railway official, who had witnessed the whole event, was heard later to exclaim, "So much emotion expended on a shabby old suitcase! Not worth dying for, that's for sure!"

Whirling stars, chaotic planets, asteroids tumbling past like giant potatoes, dark energy driving the universe outwards towards infinity: Dmitri sat on his upturned suitcase, his cello, so long absent, once again between his knees. Long shadows stretched on the stony ground as twin orange suns sank beneath the horizon. The heavy gravity made the action of drawing the bow across the strings a tremendous feat but, nevertheless, the dark, deep notes resonated wondrously and brought tears to his eyes. As far as he knew, the music was completely unknown to him and how it had come so insistently into his mind he had no idea, but play it he must!

"As the Comrade lay dying," observed the railway official later that evening to his wife, "I thought I heard music, as though someone, somewhere, were playing a lament for him. It was most touching and strange." Looking out of the window into the darkness, he added, "I shall pray for you, Comrade."

Inside the suitcase, on which he continued to sit, were wispy fragments of memory whose meaning eluded him. If only he could remember: something to do, he thought, with another place, another world, where he had been both blissfully happy and desperately lost. Then suddenly, in a split second, the universe seemed to halt its endless journey through space and time itself disappeared.

Now, there existed for Dmitri just one sublime, glorious note of music, one present instant of pure happiness where the past had ceased to be and the future would never exist: a timeless state of being where he was now sufficient unto himself.

Give Me Strength - Linda McGillycuddy

Laura gripped the Styrofoam cup so hard that it cracked, spilling coffee all over the hospital canteen table. "Damn, oh sorry, did I get you with it?"

"Not to worry only a bit, I was feeling a bit dehydrated anyway"

They laughed, and then sat in awkward silence with the ice now broken, unsure how to continue.

"Any news on your son yet?" they said simultaneously and laughed, then both felt guilty at the same time. Impossible to laugh at anything when such precious lives hung in the balance, a small tilt to the right and no more, a little shift to the left and perhaps good news...

A school trip to the Scottish highlands with canoeing, abseiling and the like had brought them to this point. She couldn't believe the enthusiasm of her normally inactive son about going; she often worried that he was going to morph into his computer. How she longed to see Ryan lounging around now with his joysticks and controllers instead of this limbo coma-land in the far north.

The coach, travelling around sharp corners with an inexperienced driver, had cut short the adventure before it had even begun. This stranger sitting beside her was the only remaining parent still as anxious as she, with his son in surgery. The two boys, previously unknown to each other, were now bound together in camaraderie of silent pain and the unknown.

"The surgeon said they should know very shortly, if they have relieved the pressure but every minute seems like an hour doesn't it," he said. "The signs seem good though. What about your boy, how is he doing?"

"They can give me no guarantees, no telling with a coma; will he waken in a minute, a month, or…"

She was grateful he didn't ask any more questions, and she excused herself to make yet another phone call. You would think that Trevor would keep his bloody mobile turned on, even if he was in France on business. Her ex never failed to disappoint and his blithe confidence that everything would turn out alright and that he was sure she could cope on her own was just another item to add to the list of why he was such a prat. A recorded message confirmed her wasted effort.

She returned to pick up her coat just as the surgeon was talking to her coffee companion and she waited until they were finished. It was obviously good news, so she approached with some confidence to enquire.

"It was a success and he is out of danger," his hands were trembling and there were tears in his eyes as he ran off to make his all-important phone call.

After sitting with Ryan for another few hours, she returned to the guesthouse, which had become her temporary home. It was all flowers and stony charm, which was lost on her at the moment but she was grateful for the warmth of the dining room and the log fire which crackled and spat. Her coffee companion came in and approached her table and asked would she mind some company?

She had always hated eating alone although she had become more accustomed to it and so smiled at him to join her. His name was Stephen. He was keeping vigil in Scotland alone, as his wife had to look after their ten-year-old twin girls and her elderly father who lived with them. It seemed strange but she felt herself unwinding from the tension that had coiled inside her since the accident three days before.

After the food and wine she could even laugh when he said that the next time she allowed Ryan to go abseiling down cliffs she should insist he get out of the coach first. "Because there will be a next time, he will recover, be sure of that." He reached out and held her hand as if he could give her the strength to make it happen. She felt her bottom lip tremble as if she were a child again, and couldn't speak. All the other diners had long gone and he led her out of the dining room and upstairs. She paused outside her room and asked him would he mind coming in for a little while, she just couldn't face being alone; he walked inside and closed the door.

He poured out some scotch for them both and they sat down on the end of the bed like two guilty teenagers. As she swirled the ice around the glass and felt the warmth of the alcohol she wondered what on earth she was doing. He leaned over and picked up her hand and rubbed it. Laura leaned against him and just breathed his scent and felt the stretch of his shirt against his chest. It was wonderful to not feel alone, she had never felt so intimately connected with another human being in her life.

His warm hand caressed her back under her shirt, and they fell back on the soft bed; they forgot the outside world and just felt the warmth and comfort that they could give each other. When they came together, it was as if a dam had broken and with all its release she felt overcome with emotion, she cried uncontrollably for her son, for herself and the years of loneliness and was grateful for the strong comforting arms holding her and his lips kissing her face and hair and soothing her with softly murmured words.

Laura awoke with a sensation of not being able to move. Her eyes adjusted to the dawn light and realised that a strong rugby thigh had her pinned down. She freed herself gently and dressed as quietly as possible. She couldn't allow herself to think of the night's events, only of Ryan and how she must be beside him at his bedside.

She arrived at the hospital to find that the Matron, looking for her, was approaching, coming down the corridor with a beaming smile. "We think Ryan is coming around, the Consultant is with him now, come with me."

Entering the room, Laura ran to her son's side and held his hand. His eyes were fluttering and eventually opened. He licked his dry lips, and said with a croak, "I'm so thirsty, can I have a coke?" They all laughed.

Laura felt her knees go weak with relief and someone put her in a chair beside the bed. She looked at her son's face in wonder and thought nothing in life would ever hurt her so much again.

Later that morning, going outside to get some air she saw an ambulance being prepared for departure and Stephen pacing up and down beside it. She was embarrassed and started to walk away but he called out to her. "I am so pleased to see you before we left, my son is well enough to travel down south to our local hospital, and so we will be on our way, but any news of your son?"

"Yes, thank God, he is awake and chatting a little. It seems that we have all turned a corner, and no hearts broken..."

They stood facing each other in the hospital car park unsure of what else to say.

He moved to climb into the back of the ambulance, and she called out, "Goodbye Stephen, I am very glad to have met you."

He smiled at her and said, "and I you."

She turned and went back inside with lightness in her heart and a smile on her face.

In Another Lifetime - William Daysh

He'd arrived early but she was already there. She hadn't spotted him. She didn't know what he looked like anyway, so he felt comfortable watching from behind his newspaper. Standing alone under the clock, she seemed bewildered and out of her depth in the bustle of Waterloo Station. She was attractive, if not as stunning as he'd secretly hoped, and young, very young at just twenty-three. He knew that much already.

Observing her slyly like this, he felt like a voyeur, a stalker, and he was uneasy about it. It wasn't like him at all, but he was curious now that she was there, in the flesh. As he watched, all the doubts he'd been brushing aside for days suddenly returned with a vengeance. If only she hadn't shown up he could have just walked away with no misgivings at all – well, no more than he had already but it was too late now. She was there, a few metres away, exactly as described, and he'd never stood up a woman in his life. Hesitating, he walked slowly towards her.

"Susan?" His voice rose higher than he'd intended.

She spun round and blinked twice, as if she couldn't believe her eyes. "Yes," she said eagerly. "Are you…?"

"…'Fraid so," he said quickly. She grinned generously and held out her hand.

"Pleased to meet you."

In spite of the confidence in her eyes, her hand felt like a frightened sparrow inside his. "Likewise." Max forced a wry smile and shook his head slowly. "You know, I've had some experiences in my time, but this one takes the biscuit."

A small thundercloud drifted over her gaze. "Well, it's a first time for me at least," she added.

Max grinned awkwardly. Meeting like this was beginning to feel like a mistake already. "Anyway, I'm pleased you came," he lied, then added brightly, "so how about a bit of afternoon tea in a quiet corner somewhere? We ought to get to know one another first, don't you think?"

"Fine, but please don't go to a lot of expense. You don't have to impress me. I'm no big deal."

He raised a hand, palm upwards, and pointed to the exit.

As they moved off, his hand reached out instinctively for her arm then sneaked back into his coat pocket. Together, they set off across the station concourse, separated by an awkward zone of detachment. In the confines of the taxi their conversation led into one cul-de-sac after another, and there was mutual relief when they pulled up outside Claridges.

Yes, Max confessed to himself, he was pleased when she seemed impressed. As they were shown to the table he'd reserved, he noticed her gaze panning the room in the hope of seeing someone famous there, and he smiled to himself. The Maitre d' gave him the young enough to be your daughter look he'd come to expect these days, and he responded with a withering glare. Once they were seated, the tension eased and eye contact became easier. Max could feel his weatherworn face being carefully scrutinised.

"We all get them, you know …sooner or later," he said with a grin.

"I know. But I like lines. They say a lot."

"Mm... Like what an old fart I am?"

"I'm not thinking that. I'm told they're lines of experience …a sort of route map of your life. I'm just trying to find the way to the real you."

"How profound! But you don't want to go there, believe me."

"That's where you're wrong. I do."

Max began to relax as she gazed wistfully around the room. "I'll bet their lives aren't half as interesting as yours."

Before he could answer, she fixed him with a hard, unblinking stare. "Well, shall we begin?" she said abruptly.

The sudden change of mood left Max's smile hanging in mid air. "OK," he said wearily, obviously reluctant. "Where do you want to begin?"

"Well, you could start by answering one fiercely burning question that has been festering away ever since I first spoke to you. Quite simply, WHY?" Max took a deep breath as Susan watched with lips pursed. He examined the tablecloth as if it were an abyss that he was about to fall into. Max knew this moment would come, but he still wasn't ready for it. He never would be. He cleared his throat nervously.

"I don't know that you'll ever understand, Susan, but I'll try to explain." He faltered for a moment. "Your…"

Her hand darted over the table and touched his arm. "Before you go on, could you tell me what I'm supposed to call you? I've been wondering about that for days."

"Max,' he said weakly. "Why not call me Max? Everyone else does." She seemed disappointed. "As I was about to say, your mother and I were not actually married when she announced that she was pregnant with you." He gave a little shake of the head. "Not only that, I had a job that took me abroad a lot." His mouth turned into an inverted crescent as he paused to gather his thoughts. The heat of her impatience began to flush his cheeks.

"Is that IT?" she snapped, spreading her upturned hands on the table. The icy tone of her voice unsettled him. "Oh well, that's all right then," she added. "That seems like a perfectly good reason to have me adopted." Max suddenly felt the whole thing about to run away from him.

"Hang on a minute. There was more to it than that …much more."

"Oh really? Like WHAT exactly?"

Max drew his head into his shoulders as if it was about to rain in Claridges. "Look. I knew all along that this would be damned difficult. I've had weeks to prepare for it, but that seems to have made no difference at all. This all happened a very long time ago, Susan. It was in another lifetime, when I was very young, and so much has happened since then. This is one skeleton I couldn't just stuff into any old cupboard. It was bigger than that. It was a tragedy, and we needed to get on with our lives. I buried all this twenty-three years ago …somewhere where I wouldn't find it again. Don't you understand? An autopsy now is the last thing I want, but I know I have to do it …for you."

There was a sudden flash of lightning in her eyes. "Look," she spat. "I'll make it easier for you. You already know that I've met Helen several times, sorry ...my mother. You know what? I really like her," she added, pointedly. "So she has already told me everything. It's simple – she fell pregnant with me, and you said that you wouldn't marry her unless she had me adopted. Then, when she did just that, you didn't marry her anyway!"

Her words crashed onto the table like shattered crockery. Max examined the pieces in silence, but she was too angry to wait for a response. "How could you do that to a pregnant woman? How could anyone that I am part of be as despicable as that?"

The words stung Max badly. He began to bristle. "Wait a minute, young lady …hold your horses. I don't have to take that from you. That's just one side of the story. There is another. You may not like it, but you should know the rest of it. When you've heard it, just remember this. I never wanted it to surface again, ever …for your sake not mine."

His gaze wandered vacantly across the room as he searched for words. When he found them, he looked directly at her and spoke slowly and deliberately. "The whole of this saga turns on this one thing. No one could prove that I was your father. The truth is that I have always believed I am not." He waited for it to sink in. Susan was visibly shaken.

"When your mother and I lived together, she was always desperate to get married. She wanted to tie me down. She tried time and time again, but I didn't want to. She even booked the Registry Office twice! I needed space, for Christ's sake! I'd only just crawled out from under the wreckage of my first marriage, and I had a small son to think about, too. What Helen and I had was very good, but it was a very on/off thing, for all sorts of reasons. In my own way I loved your mother very much, but she pushed too hard …and I kept pushing back."

Susan studied his still handsome face. It was flushed now with agitation, but she knew why Helen had clung to him like a limpet. She'd seen the photos of him when he was young, and they said it all.

"When you came along, we were living with my mother. That whole divorce catastrophe really set me back – in my head, in my job, financially, everywhere – and the ink wasn't even dry on the divorce papers. Right then, all I could think about was making a fresh start …particularly at work. I needed to catch up on lost opportunities. What I didn't need was another marriage that I might regret. It would have been a disaster. On top of that, I was constantly away on business with my new job but your mother began to stifle me again. She kept on and on about getting married, and the harder she tried, the more I resisted. Sadly, I didn't have the guts to just end the relationship. I didn't want to hurt her. She loved me a lot. I knew that but I just couldn't reciprocate …not as intensely as that. So I was completely trapped."

The genuine pain and regret in his eyes was a revelation to Susan, but she still wanted answers. "But that was no excuse for forcing my mother to choose between abortion and adoption. There was still another option …the decent one."

"Look, Susan. I don't know why Helen told you that, but it isn't true. I never forced her to do anything."

"So why was I put up for adoption then, at six weeks old?"

"That was her choice. I made mine and she made hers."

"What …like you saying to her – I definitely won't marry you if you have this baby, but I might if you don't. How bloody arrogant can a man be?"

"It wasn't like that!"

"Really? How was it, then?"

Max took a sip of his now cold tea and struggled with some painful memories. "You shouldn't have happened at all. Your mother was on the pill. How could she have got pregnant? I'll tell you. Because she deliberately stopped taking them, that's how. Don't you see? That was her means of tying me down, once and for all, but I saw through that. You were a gamble that she took all on her own without consulting me. I didn't want marriage and I didn't want a child, but she used you to change all that."

Max paused and glared around the room. Susan's eyes never left his face. It suddenly looked drained and tired. For the first time since they'd met, the flames that had been roaring in her mind began to subside and out of the ashes came the faint flicker of understanding.

"What did you mean about not being my father?" she said, flatly.

He shrugged. "Just forget that I ever said that."

"Just like that? It's a pretty devastating statement to make if it isn't true. Is it true?"

Max sighed and passed a hand across his forehead. "That was my mother. Mothers are credited with a sixth sense about these things. The first time she saw you she studied your face for ages, and said nothing. Some time later, when Helen and I were having one of our many tearful discussions about the situation, my mother took me aside and told me something devastating. She said that she had no doubt at all that you weren't mine. She told me that when I went away again after telling Helen that marriage was definitely not an option, she had a petulant fling with another bloke. I knew that anyway, because Helen told me herself. I didn't have a problem with her seeing someone else, but my mother insisted that she knew that you were this other bloke's child, not mine. I couldn't believe it at first, but then I became convinced too."

"Perhaps you wanted to be."

"Perhaps."

Susan reflected for a moment then tossed her hair. "My God, what a family! And ever since I found out that I was adopted I've been wondering what it would have been like in a normal family. How bloody bizarre! I was much better off where I was. In fact, I think you did me a big favour."

"Probably. How is it with your family life?" he said, hoping to deflect another outburst.

"Normal. Very stable. Dad is an accountant. You know, the

steady, reliable type. You know exactly where you stand with him …no surprises. Mum, too. She's lovely. All in all they've given me a good life. I've had love and a very good upbringing."

"I'm really pleased." A knot of remorse lodged in Max's throat. "So how do they feel about you seeing me now?"

"Same as they did when I saw Helen for the first time …nervous, worried, and apprehensive …but trusting. It must have made them very insecure." The lump in Max's throat got bigger. Without knowing why, he suddenly felt very proud of her.

"When did you find out that they aren't your real parents?"

"They are my real parents," she said quickly, with her eyes flashing defensively. Max shrugged his acceptance.

"I didn't know until I was eighteen. True to type, my honest, decent dad told me on my birthday …the day I had the right to know. It must have broken their hearts to do that, especially when they volunteered the news that my mother had left her address at the adoption office. Very nobly, they offered to help me trace you both, if that was what I wanted."

"And you did."

"Yes. You can't imagine how I felt. It's devastating to be told that your parents aren't really your mother and father after all. Your legs get cut away with one sentence. Suddenly, your whole life has been one big lie …and you were the only one who wasn't in on it, but you wouldn't know anything about that, would you?"

Max shook his head. It was all he could do to show his remorse.

"Eighteen?" he said, hoarsely. "Why try to find us now – five years down the line?"

"I don't know really. My emotions were in turmoil. Should I, shouldn't I? At first, I was curious about my parents. Well, you'd have to be, wouldn't you? But then I got so angry with the pair of you that I had to find you. I wanted to bang your heads together because when I was a helpless, six-week-old baby you didn't give a damn about me. You just threw me away."

Max sighed and buried his head in a hand.

"I suddenly had some new emotional baggage and no one to dump it on…except you two. But when I came face-to-face with Helen, she wasn't the heartless bitch I imagined she'd be." Her gaze dropped out of focus. "Meeting your mother for the first time is a strange experience. We got very emotional …floods of tears and all that girlie stuff but now we're good friends, and I'm glad. Now I understand why she had me adopted. She didn't abandon me after all, and she didn't throw me away. She couldn't help herself. She was forced into it by her love for you. She sacrificed her baby to have you …and she didn't. I know now that she's regretted that all her life."

Max passed a hand across his forehead. "I know, I know. God, it's strange how things pan out in life …or don't, as the case may be. Timing is everything. Perhaps if I'd met Helen at a different time in my life, if you hadn't come along when you did, if, if …it just goes on and on. It's strange really, I always wanted a daughter. But when you're young, you think there'll always be enough time for everything. I lost contact with my son. He was taken off to live in Australia. Then, when things really began to come up roses for me, I discovered that I couldn't have any more children. I won't go into the details now, but I just couldn't. So, for the rest of my life I've been standing on the sidelines watching my friends enjoying their kids growing up. So, on that one decision twenty-three years ago three separate lives got screwed up. That takes a lot of living with."

Susan could see that he was on the verge of losing his composure. She reached out to make contact. "Hey. It's OK," she said softly. "I didn't know. It sounds as though you've both had a worse time than me."

For a while Max looked at her, unable to speak. His eyes were soft and glistening. "Can you ever forgive me?" He croaked.

"Of course. I already have …both of you. I'm sorry now that I put you through this. I needed to know, that's all."

"And now here you are, face-to-face with a bastard you think is your father?"

"Yes and yes to both questions."

"After all this, do you really need me to be your father? I'm old now. All the best years have gone."

"Don't be daft. Anyway, I like older men," she added, mischievously. The sparkle in her eye faded quickly. "Yes, I do want you to be my father ...but only if you are. Are you, Max?"

"Yes," he said, hoarsely, trying to smile. "At six weeks I couldn't tell. Now I know."

She reached for his hand and squeezed until her knuckles were white. "So do I."

Max didn't know what to say, but he suddenly felt more complete than he ever had. "Darling daughter ...how I've missed you."

Darkness - Irene Hogg

Mildewed crevices in the window corners and decades of grime presented a blank canvas that screened the interior from the outside world. Every window turned the house in on itself, protected or prevented intrusion. There was no clue as to which room served which purpose. The house had encased itself but he had to know the truth of what lay within.

Grasping a clump of damp grass, Edward's gnarled hands began clawing away the grime again and again, fuelling his growing frustration and anticipation. The fresh and dewy scents of grass mixed with the mouldy spores of the crumbling wooden frames. Sunlight pierced the gloom within. Edward glimpsed a piano, bringing a flash of remembrance only to be lost as a cloud passed; piano and memory were expunged.

Age and neglect had withered the fabric of the house. Had he left it too late? Edward slid down to rest against the crumbling brickwork. The sudden exertion brought beads of perspiration to his brow. Pain speared his muscles, bones ached. For a moment his mind fought to regain clarity. Why was he here? His memory was fading. The past now belonged, lived in the present: the present forgotten in an instant.

Rested, Edward struggled upright. Gentle, soothing, regenerating rain drifted from iridescent clouds. Rays of sunlight danced and fell to the ground, dazzling, dappling moistened fields, hedges and woods. A single shaft shot above his head. He turned. The light was not repelled by the glass but pierced through to the room beyond. A flaw in the time capsule: a broken window, a way in but not for him. He needed to create his own access to his memories. Returning, to a past he had sought to obliterate, would make him whole again, wouldn't it?

Darkness meant fear. He had lived his life in the light. Even at night the darkness was not allowed to dominate. In darkness he could not be watched, and they had watched him very carefully for seventy years. Now in his eighties and released, he sought to explore the dark house and the memories he thought were there to terrorise him. Why?

Edward destroyed the lowest window: every frame, every pane of glass smashed, illuminating within, creating access and lighting his way to the past.

A kitchen, solid furniture, a stone sink filled with mould-encased dishes: rust, like old long-dried blood, encrusted metal surfaces. Floorboards creaked, and cracked beneath his weight, resentful of his presence. A pantry door swung gently in the new air, but the air could not vanquish the fetid atmosphere of decay.

Again the pantry door swung. Edward saw, briefly, the long cane within: the cane for when he was a naughty boy. Naughty boys were punished and locked in pantries.

Edward had been naughty today. He took himself to the pantry, grasped the cane. Holding out his left arm he flayed the extended hand, raising red stinging weals. His final blow broke the skin; now it was time to stop.

He was ready to face the darkness and there he would stay. Slowly he pulled the door behind him to end his life in the darkness of his memories. The same darkness that for weeks had hidden his dead parents.

Now he remembered. He had been a naughty boy.

The Treadmill Murders - Vonnie Giles

Little mice on your treadmills, that's what you were, going on unheedingly with your mousy lives, blissfully unaware of the danger you were in! And there was I looking through the bars of your cage, watching you. Running faster and faster you were – in a circle – getting nowhere, absolutely nowhere, however hard you tried.

You poor dears! Well, how could you possibly have hoped to escape – not with me on the scene, with my beady eyes firmly fixed on you both?

Of course, nowhere is precisely where you are now – as far as I know. No one in the whole world can tell for sure whether that is true or not, and now all that's left of you both are these little signs of life: a pair of your black patent high heeled shoes, Lizzie, and your pretty chiffon scarf! As for the wallet and the straw hat – well, those were yours, of course, weren't they, Henry? Here they lie in a forlorn heap, all alone, unloved and unclaimed in a buttercup field: near a river, under the cascading willow trees: on a perfect summer day. Your own fault of course, but then – you sorely underestimated your common enemy – because I'm not as green, my dears, as I'm cabbage looking, as the saying goes.

It didn't exactly take an Einstein to suss out what you two were up to – not after discovering that very unusual and very expensive chiffon scarf that now lies at my feet, tangled up in the sheets of my marital bed – and, of course, all the many subsequent little signs of hanky-panky! It must have been so frustrating for you to know that you couldn't escape from me, couldn't open the door of your cage and run off together into the big, wide world.

Of course, the one who holds the purse strings, as I do, wields the power. How you must have cursed my very proficient solicitor for his meticulous arrangement of my will, for even with me dead (and I'm sure that delectable idea had passed more than once through your minds) you would still have been trapped because, dear Lizzie, you might actually have been forced to get off that fat backside of yours and find some gainful means of employment, and you, Henry, would certainly have found yourself strapped for cash: no more expensive bottles of wine for you, no more elegant made-to-measure suits, no more luxury holidays under subtropical skies!

It was just such a pity for you both that I suddenly got bored with the idea of supporting your expensive tastes. I didn't need either of you. You were just a drain on my resources! Anyway, you needed to be punished for trying to get one over on me! Besides, what earthly good were you to me – all you both did was make my nice tidy house look messy – so why not get rid of the pair of you? So I did, and what a satisfying experience that has been! I think I must have some sort of God-given talent for murder!

However, intelligent and alert as I am, I'm unfortunately not infallible, which is why I've had to return to this buttercup field to collect these little items, these little incriminating pieces of evidence. After all we don't want anyone suspecting that anything is amiss – not just yet – let's leave that a tad longer, shall we? Though I suppose that I shall have to report your absence within the next few days but, with my flair for storytelling, I'm sure I can conjure up some plausible reason why I didn't inform the police earlier.

I just thank my lucky stars that no one walked this way during my unthinking thirty minutes, picked the items up and took them to the police station. After all, we don't want to leave any clues that might lead to your watery whereabouts before it's absolutely necessary, do we? Silly me, not to have remembered that they were here: if I'd been more methodical, more careful this would never have happened, but then I haven't ever murdered anyone before. I suppose I got rather carried away by the occasion, didn't I? Compounded by the fact, of course, that I had two victims to deal with, not just one! Another time I would be better organised…!

Oh, what on earth am I saying ? I hope I haven't suddenly got a taste for murder – wouldn't that open a can of worms! What on earth would the neighbours think? A serial killer – that nice Mrs Jensen – surely not! What is the world coming to they would all ask?   So there was I, a couple of hours ago, sitting comfortably in the branches of a willow tree, looking down upon your shenanigans. What a disgraceful pair you were and what disgusting things you got up to. And what a surprise for me – I didn't know that you had such an inventive imagination, Henry! As for you, Lizzie – well, how on earth were you able to bend that fat body of yours into such extraordinary positions? …and the language! – out in the open air too!   What if the vicar had been strolling over from the abbey church – I think his sensibilities might well have been a little offended! Though with vicars, of course, you never can tell!

Anyway, your cage was soon to be rattled and your little treadmill brought abruptly to a stop, for who should suddenly descend, Tarzan-like, from her arboreal hiding place but me, devoted wife and sister of the frolicking lovers? Yes, little mice, there I was …just like the farmer's wife, with my carving knife in my hand. My goodness me, how you did run …fortunately for me, in the direction of the river and, even more fortunately, in the direction of the weir. Hand in hand, two blind mice, not seeing the danger in front of you, so in you toppled and over you went. I didn't even have to touch you! How easy murder is!

Now, my carving knife, recently honed to perfection for the purpose by that pleasant little man on a bike, can be returned to the knife rack in the kitchen without a stain on its gleaming blade – Status quo unchanged!

It's so nice to be back home again, to be able to relax with a large gin and tonic and to ponder on today's achievements. I've already put the items back in their usual places – Henry's straw boater on the hat stand in the hall, his wallet in the bedside table. As for Lizzie's things, well, I've just dropped those onto the floor of her bedroom because that's where she would have left them. It's almost as though they've never left.

However, I have to say that I'm already missing the idea of a cage with a treadmill inside it – rather clever imagery that, I've always thought, but then, of course, I seem to possess so many talents. I wonder how the police will fare when they come up against me? "Oh, Inspector, where can they be…? It's been three days now. I'm frantic with worry, but I just didn't want to bother you! You all have so many dreadful problems to deal with, without this as well!"

Of course, I might decide to leave it for five or six days. I wonder how much difference that would make to the state of the bodies. I'll have to look it up on the Internet! Not, of course, that it would matter much in this case because I didn't lay a finger them, did I? "Oh, Chief Superintendant, I love them both so much – my dear husband and my darling sister – I couldn't live without them. You must find them for me! Please!" …all this with glistening tears in my big green eyes, my voice husky and broken with emotion (shades of Joan Greenwood there, I think!)

Perhaps tomorrow I might, just might, pop along to the pet shop and buy a pair of nice little mice, in a nice smart cage, with a nice new treadmill. A replacement, if you like, for the dear departed, but the first thing I'd have to do, of course, would be to speak to those mice very seriously, set firm rules for their behaviour, start off as I mean to go on, because I'm not sure if treadmills are one hundred per cent silent and I don't think I would care to hear little extraneous noises all day long. I do also hope that mice don't squeak and snuffle a lot!

Oh yes, there would definitely have to be very strict instructions to be learned…

"Tread mill, start! Treadmill, stop! Squeaking and snuffling cease!"

Any infringement, any disobedience by those two naughty mice and I might have to wield the carving knife again.

"Lizzie and Henry," I would say to them, "stop that noise, get off that treadmill, because otherwise I shall open your cage door and I shall cut off your tails with my carving knife!"

Though, of course, I could always drown them in the lily pond in the garden.

Carrie Cadell Reports - Irene Hogg

"For God's sake, she looks like the bloody Snow Queen. When can we call this a wrap? My feet are frozen. Is she ever going to stop farting about on that goddamned carousel? Hey, Jake, haven't we got enough footage yet?"

"I'll see what I can do, but I'm just her PR. It's up to Carrie."

Oblivious to the disgruntled murmurs around her, Carrie Cadell snuggled into the full-length white faux-fur coat, peeking coquettishly from behind her muff as man-made snow wafted around her. Footage for the TV trailer showing her riding a variety of horses on the carousel was finished; now they were on the definitive shot for the Christmas cover of Radio Times. "I have another idea. Why not shoot me sitting backward? It will be funny and different."

Geeze, thought the photographer, why can't this woman just do what I ask instead of jumping in with her 'wonderful' ideas? "OK, but this has to be it."

"Ken, I'm only trying to make it perfect."

"Carrie, we've been here since 5am. The lights are red hot and there's a crowd gathering. Remember, we're outside Covent Garden. We can't dominate the entrance for much longer. No more."

Carrie struggled into position below the carousel's canopy.

The power of the blast sent her sprawling between the cavalcade of horses' hooves. Dancing carousel lights extinguished, gentle snow dissipated by shards of glass and spears of metal shot past, and a plume of acrid black smoke billowed over her. Covent Garden was disintegrating, being blown apart, tearing itself out of existence. In the silence, flames created an inferno, rising up to clutch at surrounding buildings.

Conscious one moment, then drifting into dark terror, it took Carrie time to realise where she was. Her body lay at an awkward angle while a heavy weight forced her stomach onto another strange object. Ears ringing, she began to push, ignoring the sharp debris and grotesque limbs of broken horses. Her breath was shallow: tiny inhalations of smoke and soot. Her eyes were covered with this noxious mixture, and sightless she fought on through the pervading darkness, ignoring the splinters that scratched and tore at her body as she emerged from under the upturned carousel. She cleared her eyes and saw for the first time the Hades that had been full of light and carnival fun. Refusing to allow her retching stomach to empty in reaction to the surrounding carnage, one thought came to her: Even Oprah never got a chance like this to make her name.

Staggering between bodies, past people who appeared to scream in an agony she could not hear, she searched for the film crew. Finally she found one of them slumped behind the Outside Broadcast Unit. A rivulet of blood leaked from his shoulder and his head was gashed. Using her muff and a piece of wire, she staunched the bleed. A video camera lay nearby. Now on her knees, she pulled it to her and checked it worked. She mimed to the crewman propped against a wheel to start shooting as she crawled into the hellish mayhem behind her. She could not hear the wails of the approaching sirens or her own voice, but she began her recording to camera.

"This is Carrie Cadell reporting from Covent Garden at 7.30 am. Today one of London's great icons suffered a horrendous death as…"

Later in the day television viewers watched Carrie start her report. Many were in tears as they listened to her soft Scottish tones while her coat, now grey, began absorbing the blood she constantly wiped away from her nose and forehead, struggling to describe the events of the morning, unaware that her life blood was seeping farther into the coat with every word she uttered.

Posthumous credits rolled at the end.

Remember Me - Linda McGillycuddy

Everyone knew what had happened to Caroline, but no one ever spoke about it. Even the photos in the house had been taken down, but her wardrobe of slim-fitting clothes still stood testament to her life as if in silent homage. Angie sometimes ran her fingers along the silky dresses when she was alone in the house, trying to catch a trace of her perfume, a sense of who Caroline really was.

Mark would never talk about her. When she met this thoughtful, gorgeous-looking man, two years ago, she was intrigued by the air of sadness that surrounded him like a cloak. When they started dating more seriously he outlined briefly what had happened and how he worried about Nathan, who was then six years old. His body language told her it was not a subject for further discussion but she was determined to unravel this painful piece of history.

His close friends could see how much she cared for Mark and told her how guilty he felt, for not realising something was wrong and getting help for his wife before Caroline took her long and final sleep after months of anxiety following the birth of Nathan. The young boy was certain that it was he who had caused Caroline's stress, so he believed with all the simplicity of youth that he had killed his Mother. They now all had her constant shadow hanging over them, forever young, forever slim, pretty and forever sad.

Mark's Mother Sonia had taken over the rearing of the young boy and was jealously protective of him. Angie could feel the hostility in her eyes even when she would smile and say, "Oh, here you are again Dear, how nice to see you." It was not the most normal of families but they functioned without challenge and without joy until Angie came along.

Sonia's constant presence meant that there was always a babysitter on tap, a glorious irony now when Angie could see how much Sonia resented the time she spent with Mark. More and more Angie had managed to get him to try new things and move out of the safe rut he had created for himself – she did have a small drawer in the bedroom for things she needed for her more frequent overnight stays but never suggested that there might be more room if the second wardrobe were emptied.

Mark smiled and laughed more frequently now but then sometimes closed down on himself as if he had been caught doing something shameful. Angie hated that look, which heralded long nights of a cold back turned against her in bed. Two steps forward and one step back, is still one step forward, she would remind herself, but small steps were no longer enough.

Angie was about to take the biggest gamble of her life. She loved Mark and Nathan and would move mountains to make a life with them. She could even put up with Sonia, and that was saying a lot, but she was not prepared to live in limbo and knew that what she was about to do would literally be make or break.

Although feeling a little sneaky, she persuaded Mark to go along for a picnic on the Downs leaving Sonia behind. Nathan was chattering away a little more than usual in the back seat and, after a while, even Mark was in a lighter mood as they played silly games counting red cars passing by, anything at all that they could laugh at.

When they pulled into the car park at the same time as many other cars and families, it seemed like a strange procession that they could see moving slowly towards the sun drenched field. Some people were quiet and some were talking softly and holding hands. Mark fell silent and looked at her. The little boy picked up on the tension in the air and held her hand a little more tightly, looking at his Dad, who said, "Ok, what's going on here?" She didn't reply but, after opening carefully the boot of the car, she lifted out a large pink balloon with the name 'Caroline' written on it in beautiful silver letters. She just stood there waiting. Nathan said, "Look Dad, lots of people have got balloons too, some pink like ours and some blue."

Angie took a deep breath; "I love you Mark and I love Nathan. I believe we can be a family and be happy together, but there is something we have to do first to make that happen." She kept a tight hold of the balloon in one hand and the boy in the other and started walking. She dared not turn around but could feel her heart beating so hard she thought it would burst.

It seemed like an eternity but then she felt him fall into step beside her. Mark took the balloon from her hand... "I have to be the one to let her go."

A large circle formed with families holding onto each other but smiling at strangers new to the ritual. At an unspoken signal the people holding the balloons stepped into the circle and looked skyward. All at once the pink and blue balloons twirled gracefully into the air, some trailing ribbons which danced and bobbed in the breeze. Angie could feel the sun hurting her eyes as she traced Caroline's balloon on its journey until at last none of the balloons could be seen.

Mark pulled his son into his arms and held him tightly, the boy was crying now as if he knew something momentous had happened. She stood apart, unsure what to do, not knowing if she would be welcome. Then Mark looked at her with tears streaming down his face and held out his hand. She joined them in their embrace holding onto them both as tightly as she could, as if her future, her happiness and very life depended on it.

Little Poppets - Irene Hogg

I clasped my hands together in a failed attempt to stop the tremors that consumed me. My chest rose and fell as I gasped for air. Only my eyes functioned; my body was shutting down, protecting itself from the images on the television screen. Pictures of me hiding my face, desperately trying to push past people, to find sanctuary in my home. A hand grasped and tore my headscarf, revealing a bruised chubby face framed by dishevelled white hair. Hollowed eyes peered out in confused supplication.

Closing my eyes, muffling the sounds as I huddled alone on the sofa amid the shambles of my upturned home, I could not understand how my life of quiet happiness and innocence had been transformed. Now I was vilified, hunted down, prey to the worst traits of society and of people.

"My, how your Rosie has grown, Jenny. How old is she now?"

"Nearly five months."

In her high pram Rosie gurgled, grabbing for the tiny doll swinging from the pram hood. Eventually she succeeded, grasped the doll and immediately began sucking its foot.

"She loves that doll. It's beside her day and night. I can't believe how many generations have played with the dolls you've made. I still have mine and the other day my mum brought hers down from the attic. We were amazed; when we put them together we could see the changes to the uniforms, the length of the skirts, even the style of the shoes."

"It's something I'm good at. I enjoy it and it passes the time.

This year I have a special surprise for the new intake, thanks to the wonders of computers."

"Miss Bannister…"

"Please, Jenny. I'm no longer your teacher or headmistress. Call me Heather."

"I don't like calling you Heather. The villagers always refer to you as Miss Bannister. It seems disrespectful not to. You taught here for forty-odd years. One day this village will show you just how much you mean to us."

"Don't be silly. I'm too long in the tooth to be surprised, but not so long I can't enjoy creating something to welcome the children to their school."

"You know there's another new headmistress this year?"

"I'm sure she'll do a wonderful job looking after the children."

"And there are two more children joining the class but not until day two?"

"Oh dear. Never mind, I'll have a surprise for them as well. Something special this year. See you later. You too, Rosie, you little poppet."

I'd always managed to surprise the village with my antics. My more ambitious and physical exploits had been curtailed recently but I still had the ability to embrace the modern world. Despite this the villagers had given me a specific identity: Miss Bannister the schoolteacher: no children of her own… Such a shame, losing her fiancé in the war in Aden: a little idiosyncratic. That was me, and that was the conversation that changed my life forever.

"Mrs Taverner will see you now, Miss Bannister." The school secretary lowered her voice, "She seems quite nice but very young. They all are these days."

The new headmistress was very young and anxious to create the right impression on the village and its children. "I wonder if we could postpone giving the children their dolls until they are all here?" she said. "We could have them holding their dolls in the class photograph."

"That's no problem at all. Now I know we have two more children I'll have to work faster to have their dolls ready."

"You do know they are from America – New Orleans? They're twins."

"New Orleans! I visited there long ago. I loved the French Quarter and the jazz on Bourbon St."

"Chloe and Jacob are delightful children and I think it will benefit the school if we have a more ethnic and cultural mix."

"Pardon?"

"Chloe and Jacob are black. Do you have a problem with that, Miss Bannister?" The headmistress's tone had become chilly.

"No, no. It's just… I've been working on something special this year. There's a program on my computer and a copying process that allows me to give each child a doll with their face on it. I don't know if it will work properly with black faces."

"We can't be seen to discriminate. I'm sure you'll do your best. Your dolls have become a tradition cherished by everyone. Please call in the day after tomorrow and I'll get Chloe and Jacob to bring in some photographs. Then four days later the class photo will be taken."

Cutting out the material for the school uniform was easy, but as I had guessed, it was trying to create a true image of the children that was the problem. I used photos of black celebrities and tried them out on a variety of dark cloths but they became indistinct. I tried painting the cloths. I tried and retried everything I knew until I fell asleep, slumped forward into a sea of almost grotesque tiny black faces.

Next morning, I awoke in tears. I had never failed a child. I simply had to do something equal to, if not better than, all my previous efforts. Walking towards the classroom my stomach churned and as I entered, the village children cheered and called out my name. With the class settled again, their teacher slipped me the photos of Chloe and Jacob. They sat together and gazed uncertainly at me: beautiful children with smooth black skin and liquid brown eyes. Chloe's mop of hair in two tight bunches tied with pink ribbons: Jacob's shorter hair framing his face with a mass of frizzy curls. Sunlight lit the room and their ebony faces glowed. How could I ever do them justice, portray them as they were?

Now it was the day of the class photograph and the handing out of the poppets. Mrs Taverner gathered the class together. "This is a very important day for you and for the school. Does anyone know why?"

I knew.

Janet Clement's podgy hand shot up. "Please, miss, today the school will be seventy-five years old."

"That's right, Janet. Next week we will have a big celebration, a party for the school's birthday. Now the photographer will put you in your places then take your photograph. This nice man will ask you questions – he's a reporter, and Miss Bannister will give you all a special present."

The children cheered except for Chloe and Jacob who clung together, looking confused.

I felt so tired. For four days I had worked into the night, using the finest embroidery silk, trying to create likenesses of Chloe and Jacob. What no-one knew was that for every poppet doll I had made over the years I had created a replica. My seventy-fifth birthday would be in two weeks. My gift to the school would be these dolls who represented generations of children over fifty years, most of whom were now parents, grandparents, and even a few great-grandparents: each in their class just as they had been all those years ago.

"Miss Bannister, if you would be so kind?" Mrs Taverner ushered me forward. One by one I handed out the dolls. Finally, one in each hand, I offered Chloe and Jacob theirs.

"They're different," said Jacob, looking at the rest. "I don't like them. Take them away." At that moment Chloe let out a scream and threw her doll at me. A tiny pinprick of blood was forming on her finger. "Voodoo doll, voodoo doll," Jacob started to scream.

The rest of the children became hysterical, crying and screaming. Chaos was everywhere. The photographer, madly clicking his camera, came closer to capture the expressions of terror and horror on the children's faces. Staff tried to calm the children while the reporter studied my every expression.

Jacob ran at me, kicking and screaming, "Evil, evil juju."

I fell, and it seemed as if a regiment of tiny hands and feet lashed out before I lost consciousness.

A low murmur of distant voices and occasional rustle of paper dragged me back to awareness. My body felt pain. I lay uncomfortable on a hard bed. My face felt strange. Something hard pressed over my nose and mouth.

I prised open my eyes and squinted against the bright strip light, I moaned and immediately a woman in police uniform was by my bed pressing a button.

"Do you know what has happened to you, Miss Bannister? Why you are here?"

A nurse scurried in, taking pulse, blood pressure, checking oxygen. A doctor appeared by her side. "I don't think the patient will be fit for questioning tonight. We'll keep her sedated until morning then check on her progress."

I heard the policewoman ask what would be said to the reporters outside. "I'll give them an update on her physical condition. After that they will be asked to leave the hospital grounds."

I felt a sharp prick in my arm and again retreated into oblivion.

When the policewoman returned the next afternoon, the doctor insisted on staying and the Reverend Smythe held my hand throughout the questioning. His hand and presence were a comfort.

"A neighbour let us into your home last night, Miss Bannister. How do you account for those miniatures, dated replicas of all the schoolchildren past and present?"

I tried to explain but I could see she sought a more devious reason.

"Can you account for the dolls of the village children being created in a different way from the black children?"

Tears rolled down my face, my voice lost in sobs, my mind cramped, unable to find words to explain.

"You should know the story is now nationwide and you seem unable to provide satisfactory answers. The doctor says you will probably be fit enough to leave hospital tomorrow. We can't protect you after that."

"Heather." It was the Reverend Smythe. "There will be a community meeting in the church tomorrow night. Maybe you can get home then. I'll come and tell you what is decided. Have faith. This is all a misunderstanding."

Faintly I heard my voice ask for a newspaper. I needed to know, had to know, how were the children.

"No, Heather, I'll come to you after the meeting."

So here I lie, huddled against the world but watching myself on a box in the corner, observing the scene a few hours earlier, still hearing the howls and jeers over the noise of the rampaging media.

Reverend Smythe's face appears; there are placards around him. As one microphone is attached to him, others are thrust forward. The faint sound of singing serves as a background to his words. "Today in this world we are too quick to see the bad in people: to attack the innocent because we cannot believe there are those whose innocence and goodness protects them from evil. In their world evil in deed and thought does not exist.

"Heather Bannister is one of those people. Tonight I will lead a congregation of villagers to Miss Bannister's home. There, we wish to show our gratitude for the selfless giving of herself to others. There is no story here of evil but rather we will build an extension to our church in which each and every person can see themselves as children, innocent in mind and body and be thankful she chooses to live among us." As the television cameras pull back to show the procession making its way towards my home, I close my eyes for the last time.

The Rose Giver - Linda McGillycuddy

It started with the roses. Innocent enough, you might think: Sophie was delighted at first, flattered really. The rose seller would offer her a red rose with a smile, in one of the many bars and restaurants in the Costa Blanca Town where she lived and worked, and Sophie would smile and say thank you, laughing it off as an offering from the rose seller on account of her incredible beauty, but he would shake his head and point over to the doorway where only the back of a man exiting the premises could be seen. Aha, so she had a mystery admirer. How exciting! Every night she was out, the roses kept coming but never a glimpse of the buyer, and then little gifts and flowers started to arrive at the Estate Agents where she worked. The other girls were a little piqued that they were not singled out for such special attention but her boss, Martin who was near retirement and had seen it all regarding conmen, clients and nasty surprises, warned her to be careful.

He was right. Facebook messages soon followed, swearing undying love and how they would soon be together. It became more than a bit tiresome when text messages came around – one or two a day; her number was easily available because of the office. Sophie replied to 'The Rose Giver', as her admirer called himself on Facebook, and asked him to stop, telling him she wasn't interested in a relationship right now… When the increasingly intense and sometimes obscene messages became several a day, she told him she would report him to the Guardia Civil, uncertain if they could actually do anything but hoping he would get the point and leave her alone, but he didn't. When she then closed down her Facebook account and changed her mobile number she began to sense someone was following her. She went to a self-defence course and stopped going out after work.

Martin had always insisted that when any of the girls went out on a viewing, he knew who they were meeting and where they were going but he took special care with Sophie as he told her he was very worried about the developing situation. Six months of unrelenting attention from 'The Rose Giver' saw Sophie's nails bitten down to the quick, her hair starting to fall out, and everyone remarking on how thin and pale she had become. She was tired and worn out from looking over her shoulder all the time. The police could not help her, because all she ever saw was a glimpse of a man behind her and no offence had been committed.

The situation could not continue any longer, her health was breaking down and she was a nervous wreck. She gave in her notice at work and moved to a bigger town farther up the coast. Martin helped her to find another job with an old pal of his and Sophie used her middle name, Marie, to start again: anonymous: giving no old friends her new address and new name.

The work was demanding, and she was good at her job. Her new boss was under the impression that she had fled an abusive husband and agreed not to reveal her details to anyone. Sophie/Marie's nails started to grow again and she picked up a bit of a tan as she could now venture out into the sun to sit at one of the seaside bars, enjoying a coffee. The first few times when rose sellers walked near her she would flinch, but they just passed her by, no roses this time. How she hated the smell of roses, the very look of them.

Her little apartment became very comfortable as she added her own personal touches, feeling settled at last. The pokey bathroom had no window but her bedroom had a nice view. She had strong locks put on every door, even internal ones, and the handyman did not even raise an eyebrow when she asked him to put one on both sides of all the internal doors.

When the news came that Martin had died suddenly, she felt very sad, he had acted protectively towards her, like her father would have, but her parents were long gone. Her new boss took the news of his friend's death very much to heart and announced his retirement, confiding in Sophie/Marie that he did not want to die at his desk and was off to enjoy a world cruise. All links to her previous life had now disappeared and with this a change came over her. She walked more confidently, held her head higher and dared to look people in the eye. She became even more successful at work and started to build up quite a bit of money. Life was looking good...

It was one of the many fiesta holidays. She had been out with a few colleagues from the office and was a bit tipsy after the wine. She kicked off her shoes as soon as she got home: man, those stiletto heels were killers! She lay down on her bed without undressing and fell asleep.

It was just a scratchy noise at first, just to waken her slightly, then a footstep outside the door brought her immediately awake. All her fears came flooding back as she realised someone was in the apartment. She knew it was him, 'The Rose Giver'. The door opened and she could see a man silhouetted in the light from her hallway. "Hello Sophie my darling, at last I have come for you." He grabbed her from the bed and dragged her roughly outside into the light.

She was face to face with her tormentor. She forced herself to take a deep breath and use all the techniques she had been taught. She looked into his crazy eyes but, instead of fear, she felt her confidence coming back and her anger rising. He intended to kill her and she had to stop him. She recognised him as one of her early clients, a charming and nice-looking man who had asked her out, but she'd turned him down. She didn't know why exactly at the time; he had seemed just a little too charming.

"It is you, is it?" She asked quite calmly, as she took a step back.

He may have been surprised to see her so composed but he sat down and looked around casually as if this were just an ordinary visit or a date they had organised. She remembered what she was taught at the self-defence class she had attended. 'You are less likely to become a victim if you don't act like one!' Another titbit came back to her as well – The forehead is the toughest part of the body but the temple, well that's a different story...

"Why don't I pour us a drink and we have a little chat, ok?" I'll just tidy up these things..." He sat back in the armchair and smirked as if things were going his way. She picked up one of her shoes and swung it with all her strength at the side of his head. The stiletto heel struck and she leaned down hard on it, with all her weight, against the side of his head. She didn't know if he was dead or not and didn't care ...after dragging him into the bathroom she locked it from the outside. She listened for a while outside the door but all was silent as the grave.

Her heart was pounding as she took from under her bed a case containing all the 'quick exit things' she'd kept as a matter of habit. She changed her clothes, checked her money, then locked the flat behind her and stepped out into the street. Sophie breathed in the cooling night air and steadied herself as she started walking. Fiesta weekend meant that the streets were still busy with late revellers; certainly no taxi driver would remember driving her to the train station.

She passed a couple of rose-sellers chatting on a corner and smiled at them. Now she was truly free.

Fancy Seeing You Here - Jennifer Nesteroff

Janet knew Tom was having an affair. She just didn't know with whom. It wasn't a 'lipstick on the collar' kind of revelation or a faint odour of perfume on the shirt: not even the usual long blonde hair (or brunette, auburn or black, according to the flavour of the month) clinging incriminatingly to the jacket. These were the 'signs to look for' exhibited by the habitual rover, grown careless. No, Tom wasn't that kind of man: he was steady and dependable, always there for her, always ready to assist her in any way – and that was just it. Lately, he had become even more attentive and caring. There could only be one reason for all this. The man felt guilty!

Janet was a quiet and efficient woman. If there was a problem she would handle it as simply and calmly as possible. There would be no need to involve Tom in this, no need for nasty, tearful scenes, no hurt and heartbroken looks. She would tackle this problem and eliminate it in her own way, when she discovered its name.

"Tom, I'm off to the hairdresser. She's not too far away, so I won't take the car. Shouldn't be longer than two hours. Oh, by the way, don't forget to email the Accountant about the insurance".

The hairdresser was in a solemn mood when Janet arrived. It seemed that her grandson was quite ill and she felt that she really would like to go and see him, but didn't want to disappoint her customers. Besides, there wasn't much she could do. "Tell you what," said Janet, "Why don't you run over and see him now for a while. My hair can wait until another day. I have enough to do at home, anyway".

On her return, as she entered the house, she heard Tom laughing and joking on the 'phone in the lounge. He was talking to his fishing buddy, Jack, with whom he would be going on a three-day fishing trip to the coast next week to catch 'some big ones', as they always put it. Passing the dining room table, she noticed Tom's laptop standing there, still open at an email he had just finished typing. She stopped in amazement as her eye caught the first line. 'My sweet Hot Lips' it began. "Well, well, this is not mail to the Accountant, is it my Tommy? I do believe I have you!" She quickly noted the address, which was that of a Company. "Still don't know who you are, do I?"

The letter said something about the fishing trip, which would prevent Tom from seeing his `kitten` next week, but that he would meet her at the lake at 4 o'clock the following Saturday ...and, yes, of course, he had signed himself Hawkeye. "Imagination is not your strong point, is it? You are certainly no Browning." Then she quietly left the house again and went for a nice, long walk.

Jack was in high spirits when he came to pick Tom up the following week. He liked driving almost as much as fishing and couldn't wait to get underway. "Let's go and catch some big ones, Tom, old boy!" he shouted, as he pulled into the drive. Janet wished them luck and waved them off. Returning inside, she sat down in front of Tom's laptop and composed an email from him to Hot Lips.

The drive out to the lake was beautiful. Tall poplars lined the narrow road, hints of autumn's approach yellowing some of their leaves. Soon the whole forest would be ablaze with the last, bright colours of the year. The lake came into view between the trees ahead, sparkling and dancing in the afternoon sunshine. "Ah, such a romantic spot," thought Janet wryly. She parked the car in a clearing some distance from the lake and walked toward the path leading to the shore. She was deliberately slightly late, wanting to have the advantage of seeing her rival first. As she rounded a bend, the sight of a very familiar figure sitting on the grass by the water's edge confronted her.

She stood staring for a moment, the shock erasing from her mind all the bitter, hopefully clever things she had thought to say to this woman. Then she collected herself. "Well now, fancy seeing you here. Waiting for someone, Kitty?" At the sound of Janet´s voice the woman scrambled to her feet.

"Janet! I…I thought…"

"That Tom was coming. No dear, Tom´s away on that fishing trip you thought had been cancelled."

"You sent that email!" Whispered Kitty, "you found out!"

"I did, indeed. Right on both counts. Good for you! You never were very bright in High-School, I remember, except when it came to collecting boys …other girls´ boy-friends. You know what they used to say behind your back, don´t you? 'Pretty Kitty, 'tis a pity her brain´s so itty bitty'..."

"I had friends enough," retorted Kitty.

"Yes, mostly the kind who weren´t hoping to have intelligent conversations with you."

Janet pulled herself up. This confrontation had immediately descended into a ridiculous schoolgirl spat! Strange how the sight of this old acquaintance had caused her to revert to childish bickering! She regained her calm and gave Kitty a disparaging look. "Well, those days are over. Now it seems that Pretty Kitty has graduated to other women's husbands. Got a large collection, have you? Don´t answer that! I do not want to know about your present state of affairs. I´m only here to rescue Tom from your clutches."

"Oh and how do you intend to do that?" Kitty enquired, a look of defiance creeping into her expression.

Janet suddenly realised she had no idea! Had she really thought she would be able to scare off some rival with sharp words and alarming threats? What words, what threats? She had been too clever by half and now she was in danger of making a fool of herself. Then a memory flashed across her mind. Kitty couldn´t swim! She hated water, was terrified of it. At school she had refused even to try to learn to swim and in the end the coach had given up on her. Now here was Kitty, standing close to the edge of the lake and a nice, deep lake it was too, Janet thought.

She rushed at Kitty and pushed with all her strength. Kitty screamed as she was knocked backwards into the water. She surfaced, spluttering and thrashing, the fear of God reflected in her eyes. "Please Janet, what are you doing? You know I can't swim!"

At dinner on the night Tom arrived back, Janet had a funny story to tell him. "I read in the paper yesterday about a woman who found out that her husband was having an affair. While he was sleeping she cut off his wandering little friend and fed it to the dog." Tom looked horrified.

"My God, that's gross! You couldn't do anything like that, could you? No, of course you couldn't. Anyway, ha ha, we don't have a dog."

Janet smiled at him sweetly.

"We could get one."

A Christmas Quandary - Irene Hogg

"Close front tabs. House lights on. Working lights on… and not a word from you actors until you're in your dressing rooms. You're supposed to be training as professionals."

I envied the cast as they left the stage, celebrating the last night of the Drama Academy's annual pantomime. A squealing Princess Aphrodite was trying to stop Prince Caspian upending her crinoline. Stage glitter was still falling from the flies above as someone shouted "Heads!" warning everyone that they could be knocked unconscious by flying scenery.

Eventually, with hugs and kisses the actors departed, their work finished. They left it to the stage crew to remove every trace of the magical kingdom.

With the audience gone, I slid behind the scenery to the stage manager's desk, hoping for a quick chat with John who had been controlling the lighting from the back of the auditorium.

"How many warns did I give you, John," the stage manager growled, "about that special lighting effect and you still got it wrong? Stay right there. I'm coming up. Blithering idiot. I'll call you worse than that when I get there. And as for you, Quizzy, are you on props or are you going to stand there all night?"

"I'm moving, sir." That had blown it. Any chance I had of sympathising with John had gone. Poor John. I really liked him. From day one we had clicked. Opposites attract, I suppose.

Three weeks into a Drama course I had been christened Quizzy. Stupid name but apparently I was always asking questions and never shut up, and when I did keep quiet they told me I had a quizzical look in my hazel eyes. I also had a mop of frizzy blonde hair – hence Quizzy.

John was just John – nothing very special about him. In classes he was quiet, a bit intellectual at times, but we had fun. We enjoyed being together. Nothing romantic: simply good friends who happened to be male and female. When I made him laugh his brown eyes responded to my silliness. He helped me understand the meaning of some of the plays that were beyond me, never once saying anything about dizzy blondes.

One thing he did really well was act. He seemed to absorb any character he played but the acting profession is so competitive that sometimes parts that should have been his went to others. He was still a bit awkward, all knees and elbows as his body tried to catch up with its six-foot-three height.

I'd better get on with my work, I groaned, as someone on the sound system sang, 'Tis the season to be jolly'. Like students everywhere we were set on making merry big time before returning to our various nests and fulfilling family obligations. The actors, now disrobed, leaving black beards, swirling cloaks and gossamer dresses behind them, headed for the nearby hotel bar, but I was still ducking under shell thrones disappearing into the wings as I dismantled the Demon King's Sea World.

David Essex pounded out 'Gonna Make You a Star' as he had done all week. The hotel bar we called our own was noisier than usual, invaded by office crowds because it was handy for the station and only a short distance for present-laden revellers to lurch unsteadily to their trains.

Were any of the usual crowd here or had they gone elsewhere? Drama students are not happy when pushed from their familiar bar-stools by office workers.

Over the tangle of Christmas hats and party squeakers, I thought I could see John, head down, inconspicuous in the far corner. I knew he had seriously annoyed our Stage Management lecturer and actors, so some friendly distraction might jolly him out of his despondency. Squeezing my way through, I finally reached his hunched back, placing my hands over his eyes. "Guess who?"

Slowly his head lifted and he swivelled round. Just as he placed his hands over mine, entwined them and drew our arms down, my jaw dropped.

It wasn't John.

"Oh…er…" What could I say?

Pressed up against a complete stranger, my hair still full of stage glitter, a garish lipstick pout imprinted on my cheek, I stood breast to breast with a well-known politician whose name I could not remember. "I take it you're a Drama student." The smooth rounded tones of a public speaker wrapped themselves around me. Dark twinkling eyes questioned me from above.

Being one of a select few to gain entry to the Academy, I was of course erudite, engaging and oozing confidence. "Er, yes," I mumbled.

"I thought so. I'm waiting to meet your Director to discuss funding."

"Uh, huh," I nodded.

"Perhaps you'd care to join me?"

"I…er…" How could I possibly have mistaken this Adonis for John? Yes, they both had dark brown hair and black polo necks but there all similarity ended. John's polo was cotton and fraying at the cuffs, not soft cashmere sculpted onto a perfect male physique topped by immaculately styled hair. A slight greying at the temples and musky cologne combined to overwhelm me. He was so masculine all I could do was gawp.

"Tell me, what do you do? That is, apart from holding hands with strangers?" Oops. Our hands were still entwined. I slowly extricated my fingers and stood before him like a naughty schoolgirl, hands now by my sides. "What would you like to drink?"

My usual was the pint of lager beloved by students, but that seemed inappropriate. I was recovering fast: sophisticated, in control, one of those screen goddesses capable of withering the paparazzi with a glance.

"Cinzano on the rocks. Thank you."

He raised an eyebrow and ordered the drink which I managed somehow to sip. We exchanged incongruous conversation. He was booked into the hotel for the night ...uh, huh! He would be flying to Melbourne for an Arts Funding meeting the next day, but returning here. "Oh, yes."

He wanted to know more about life in the Academy and my personal ambitions.

Trying desperately not to witter on or present myself as a Drama 'Daahling', I outlined how broad the subject base was, which partly explained my weird appearance. "But I really want to direct. I don't think I'm suitable acting material." Based on my performance since meeting him, I could only imagine he agreed. His expression was more amused than interested.

Then the music changed and, as Barry White was telling me I was 'His first, his last, his everything', I stood there in silence, gazing into the distance, imagining those words were meant for me. Then I realised I no longer had his attention. Our Academy Director was pushing his way through the crowd and bearing down on our corner as only he could. He was a bear of a man with a shock of white hair, barrel-chested and with eyes capable of dissecting one's every thought. I was suddenly intimidated, as if caught with my hand in his candy jar.

"Hey, Quizzy," the barman was yelling in my ear, "what are you doing here?"

Eh, what? I thought to myself. What am I doing here?

"How're ye gonna get home? The trains is off. Flooding in the tunnel."

My jaw dropped for the second time that evening.

"Quizzy?..." my politician questioned.

"Elizabeth, actually," I blushed.

"… doesn't need to worry about that." The suddenly clipped tones dismissed the barman. "I'm sure we could both be very comfortable here." He raised an eyebrow again.

Well, the possibilities were endless. An eminent politician's wife, or would it be a mistress? a man with influence and with an interest in the Arts: a Drama student desperate to become an acclaimed director: a good-looking man and a glamorous future awaited.

"Quizzy, are you stuck as well? Good evening, Duncan. Sorry

to be late but I had to make provision for our poor stranded students. Like Quizzy here. I hope she's been keeping you entertained."

"Of course, Charles – a charming young lady." He smiled knowingly and looked benign.

"I…think I'll go back to the Academy, sir, if some of the others are sleeping there."

"No problem. The caretaker will let you in."

"I hope to see you again soon, Quizzy."

"Oh yes, of course."

As Elvis sang 'It'll be lonely this Christmas', I left the bar to head for the Academy, having decided that's where I would sleep.

In the hotel lobby, Duncan (I now knew his name courtesy of the Director) caught up with me. Hand on my shoulder, he whispered, "I hope I won't be lonely." He looked up at the sprig of mistletoe dangling over us.

I smiled. "I'm sure you won't."

He closed in to claim his kiss. I could feel his hands grabbing at my backside as he practically swallowed me.

Impressionable, gullible, yes... a dreamer, yes, but I was not ready for whatever that particular politician had on his agenda. Though I did think about it! I also thought of the reaction of the Director. He would not be pleased.

With a degree of uncertainty fluttering in my stomach, I trudged up the marble steps of the Academy and down into the chilling cold of the basement, movement studio, where rubber roll-mats and discarded stage curtains would dampen any thoughts of passion. Other railway refugees were debating the best strategy for maximum heat, from 'multiple occupancy' to wrapping themselves into bundles like cocooned caterpillars.

Checking that the lone mound in a corner was definitely John, I huddled down beside him. "John?" I ruffled his wavy hair. His familiar smell was like a comfort blanket.

"Go away."

Snuggling closer I whispered, "I have a problem and it's your fault."

"Yeh, I know. I messed everything up tonight. I'm just one big problem." I let out a sigh, then a little sniff and another more audible sigh. Eventually I nudged him again. "O K. What is it?"

"Well, there was this guy and I thought he was you and..."

In the increased darkness I couldn't see John's reactions. I could only hear the occasional, "You what? He what?" of incredulity. Finally he rebuked me with, "How could you be so stupid? So naïve? You need glasses."

"Yes, I know, but what am I going to do? If I go back perhaps I could apologise..."

"You're not going back to that hotel."

"But if I don't go back he might tell the Director I led him on and then I'll be in trouble. He might cut our funding and I'll be in even more trouble." Now I was really sniffing.

"Don't be such a Drama Queen. I'll sort it out."

"No, no. What are you going to do? Hit him? You'll get chucked out of the Academy."

"You stick to acting and let me manage the situation. You know, you can be a real idiot at times."

John was clambering over sleeping bodies towards the door. I tried to stop him but expletives and threats from the other occupants had me diving back to the security of John's sleeping area, huddling into a ball in anticipation of what might be happening in the hotel.

Exhausted, I fell asleep curled up like an embryo. It's a wonder I didn't suck my thumb – a throwback to childhood whenever I was caught misbehaving. Something was tickling my nose. I brushed it away and back it came. This time my ear was being tickled. I sat up in the semi-darkness and hands covered my eyes.

"Guess who?"

"John!"

A match flickered, lighting a small candle. John held the candle in one hand and in the other was a sprig of mistletoe. "All sorted. Do I get a kiss?"

As I wrapped my arms around him he blew out the candle. Between kisses I was told in no uncertain terms there was only one man I could play 'Guess who?' with, or kiss under the mistletoe, and as soon as possible he was taking me to see an optician.

Harry - Jennifer Nesteroff

Harry was puzzled when the door didn't open. Jock always got up at this time every morning; Harry knew that by instinct. Jock should be coming out by now, calling his usual greeting, "Right Harry lad! Let's go!" Then they would be off for a brisk walk before breakfast.

Jock was almost the first person to be kind to Harry. Before Jock there were others, though when he had been born there were no people around, just his mother and his three siblings. They lay on an old piece of rag in a cold damp shed. It was the only decent shelter his mother could find when she needed to give birth, but even this was a very inadequate place for a starving bitch with a newborn family. They had been there for two days when it started to rain. Freezing wind and sleet buffered the shed and water began dripping through the holes in the ancient roof. By the third morning, two of Harry's siblings were dead.

Later that day the noise of an approaching truck made Harry's mother stiffen in fear. It stopped outside and the half-open door was thrown back as two men entered and started removing some petrol drums that stood just inside. They were about to leave again when the frightened eyes of the dog cowering in the corner caught one man's eye. "Hey Jim, look at that!" he exclaimed. The other man paused to look and then shrugged his shoulders.

"Yeah, so what? It's just a stray dog sheltering from the rain. Come on, we've got to get going."

"Hang on, I can see a couple of little pups over there. She must have just had them, poor thing!"

"Well, that's her problem. Let's go. I want to get home before dark."

"Aw, we can't just leave them. Ah, there are two more dead ones here. Look, we practically pass that Dog Shelter on the way home. Surely we can drop them off there." He began to talk softly to Harry's mother. She edged slowly towards him, anxious about her pups and sensing that this man might help her.

"Gawd, you're a soft blighter! All right then, if you can get them in the truck, but hurry up!"

It was warm in the Shelter. As time went by, Harry's mother began to put on weight and become healthier. The two pups grew bigger by the day and they were soon playing with each other and feeling very much at home. Then, one morning a plump woman with an even plumper son came and looked at them. "I want that one!" shouted the child, pointing at Harry.

"All right, Darling, that one it is!" The woman turned to the Shelter Manager. "It's Richard's birthday, you know and he does so want a puppy. Mind you, his father is not so keen on the idea, but I'm sure he will just love this pup. I believe Richie has already thought of a name. Tigger, isn't it, Darling? Isn't that sweet?"

So the fat woman with the even fatter son took Harry home. He never saw his mother or sister again. In the weeks that followed, Harry, or Tigger, as he was beginning to learn that his name was, settled down well in his first real home. He had plenty to eat and a good bed and Richard played with him and took him for walks a great deal. He had only one problem, Richard's father. This man did not love him at all, as Richard's mother had predicted. He hated him. Harry soon learned to keep out of his sight as much as possible.

For Christmas, Richard received his usual load of presents. Among them were several fascinating video games. Richard loved these and played them almost continuously. Harry began to get forgotten more and more. Richard's mother often had to remind him to feed 'Tigger' or to take him out. Sometimes Harry had to wait so long that he was forced to dirty the floor, in which case, Richard's father would fly into a rage and shout and kick at him: then came the holiday to America.

"Well, we shall have to put Tigger in Kennels, won't we, Dear?" Richard's mother tentatively asked his father.

"There is no way I am going to pay good money to keep that damn mutt in luxury. I'll take it out somewhere and drop it off. Someone is bound to take it in, so it will be all right."

"But Dear, Tigger is Richard's pet. What would we tell him?"

"Your spoilt Richard lost interest in his so-called pet long ago. Just tell him it got sick of him and ran away."

Harry couldn't understand it. Richard's father had bundled him into the car and had driven off with him for what seemed a very long time. Then the car had stopped and he'd been roughly pushed out and left on his own while the car sped away down what turned out to be a country road. He'd tried to race after it, but soon became too tired and had to stop. Where was he? Why had this been done to him? He was cold and frightened and had no idea where he was. There were trees all around him and it was getting dark. Forlornly he began to walk along the road, not knowing what else to do.

Days went by. Harry walked and walked through the forest. Sometimes, tired out, he lay down to sleep under some bush or tree, but hunger and, above all, thirst soon had him on his sore feet again. He saw no one. At last, he was unable to go any farther and he sank down on the ground and closed his eyes. Just as he was lapsing into unconsciousness, he seemed to hear a voice speaking softly above him.

"Oh, you poor little fellow! I bet some bastard threw you out. Well, let's see what I can do for you." A tall, rugged man was bending over him, stroking him softly. Before Harry could react, the man picked him up and started carrying him to a road that led to a house on the outskirts of a small town. This would become Harry's last home. The man, Jock, nursed him back to health and soon became his adored friend. He christened him Harry. They went everywhere together. Harry especially loved the long walks they took almost every day into the misty hills that surrounded their home.

During summer, Jock would walk to the Pub in the village, accompanied, of course, by Harry who soon became known to many of the village people. On winter evenings, Harry would curl up at Jock's feet near the open fire, dreaming of the rabbits he had chased across the fields during the afternoon walk. So life went on for Jock and Harry, year after year and year after year, they both grew a little older and a little slower.

Harry used to sleep in Jock's room, on his cushion on the floor next to the bed, but of late the cushion had been moved to outside the room and the door was kept shut. "Sorry, old lad," Jock had tried to explain to him, "but you're getting too noisy in your old age! All that snoring and grunting keeps me awake." So Harry, after some initial surprise and protest, had settled down in his new sleeping place and was waiting each morning for the door to open and Jock to appear with his usual jovial command.

However, this morning was different and Harry couldn't understand it. He began to whine and finally got up and began scratching at the door and barking loudly. At last, he heard a response from Jock. The voice was quavering and feeble so that Harry, who was becoming rather deaf, had trouble hearing it. He knew that there was something quite wrong, though. He kept barking and whining anxiously and trying to somehow get the door open, but to no avail. Suddenly, the sound of a voice outside the open window in the sitting room caught his attention. "What's all the fuss about, Harry?"

It was young Brian Cameron from down the road! Harry knew him very well. He ran to the window barking loudly, then back to the bedroom door and then to the window again. "What are you trying to tell me and where is Jock? I guess I'd better come in take a look." Brian clambered in through the window and went and opened the door to Jock's room.

Harry pushed past him and ran to where Jock lay on the bed. Jock stroked Harry's head with his right hand. His left side was immobile and saliva dribbled from the corner of his mouth. "That's my good lad," he whispered. The Ambulance arrived quickly and the Para Medics prepared to take Jock to the Hospital.

"What about his dog?" enquired one as they were leaving.

"Don't worry, I'll take him to my place, but I have to go into town first. Lucky thing, that. I was just calling by to see if old Jock needed anything. Anyway, I'll come back later for Harry."

"Better close the window, then, or we'll have him chasing after his boss all the way to the hospital!"

Harry felt distressed. Where had they taken Jock and why couldn't he go too? He stood by the front door barking and whining for some time and then, finally, giving up, went and plopped down on his bed. He felt so very tired. He sighed and laid his head between his front paws. He was drifting off to sleep when he heard the call, "Right Harry, lad! Let's go!" He bounded up, full of energy now, and went racing out across the fields, his heart full of excitement and love, to where he could see Jock standing and calling to him from within a cloak of swirling mist.

My Brother - William Daysh

The hairs on my neck stiffen with expectation. I see the autumn sky darken and thicken with rain. I know he's coming. He returns each year, my older brother, regardless of how many years have passed since he left with such finality.

Always reluctant to come in, he stands there in the pouring rain, tapping the window for me to come out. Excitedly, I rush out to greet him. Always in the rain, that is when we take our annual walk together and talk incessantly all the while. Passers-by stare at us, some smiling benignly, others clearly convinced that we're mad, but we don't care. We're together again. I, for one, treasure these precious moments. I miss him so much and tell him so, pleading with him to come home, but he just shakes his head. He knows that it saddens me when he has to say that he can't, but I have to ask. So we walk on, and he continues with his unbelievable tales of life, and war: 'the war to end all wars' they said it would be.

He seems thinner, paler, these days, but lucid none-the-less: coherent and stronger than he was when he left. His stories then used to pour out in many different languages. Words and subjects were all tangled up in a colourful tapestry of bewildering confusion. Infinite patience was needed to listen, but I had it in abundance, for him. I didn't even consider that it was a debt repaid for taking good care of me in my earliest days. After all, Ben was the willing pilot who guided me safely through the shallows of my youth: the selfless life-boatman who risked all to rescue me from my storms: my clear, bright window to a world I had never seen. No, nothing could repay him for all that.

I remember clearly my sadness when he went off to the war. He went willingly, believing that in doing so he would save us all from catastrophe, while I, too young to fight, was left at home to wait. The next time I saw him he couldn't talk about it. He couldn't tell us of his bravery at Verdun. He couldn't even remember it. The truth came much later, of how he'd struggled back through rain and thigh-deep mud, hell-bent on rescuing wounded friends, and it was there in the crater of Hell that a shell-burst changed his life in one brilliant flash. He survived and came home, calling the names of dead comrades, rallying them on, though they were all under the ground. The tiny fragment of shrapnel that pierced his forehead had turned his world into a black abyss. Unable to see or remember, all he had left was touch. He talked with his hands. The right spoke of romances, the left of soldier's memories.

Now it is different. His eyes are no longer dry buttons that fasten the skin of his face. They are clear and bright as he talks to me. We walk the streets with the rain washing the tears from our cheeks, ecstatic at being together again. Then, outside our front door, he bids me farewell once more and walks away to nowhere.

Inside, back in this lonely consciousness, I feel the icy hand seizing my heart once more. Re-entry is painful but I force myself to remember. Until next autumn when he'll come home again, Ben is resting beneath the forest of stone on the hill, where we walk each year and he shows me his name.

Indra Slays the Dragon - Irene Hogg

Rotting fruit pummelled the old man. His singing died as a brick felled him. Blood spurted from his temple, mixing with the rivers of Indian detritus flooding the cobbled street. Screams of abuse spewed from street vendors crouched beneath the sodden awnings. Curses, obscenities descended on the unconscious being at my feet, while langur monkeys leaped from fading pink rooftop shelters to scavenge around him.

Instinctively I knelt at the old man's head, trying to staunch the blood.

"Leave him. Old fool. Wrong place, wrong time, wrong song." The western-clad stallholder looked down on my feeble attempt at first aid. I cradled the wizened head, then realised I held a corpse.

"Why? He was singing, happy."

The shopkeeper took pity on me. "Come inside."

Shivering, I huddled amidst flaming saris, watching as a tattered tarpaulin masked the corpse. Visions of the old man's blood running through the pink city of Jaipur, the viciousness of the attack, the avarice of the langurs: all kaleidoscoped in my mind.

I asked again, "Why?"

"It is the rain."

"What?"

"Let me explain. When I was young we prayed and sang to the god Indra to slay the cloud dragon, giving water to the land and cleansing the earth."

"The old man was singing for rain? More rain?"

"Today some, the city dwellers, curse the rain. Streets run like sewers. Vendors can't display their wares. Poverty increases; for them the rains are a curse."

"That's why they killed him?" He nodded. "For singing to bring rain? Why didn't he stop?"

"Let me get you a taxi. No trade today. I'll see you back to your hotel."

In the rickety yellow tuk-tuk he told me the story behind the old man's singing. Piece by piece I tried to make sense of it.

With the expansion of the city and its industries, natural streams and rivers became polluted or diverted. Crops failed, water was scarce or disease ridden. Women were left to provide every need for their families, maintaining crops, cattle and land. The men had left in search of work. Many never returned.

The old man, too frail for industry, remained with his daughter and grandchildren. One by one, the children died, until only his youngest granddaughter remained. Knowing the need for water, the child had begged her grandfather to sing old songs from another time, of good defeating evil. He sang the child to sleep, he sang in the field; whenever they were together he sang the rain song. His daughter prostituted herself in the city.

"Will someone tell his relatives?"

"They will know. They always know."

"But why was he singing today? There was no child with him."

"Her grandfather sang at her funeral and when he sang she was close to him."

So, I sit, surrounded by smells of dampness and the clatter of the monsoon. I ponder over the rains of India and the givers and takers of life. I wonder if, somewhere in the city, raindrops are mingling with the salty teardrops of a daughter.

I Remember - Jennifer Nesteroff

I remember how dark it was that night. There was a thunderstorm brewing on the southern skyline, but its distant flickers of lightning and rolls of thunder did nothing to diminish the darkness of a typical moonless night in the Australian bush.

I was a teenager, home on holiday from boarding school. My father was away on business for a few days so my mother and I were alone in the homestead of our somewhat isolated property: situated 30 miles from our nearest town and about 6 miles from our nearest neighbour. We were sitting together in the kitchen chatting about anything and everything that came into our minds. We had much in common and always enjoyed discussing subjects that particularly interested us.

In the midst of our conversation, we heard a tapping sound coming from the front of the house. We thought it must be someone knocking on the front door, which was odd so late at night and especially as we had not heard a car arriving. We thought, perhaps, that someone may have walked up to ask for help, having had car trouble on the main road, which ran through our property about a mile away from the house. However, when my mother went and opened the front door, there was no one there.

"We must have misheard," she said as she returned and settled herself again by the warmth of the stove. We continued talking and laughing for a few minutes then, suddenly, the knocking sound came again. Tap, tap, tap, tap. We looked at each other in surprise. Now, that was certainly someone at the front door. My mother went again to open the door. There was no one.

This time she looked worried and somewhat perturbed, though I could see that she was trying not to appear so for my sake.

After the third bout of knocking and finding no one there, neither of us could pretend that we were not completely alarmed. We wondered if it might be someone playing tricks on us, someone drunk or mentally disturbed. He must be knocking and then hiding around the corner of the veranda in the dark, or some such thing. We had a veranda surrounding the house on three sides. I knew it well! On dark nights, it was pitch black there and when I was little, it had scared me to death.

Although I knew, naturally, that there were no such animals in the Australian bush, I always had the feeling that, if I ventured around it, some animal, a lion or a tiger or even a great, brown bear might spring out at me from round one of the corners. Not wanting to be a frightened baby, I would make myself walk that dark, dreaded distance, my heart throbbing and my knees shaking with every step. As I arrived back in the light of the kitchen, I never ceased to feel relieved and somehow a little surprised that I had not been torn to pieces on my journey. Now I had that awful feeling again, only this time I thought that there could be a real source of danger waiting out there.

We listened in awful apprehension as that mysterious knocking sounded yet again. There was nothing else to do but to seek out the cause of this once and for all and to try to deal with the consequences as best we could. My mother was a strong, sensible woman who usually suffered no nonsense. Now, she suppressed her fear with a show of anger. "This can't go on. It's ridiculous!" She stood up and strode determinedly along the hall to the front door with me trailing in her wake. Even though she had told me to stay back, I was not going to let her conduct this investigation alone. As she passed by the guest bedroom near the front of the house, she suddenly stopped. "The sound is coming from in there," she exclaimed, as we heard tapping again.

She threw open the door of the room and switched on the light. And then we saw it! A black nose and two brown eyes with a sheepish expression in them were poking out from under the bed! There lay one of our dogs, the one that was always afraid of thunder, anxiously thumping his tail on the floor. He knew he was doing wrong as dogs were not allowed in the house, but his fear of the thunder had overwhelmed him. Obviously, when we raised our voices or laughed while we were talking, he reacted by wagging his tail. We didn´t scold him. In fact, we patted and hugged him in huge relief.

Where were you last night? - Jennifer Nesteroff

Tabitha stood up and stretched herself, sending the children, who were still enjoying breakfast, flying. The squeaks of protest did not impress her.

"Oh, pipe down, you greedy little critters, I've been stuck with you all night and I've had enough." Suddenly, a sleek, golden vision of confidence appeared on the windowsill. "Ah, decided to come home, have we? Well, don't just stand there doing your Monarch of the Glen thing. It doesn't do a lot for me, nowadays. Motherhood puts a real damper on that sort of excitement. How about jumping down here and giving me a hand with the kids."

With a languid flourish of his long, graceful tail, Charlemagne alighted on the floor next to Tabitha. "Now Tab, my lovely, don't be like that. Had a hard night, have you?"

"The usual, of course. Kids all over the place, wanting to play and snack, but never mind me. Where were you last night?"

"Oh, out and about, here and there, admiring the moon, taking the air. What a poetic phrase that was! I do amaze me!"

"Well, you don't amaze me and I know just what you were admiring and taking."

"Now, Tabatha, there is no need to be coarse. What has happened to that sweet little white bundle of fluff I found cowering and crying in a doorway because her family had moved house and had conveniently forgotten to take her with them? Homo sapiens! You know I was so taken with you that I decided to bring you home with me. I knew my Old Dear wouldn't mind. She isn't called `the cat lady' for nothing and she has even allowed you to stay in the house with the little ones.

"Yes and that's just it. I'm in the house while Charlie the Charmer checks out the scenery ...and that's called alliteration."

"Alliteration, indeed! I should think that you would be more acquainted with litter, and kindly refrain from calling me that dreadful sobriquet. The name is Charlemagne, if you please!"

"Right, Your Highness. I'll try to remember."

Charlemagne glanced around the room. "Now, where are my enchanting children? Ah, here comes my petit choux, my little Fleur de Lis. No, do not play with Papa's tail, Cherie. We do not want it to become all milky and chewed, do we? But where is my first-born, my Dauphin?"

"He's over there shredding your dear, old homo sap's curtains."

"What an adventurous little fellow he is! I cannot wait until he is old enough for me to take out and present to the local feline population. Everyone will be so impressed! He will be such a chip off the old block, as they say!"

"Good, Charlie boy (oops, there I go again!) You hold that thought while you're minding your illustrious offspring. I'm going out."

Charlemagne looked horrified. "I can't stay here on my own with them! Why do you want to go out, anyway?"

Tabatha sprang onto the windowsill. "I'd like to do a little checking of my own. They tell me there's a new guy in town, jet black with the most hypnotic green eyes..."

"But Tabs..."

"Back in a while. `Bye, kids. Enjoy yourself, my Monarch!"

In a white flash, she was gone.

"Oh dear, how I hate baby-sitting! Hey, you little brats, I've told you, not the tail!"

Devotion - Gail Tucker

Nobody looked twice at Angela that Thursday morning when she left the church after mass and headed for the supermarket. The stout woman, in her late sixties with dark streaks in her otherwise white hair, pushed her trolley ahead of her through the aisles of biscuits and cakes. It was Father Kelly's day for tea, and the devout woman always made sure she had something special for him. For nearly seventy years she had been at the beck and call of her men; her duty had been well embedded by her equally devout mother.

Halfway home she remembered that Jack had told her to fetch another bottle of weed killer and some of the special ties for his prize dahlias. Looking at the darkening sky the weary woman hesitated a moment, before retracing her steps and ducking into the ironmongers, just as the first big spots of rain hit the pavement.

Angela let herself into the empty kitchen and dripped on the mat. She thrust her shopping bags among the dirty breakfast dishes on the draining board. Jack had not stirred from his computer since she went out; years of resentment finally surfaced. She dried her dripping hair and put on the kettle, a nice cup of coffee would put it right. She breathed steadily now as she reached into the cupboard for the jar of decaf' they had to drink these days on account of Jack's high blood pressure, and spooned the powder into the cups, well aware that if he'd not thrown salt on every meal she'd cooked over the last forty-six years, before even tasting it, they might still be enjoying proper coffee. She couldn't see that the decaf did much good anyway. Jack complained it was so very bitter, and took so much sugar to counter this, that Angela expected diabetes would be next on the list of her trials and tribulations to be offered up to the Almighty.

Beyond the steaming cups she caught sight of the chaos on the draining-board. With icy deliberation Angela measured out two teaspoons of dark brown liquid from a bottle in her shopping; she could predict accurately that Jack would not be distracted from his surfing as he drank the coffee his dutiful wife put at his elbow.

With a firm hand she clicked shut the door on the last plates in the dishwasher. As she pressed the start button, Angela knew that Father Kelly would give her absolution.

Checking the Facts - Mai Griffin

I really would love to be a writer, but writers have to know things, like what they do when they sit at a piano – practise or practice, c or s – and that the other is, or definitely is not, what a doctor has.

Actually, I tried looking that up once. Tearing myself away from my word processor and the gripping plot I was devising, I searched the bookshelf for anything musical or medical – no luck! While I looked through a heap of magazines, continually sidetracked by letters written by desperate housewives to the problem pages, the electricity failed. Naturally I read on, happily unaware that because I hadn't "SAVED", my words were lost and all my devoted research a waste of time!

When I gave up fuming and sat at the keyboard again, trying to reconstruct it, everything was working except my brain! I seriously thought I must have dreamed about having written the perfect outline for the great masterpiece of the century – the one that would be awarded a prize for 'Best Selling First Novel By A New Writer' or something, because I had totally lost the plot ...and it had been a brilliant opening line! Then I saw that the time on my watch didn't agree with the electric clock – the one I had been keeping an eye on so that I wouldn't be late with the lunch again!

The rattle of keys and the front door slamming sent me into an immediate panic. Switching off the computer and restoring his desk to its usual state – littered – I almost broke my neck to reach the kitchen and look busy before he emerged from the hall cloakroom. When I am a Best-Selling Author, I'll have a cook/housekeeper!

I never did remember all the brilliant twists and turns of the story I worked out that morning but the outline I decided to be happy with, proved disastrous. Why I decided to weave my story around life circa 1920 I shall never understand – history was never my strong point at school, although it was marginally better than my geography which ranked low, alongside science and maths. I suppose I had imagined that having living links to the era, through a heap of elderly relatives, it would be easy to sound convincing.

In an attempt to revive my enthusiasm for the story, a brilliant idea popped into my head. I could take my tiny unobtrusive cassette recorder on visits to old aunts and uncles who would welcome me as a diversion from their usual boring chores and willingly sit for hours, talking over old times.

Starting with my parents because they lived close by, I rang to tell them my plans and said I'd be round in twenty minutes. I could hear mum explaining it to dad, sounding suitably excited and his reply, which wasn't flattering so I won't repeat it.

To be fair, I know that in the past I have started a good many schemes and embarked on projects that were never completed, but this time is different. I am determined to write a book. I heard him reminding her that she wanted him to dig up some potatoes but she, always eager to encourage me, told him, "Never mind, we'll have a tin of spaghetti for lunch," and to me, she said they were both thrilled to help and she'd put the kettle on straight away.

Later, while we drank coffee, dad relaxed and they both giggled as they recalled their courting days. They revealed quite a lot about the years of their youth in the early decades of the century and I was so enthralled I forgot about the recorder until mum said, "I'll just clear away the tray then we'll get down to work."

When she came back I showed off the dinky little gadget, switched it on and set it facing them where they sat together on the settee. They did try to get back into the mood but it was hopeless. After ten minutes of embarrassed elbowing and throat clearing, dad said he'd better get the spuds after all ...it looked like rain!

The following day I took my recorder to visit Aunt Amy and Uncle Jim. They are in their eighties so I didn't bother to ring first. I did not want them worrying about my visit, or fussily making a special event of it; better to surprise them, I decided.

Instead of looking delighted when she saw me on the doorstep she said, looking distinctly upset, "I thought it was Freda at last! We are all waiting to play – the morning will be gone at this rate! How is your bridge child?"

She clucked with disappointment when told it was non-existent and not at all enthusiastic when I explained the purpose of my visit. She said I could ask Uncle Jim for his help, he had more spare time than she did but I'd have to come another day – he was out at a stamp-club auction.

To avoid a wasted morning (in spite of my aunt's panic it was still only 10.30!), I caught a bus out of town to the old peoples' home where the Godfather of our clan was winding up his days. Grandfather used to tell us kids stories by the hour. He was never too tired at the end of his working day to take one of us on his lap and talk about the funny, naughty things he'd done at school. Pranks that he and his friends had played on their teachers were high on our list of favourites and we believed every word as fervently as we did the Gospel. Actually, I had intended saving Grandfather for the last, sure of his enthusiasm and full co-operation, but I was in dire need of a mental boost before my own interest in the subject waned.

He was really pleased to see me. An orderly wheeled him out into the garden to enjoy the unusually sunny day and we settled down for a nice private chat.

As he was able to walk, he was upset about being in the chair and used up fifteen minutes telling me how fit he actually was and how they insisted on cosseting him, just because he was ninety-eight! They just wanted to show him off when he reached a hundred he said. "They think they are all going to be interviewed with me on television... only another eighteen months to go you know, and I'm as good as ever I was – well nearly!"

Not sure how to interpret his nudge-nudge wink-wink, I hastily produced my recorder and explained why I wanted to talk to him. The miniature wonder fascinated him so much I had to show him how it worked. He spent the next ten minutes playing with it and succeeded in wiping the admittedly few comments I had actually managed to record!

The matron, although warning me not to tire him, had graciously given us an hour together. Half the time had already gone and I was exhausted. He was as bright as a button and, having pressed to record, he held the thing an inch from his nose and proceeded to shout into it.

Forcibly pulling his hand farther away from his mouth (and turning the volume down) did not noticeably interrupt his flow as he embarked on his life history. I was suddenly optimistic that usable material would result from what, so far, had been a fiasco.

My hopes were dashed when he reached ten years old and got stuck in the old groove of school scrapes. "Very funny," I interrupted yet again, "but what was your home like? What did your parents do for evening entertainment or at weekends? What was their life like?"

He looked at me in astonishment and sniffed – "Life? Oh, their life? Ordinary, same as everybody else's. Now school – that was exciting! Didn't learn a lot, me and my mates, but we had a great time! Did I ever tell you about the time we locked the headmaster in a cupboard?"

Last week I had a brilliant idea for a new plot and, if ever the bus comes, I'm on my way to the library to check up on a few things. That's what I mean – real writers don't have to waste time going out for information, they have all they need in their heads. It is such a waste of time standing here when I could be enjoying myself at the computer – moving paragraphs around, inserting, deleting and finally counting how many words I've written. There is nothing more gratifying than seeing the word total growing by thousand after thousand.

Still no bus: I'm going home! I know that quality is more important than quantity – I'm not stupid, but surely whoever edits it will correct spelling mistakes and make sure the facts are right... Isn't that what editors are for?

The Do-Gooder - Jennifer Nesteroff

"Don't sit there," she commanded, "that's the cat's chair."

Allison, who detested cats, had no trouble obeying the command. She seated herself as far as possible from the said chair. "You must be very fond of your cat to give it its own chair. I'm afraid I am not very enthusiastic about cats, myself, Miss Simpson."

The small, elderly lady sitting opposite her smiled. "Oh, that's all right, dear. He won't bother you and he may not be here long. I foster cats, for the local shelter you see, and when I find them good homes, I pass them on. Been doing it for some time and the shelter people are really quite pleased to have me as they get so many strays. They do think me a bit strange, though, as I only take black cats. They bring you luck, you know and I had a beautiful black cat myself when I was a child. I like to make them as comfortable as possible while they are with me – but enough about cats. You have come to see the room I have for rent upstairs, haven't you. Let me show it to you."

The room was very pretty. It had blue frilly curtains and a matching bedspread. A floral covered sofa stood in the corner. "Oh, this is very nice," exclaimed Allison.

"Yes, I like it." Miss Simpson replied. "I decorated it myself. I used to be a seamstress, you know, and a tailoress. I was always clever with my hands. You'll be pleased to know that I cook rather well, too, so I think you'll be quite satisfied with the meals, should you decide to stay."

Allison moved into Miss Simpson's spare room the next week. Everything was to her satisfaction. The newspaper office at which she worked as a journalist was within reasonably easy reach and Miss Simpson proved to be very sweet and an entertaining companion. Their meals together were always agreeable. Miss Simpson would often regale her with stories of her early life. She had been born here and knew everything about the district and its history. Occasionally, she would make her special rabbit stew, which Allison found delicious. It was a recipe handed down from her mother. "It's the particular mix of herbs and spices that give the unique flavour to the dish, you know." Miss Simpson informed her. "We were quite poor during the war, but my mother managed to feed the family adequately. She was a clever woman."

One day Allison found that she was not feeling well at work. She thought she might have the beginnings of 'flu and her editor, feigning sympathy, advised her to go home. Of course what he really thought was, "I don't want you passing your germs on to the rest of the staff, although you probably have already, damn it." He suggested that she might think about something interesting to write for the paper while she was convalescing and wished her a speedy recovery.

Arriving home, she found Miss Simpson in the company of a young man who, apparently, was delivering a large cardboard box. The cellar door, which Miss Simpson usually kept locked, stood open. This seemed strange, as Allison was sure that Miss Simpson had said the cellar was just full of old junk and that she hardly ever went down there.

"Good heavens, dear, what are you doing here?" exclaimed Miss Simpson as Allison walked in. Allison explained that she was not feeling well and that her editor had kindly sent her home. "Oh dear, what a shame. You must go straight up to bed and I shall come and see how you are directly. This, by the way, is a nephew of mine, John, who brings me material to make into clothes for the needy. That's another little hobby of mine to helps the less fortunate in our community, you know. Now, off you go to bed!"

Allison realised that the cellar must be where Miss Simpson did her sewing. Why had she never mentioned this?

During the next three days, Allison stayed in her bed feeling quite wretched. Miss Simpson came to see her with offers of chicken soup and sympathy and generally fussed over her. During the third night, Allison suddenly woke up. She found that she was feeling a great deal better. Then she became aware of the sound of someone crying out from somewhere downstairs. This must have been what had awakened her. Miss Simpson! Scrambling out of bed, she hurried downstairs.

She saw that the cellar door was open and heard Miss Simpson calling from below. She could see her lying at the bottom of the cellar steps, cringing in pain. "Oh, there you are, dear, I'm so sorry I had to try to wake you, but I think I may have broken my leg. I can't move it and I'm in rather a lot of pain. Perhaps you might give me a hand to get up the stairs. No! Don`t come down here, just give me your hand so I can pull myself up."

"Nonsense, I'll come down and try to make you more comfortable and then I shall 'phone for an ambulance."

"No, no! Please don't come down!" ...but Allison was on her way. As she entered the cellar, the sight that met her eyes almost made her forget Miss Simpson and she gazed around in horror.

There, hanging limply from the ceiling, the wire noose cutting into its neck was the new cat that Miss Simpson had acquired only the week before. On a table nearby lay several knives. A cardboard box, obviously the one that John had delivered, stood open on the floor. The smell of the freshly tanned leather rising from the small, black pelts inside, made Allison's stomach heave. This was, indeed, where the old woman did her sewing. A sewing machine stood to one side and next to it on a dressmaker's dummy hung a half-finished black fur coat. Allison stared at Miss Simpson. "My God! You're in the cat fur trade!"

"I told you not to come down here."

"Did you kill and skin all these cats?"

"No, of course not, only the ones I get from the shelter. John supplies me with the rest and he tans them all."

Just then, Allison noticed the freezer standing in the corner. Steeling herself, she went over and flung it open. The skinned carcases of several frozen cats lay inside. She imagined that some of the poor, dead eyes still held the agonised, pleading expression they must have shown in their last moments and she burst into tears.

Miss Simpson now became defiant. "There's your rabbit stew that you enjoy so much. I did get the recipe from my mother, though. Did you really think we could afford to buy rabbits during the war?"

The Rebel - Gail Tucker

The child swung upside down in the tree – if only she had feathers, just a few, she knew she could fly. She swept her arms out wide, willing herself to swoop away. Concentrate on the fingers, or perhaps the shoulder blades that's where angels grew wings after all.

"Rosie!" the anxious call was so close it almost dislodged her. Nanny had spotted her from the nursery window. "You'll catch it, Miss Rose, if your mother sees you up there again. You know what happened last time."

"She's out Nanny. Don't worry, they're at Newbury this afternoon and I heard Pa tell her to take a coat for later, so they'll not be back for ages."

Minx! Nanny didn't envy the school that one went to, but they'd seen it all before too, she knew that.

"Ring-a-ring-a-roses a pocket full of posies..."

Leaning out of the window the elderly woman could see the other girl playing with both dollies. Georgina had propped them up against the mounting block and was attempting to interlace their hands to join her in a circle. The Labrador kept patient guard at a distance from where he could watch both his charges.

"They're back." On the upswing Rosie had just caught a flash from the metal mast that must be the support for the big tent, that open-sided tepee, which housed the main stage where all that wonderful noise came from last year. She remembered her mother's headache that had lasted all weekend. She remembered the thrilling vibration through the brass bedstead as the drumming and thrumming reached crescendo after crescendo ...it seemed, all night long: utterly thrilling.

Rose slithered down the tree, tore across the grass and tugged at the only dancer in the circle, "Come on, I'll show you something!"

"Oh Rose, you've spoilt it now. You always spoil things."

"Never mind that, Georgie, come and see this." The younger child had no choice, her legs flew over the gravel, forced to follow the trailing arm of the bigger girl.

"Where're we going?"

"You'll see."

As he reached the gap in the hedge, the old dog looked back at the house but there was no command forthcoming so he too followed Rose out of the stable yard, across the paddock and into the lane. By the time he had caught up with his charges they were leaning over the top gate to the ten-acre field below the lodge – or rather, Rose was leaning over the gate and Georgina was jumping up and down trying to see.

"Here, climb up the bank and catch hold of the post. See now?"

"Yes," Georgina hauled herself into position leaving a trail of devastation through the carpet of primroses, this child was not born an eco-warrior.

By now the field was abuzz with activity. Campervans were parked around the perimeter; trailers bringing portaloos shuffled around at the far end and small groups of hikers, carrying lumpy backpacks, were arriving in a steady stream. In no time at all, strange twanging and booming sounds began, interspersed with nasal-voiced, "testing...testing...one, two, three." Years later Rose would identify this as the moment when she learned to fly.

In the meantime Nanny was right, she was a challenging pupil. Quite early on, her Housemistress had received a tart phone call from the Head who hoped that The Remove were not intending to spend all Sunday afternoon hanging, like so many bats, upside-down in the trees behind the cloisters but, if they were, perhaps someone could check they were at least wearing their bicycle helmets.

The phrase 'a tendency to turn everything upside down',

which appeared in her first end of year report, had become 'a healthy anarchy' by the time Rose reached the Sixth Form. All this mild rebellion was tolerated by her father who, in the absence of any son, loved her unconditionally. Her mother took solace for her own failure in the biddable Georgina whom she refused to send away to school and who did not miss her unnervingly remote sister.

Rose who gave every semblance of being happy and gregarious never allowed anyone to get truly close. She might have been the leader of activities but she grew the aloofness of many born to lead. Indeed, no one ever knew where Rose built her bendy. Others might have their shared illicit hideaway, with its cache of export lager and Silk Cut, occasionally brought to light by zealous groundsmen, or a history teacher's dog, but Rose maintained her secret for three whole years. Indeed, it was never found in her lifetime.

Rose met the anarchist as she swung through the trees away from the police cherry-picker. He had reached down to whisk her to safety. She was smitten. Not, of course, by his looks – they were hidden beneath the balaclava – it was the instant recognition of a superior flier that did for her. For his part, it was the trusting gaze from between the scarf and the cycle helmet that was his entrapment. In that instant something very like nobility shifted from its hiding place in that erstwhile common man.

They became an efficient fighting force disrupting what the media called 'the progress' of the by-pass; they survived for longer than most at heights beyond the reach of the police and regularly managed to disable unattended machinery. When they realised that Rose was pregnant it was he who climbed down and forced her to give it all up. One night he said, "Come on, I'll show you something." Then, for the first time in her life, Rose began to pretend.

She pretended to like the cracker-box semi on the housing estate. Raised amongst one of the finest private collections of early English Renaissance, she pretended to like what he called art. She even pretended to love this man she now saw had feet of clay and, for the sake of the child, she pretended to like the cat she had bought to keep the birds away.

No one can pretend forever. One day, as she pushed the pram past the park swings she heard a fluttering. Behind the hedge she found the neglected aviary where disconsolate canaries pecked at dirt encrusted perches. Rose stood still. From near the swings unseen voices chanted, "Ring-a-ring o' roses..." One dirty yellow feather landed on the pillow.

It had to stop. The mundane had proved unbearable.

She had to stop. Now, before it was too late. If she could leave Josh somewhere to be rescued perhaps it would not be spoiled for him. The man who used to be a flier would surely let their son go where her pride could not. She snatched the child from the pram and headed out beyond the by-pass.

Dante's Revenge - William Daysh

In the twenty-five years that he'd been dealing with corpses, Mr Willard had never before encountered a case of post-mortem megalophallos priapism. This was patently obvious to the GP on the phone. The good doctor realised at once that Willard understood nothing of what he'd been saying and, having better things to do, passed it off quickly by saying that it was an extremely rare condition. Before ringing off, however, he added that even as he spoke, such a case was winging its way to WILLARD'S PARLOUR FOR THE DEAR DEPARTED – *'Dedicated to making your funeral a memorable occasion and fully compliant with the Funeral Ombudsman's Code of Practice'* – in the form of Mr William Dante, or 'Big Willy' as he had been affectionately known on account of his prominent stature.

"My dear doctor," crooned Willard dismissively, while using his reflection in the framed photo of a Rolls Royce hearse on his desk to straighten his tie. "We at WILLARD'S have seen all manner of strange things in our time. I'm confident that we'll cope, but thank you so much for warning us. A very good day to you, sir."

Patting his abundant silver hair, he rose to make his way to the staff rest-room. Just then, he saw the bright livery of Nailby City Hospital sail past the window as one of its ambulances slid like a bicycle pump plunger into the tunnel-like passage beside the parlour. Hastening through the building, Willard flushed his two assistants out of their well-worn armchairs and chivvied them to the tradesman's entrance. Joined by Cedric the embalmer

– a precise, school-masterly man – Willard and his three members of staff waited there in a line of anticipation as the ambulance driver reversed carefully into the yard and clambered out. Grinning from ear to ear, the man approached Willard with a clipboard and pen.

"Bit of an odd one here, Mr Willard," he said cheerily. "A Mister Dante … a rather prominent gentleman, if you ask me. Sign here please."

"No one asked for your opinion," muttered Willard, waving the driver's chewed biro aside and signing with a gold-plated fountain pen drawn from inside his impeccable black jacket.

The corpse was then ferried to the embalming room where the four men gathered to examine it under the harsh beam of an overhead inspection lamp. In the background, they could hear the ambulance purring away with none of the driver's usual light-hearted banter. With the exception of cheeky Charlie Smythe, who sucked his teeth noisily, the four men stood silently in awe of the size of the body on the table. Cedric read the label attached to the zip.

"William Dante. That's Big Willy isn't it? I know him," he added, dreamily.

"So you should," said Willard sharply, frowning at the bag that overhung the trolley at both ends and reflecting upon which of the twelve coffins in his glossy catalogue would be large enough for it. Cedric made some comment about the midriff bulge in the bag, suggesting that Big Willy had a substantial paunch.

"We buried Dante's third wife a number of years ago, if you recall," Willard went on, looking as if he had a bad smell under his nose. "I'll never forget him and the long-running dispute we had over his wife's funeral arrangements. It all began when I was going through our catalogue of background music for viewings. Dante insisted on having New Orleans Blues. I ask you! Naturally, I refused, of course, and he was obliged to settle for something more tasteful. Then, after the funeral, he flatly refused to pay the bill in full, and when I remonstrated with him he called me 'a humourless old faggot'!

"The argument went on for months. In the end, I had to take him to court. Then he was forced to pay up. My God, you should have seen him. He went purple and shook his fist at me outside the court. He cursed and swore that he would get even with me. Do you know what he did? He got Securicor to deliver the money in small change – several heavy bags of it. It gave me a hernia taking them to the bank. No, Dante was a dreadful, objectionable man. I'd be a hypocrite if I said I would shed a tear over him now."

Willard's sharp outburst had them all grinning behind their hands.

"Well he must have flourished on hospital food," Cedric noted, surveying the mound in the body bag. "He's always been lanky, if I recall correctly ...tall but quite thin. Big fellow, isn't he?"

It was always Cedric's practice to refer to the deceased as if they were merely asleep. Charlie, a chirpy character who was never stuck for something to say, piped up brightly. "Well, 'e must be full of wind then, Cedric, because 'e ain't as 'eavy as 'e looks. Funny that. Shall we 'ave a look then, Mr Willard?"

Not waiting for a reply, Charlie unzipped the body bag with a single sweep that required him to sidestep the length of the body and the white shroud beneath was revealed. Solemnly, Willard stepped forward to lift one side of it, but withdrew as if stung when something stirred under the shroud. The four men watched wide-eyed with disbelief as the middle of the shroud rose slowly, as if elevated by a silent electric motor. It rose higher and higher until it came to rest at a seemingly impossible height.

Furtive glances of disbelief shot between the four men. No one spoke. As could be expected, it was Charlie who eventually broke the stunned silence.

"Naaah," he said, in a long, drawn out way, looking less sure of himself than usual. "Someone's 'avin' us on."

He nudged Willard.

"Go on, Mr Willard. 'Ave a look."

As one, a row of expectant eyes fell on Willard. His cheeks began to flush. Wishing to appear manly, but clearly apprehensive, he hesitated to step forward. He lifted one side of the shroud and peered inside.

"Good God!" he gasped, tossing it back and stepping away. He was visibly shaken. "Is that real?"

Cedric, with all the casualness of a man whose livelihood is cadavers, donned the surgical gloves he always kept in the pockets of his white coat and bent over the megalithic symbol of Dante's manhood. He examined it studiously through his gold-rimmed, half-frame spectacles.

"Yes," he pronounced, arching his eyebrows as he straightened up. "It is indeed real." He lowered his head and peered at the others over his spectacles. "A magnificent specimen, if ever I saw one. It's a bit black now, naturally, but it's quite splendid all the same."

"Cerne Abbas Man," said Willard, vacantly, recalling a weekend break in Dorset. The observation was wasted on all but Cedric.

"Caw," exclaimed Charlie. He was obviously full of admiration. "I've never seen anything as big as that. The lucky old sod!" His mind was working overtime. "They must've stood on that at the 'ospital to get the zip done up. No wonder Fred nipped off a bit smartish in 'is ambulance. It's not like him to disappear like a rat up a drain-pipe."

"Quite so," said Willard, covering his burning cheeks with his hands. He now realised why Doctor Jones had bothered to phone, and was wishing that he'd paid more attention. "It's called 'Mega Fallopianism'," he said knowingly. "A very rare condition."

Cedric pursed his lips and gave Willard his disenchanted headmaster look.

"It's simply a matter of blood being trapped in the extremities at the time of death," he said flatly. "It can be quite a sight."

Willard's eyes widened.

"Quite a sight? It's more like a bloody exhibition. That is enormous!" he added, breathlessly.

Charlie's jaw was still hanging down.

"Blimey," he said. "One of them nurses must've been bendin' over by 'is bed when 'e snuffed it. That's probably what did it.

'Ere, maybe 'e was on that Viagra stuff."

Willard rolled his eyes to the ceiling.

"That's quite enough of your medical speculations, Charlie. It hardly matters how it came about. It happened, and the problem is ours now."

"The question is," said Charlie, his eyes still glued to the spectacle on the table. "What the 'ell are we going to do with it? Looks to me like the old boy's too long for our boxes anyway …but with that thing stickin' up like a flag-pole there's no way we'll ever get a lid on."

"Well, you'll just have to …somehow."

By now, all sorts of commercial considerations were running through Willard's mind. Charlie cast a professional eye over the body and then reached his own conclusions.

"Can't we sort of bend it a bit …or chop it off and hide it somewhere?"

The suggestion drew a sharp intake of breath from Cedric.

"Good Heavens, no," he gasped. "That's contrary to the Code of Practice. The Ombudsman would have our guts for garters if we did that. No, we can't do that."

He thought for a while.

"I suppose I could try letting some of the blood out of it …but it's already too late for that I fear. It's very rigid, you know. Go on, feel for yourself."

Charlie fanned his hands in horror.

"Not me mate. That's your job. I'll stick to the boxes."

Without realising it, the four men fell into a ring and began to walk slowly around the table, chins in hands and wracking their brains.

"Cedric is absolutely right," said Willard, finally. We're not at liberty to mutilate clients. Not even this one. As licensed undertakers, we are committed to seeing that our customers are buried in the condition we receive them. They didn't chop anything off at Nailby City, did they? No. Therefore we shall have to accommodate it. Are you sure it won't go into a No.10? That's the tallest one we've got, isn't it?"

Whipping a steel tape measure out of his back pocket, Charlie stepped forward and checked the overall height of Dante's protrusion, then shook his head.

"Nope. It's six-and-a quarter bigger than that," he said – gleefully it seemed to Willard. He rejoined the group circulating around the table.

George the pallbearer, a sallow man of few words, was suddenly moved to make one of his rare observations. The others waited as it rumbled up, gathering momentum as it came.

"No wonder they used to call him 'Big Willy'," he said, in his usual droll monotone.

They all stared at him at once.

"I mean, just look at the thing. It's like the Eiffel Tower!"

"But I bet it kept 'is missus 'appy," speculated Charlie. "Married four times, 'e was. The last one's a cracker too …exactly 'alf 'is age."

"And she wants to see him again before he goes," added Willard, curtly, before giving a despairing sigh. George, in a world of his own, had another of his rare thoughts.

"Well, Charlie, you'll have to make a special coffin for him."

Willard began to look agitated.

"We can't do that," he said. "Think of the cost. I've already quoted for one of our standard coffins and I can't go back on that. We'd go out of business if we provided custom-built coffins at those prices. Anyway, it would look grotesque …a great pyramid instead of a lid."

"Cost you a fortune that, Mr Willard." Charlie grinned mischievously. "I know what. I'll cut a hole in the lid of a No.10, then Mr Dante could just poke through."

Willard gave him a look of disgust.

"That's a very good idea, Charlie," droned George, with an unusual burst of enthusiasm. "We could get Mrs Collins over the road to make one of her floral tributes …to cover up the end, like." He thought about it for a moment, then added, 'But then, that wouldn't do because tributes have to be taken off in front of the bereaved."

Entirely out of character, he began to titter quietly.

"Unless we made it one of them fixed tributes," he added,

quite carried away with himself. "You know, one with a candle. We could get a big candle, hollow it out, and put it over the end of Big Willy's…thingy. Then we could decorate it with a floral tribute and glue the whole thing onto the lid. Sort of camouflage."

George's imagination drew him inexorably into a fit of titters. In an instant, he was giggling like a silly schoolgirl and Charlie had lost his battle with the mirth bubbling up inside him. One shared glance was all it took for waves of helpless belly laughter to break over them, made all the worse by Willard's indignant expression and despairing pleas for reverence and decorum on behalf of the bereaved.

"Well," choked Charlie, dabbing at the tears streaming down his face."Perhaps we could rig a sail on that mast of 'is and sail the box to the cemetery on the river. Mister Willard could steer. Hard a' starboard! eh, Mister Willard?"

By now, Charlie, George and Cedric were in convulsions of belly-laughter, the like of which the embalming room had never experienced before. Willard, indignant and frustrated, realised that nothing constructive would ever come of discussing such a delicate problem with men in this state. He stormed off to find peace in the serenity of his office. The other three retreated to the rest room, leaving the problem of Dante's rise unresolved.

In the end, it was Cedric who came up with the most sensible, viable solution. In view of Nailby City Hospital's success at cramming Dante into the body bag and zipping it up, he thought it just possible that he could do the same for a No.10 coffin. Dante, with his feet planted flat against the base-board and his head reverently tipped forward on a satin pillow, would just fit into a No.10. However, his northern elevation, as Charlie had astutely noted, would not. So, while Charlie was modifying the lid of the coffin by sawing it in two, to allow the lower half to be screwed down securely while the top half remained open for the private viewing, Cedric ingeniously prepared the body for the after-life.

By means of a hair-dryer and an entire roll of parcel-tape –

not to mention infinite patience – he constructed an elaborate 'A-frame' out of plastic tape, which he secured to Dante's hips in the manner of a truss. Then, with several loops of the tape, he lassoed Dante's obdurate extremity and inclined it at a more convenient angle. Although inherently suffering considerably from tensile stress, the device, when finished, seemed quite capable of restraining Dante's wayward member so that he could be fitted into a No.10.

It was then decided – by whom no one can remember – that as relatives, fortunately, would never again clap eyes on the lower half of their dear departed, his trousers could usefully be dispensed with. It was either that or a specially modified suit would have to be made. Dante was therefore laid reverently in his coffin, trouser-less, with his top half dressed fit for a dinner-party. Thus immaculately clad in a black jacket, crisp white shirt and black tie, Dante radiated serenity, and his mourners were presented with a picture of sublime normality.

The viewing and subsequent service went as well as could be expected. Willard fussed about in the background all the while, wiping small beads of anxious sweat from his forehead and glancing nervously at the coffin. When the lid was finally screwed down, he gave a great sigh of relief which he managed to disguise as a clearing of his throat.

At the cemetery, he watched nervously until the coffin found solid ground at the bottom of the grave, and then went to stand with the two gravediggers waiting unobtrusively some distance from the graveside, but not until the service was over did Willard feel the weight of the world lift from his shoulders.

As the mourners, the vicar and Willard's men dispersed, Colin and Jack, the diggers, moved like busy dung beetles to the now silent grave, ready to fill the hole. However, as the first shovel load of dry earth fell lightly over the coffin, a strong gust of wind plucked Jack's heavily soiled cloth cap from his head and hurled it into the grave.

"Shit! Hang about, Colin. Me bloody cap's gone in th'ole."

Colin leaned wearily on his shovel as Jack lowered himself gently onto the coffin. Bending to pick up his cap in the earthy silence of the hole, Jack's attention was drawn to a strange renting noise inside the coffin. Alert, and with his ears finely tuned, Jack listened carefully. Just then, two resounding thuds sounded under his feet as Cedric's Heath Robinson construction of parcel tape succumbed to the strain of its purpose. Jack immediately took this to be the occupant tapping on the lid with his knuckles and shot out of the hole like a scalded cat to stand saucer-eyed in the daylight.

Colin stared at him with a mixture of alarm and bemusement.

"Jesus Christ, there's somebody in there!" croaked Jack.

"Well of course there is, you great prat," scoffed Colin. "He's bloody dead. That's why we've got to bury him."

"No, I mean there's someone still alive in there. He's tappin' on the lid."

Colin's jaw dropped.

"Are you serious?"

"Dead serious. It scared the shit out of me."

"Well, we'd better get onto the Police right away. Come on, run for it, before he snuffs it. I'll get a screwdriver and take the lid off."

While nowhere in the cemetery offices could Colin find a screwdriver, Jack did get to a phone. Within minutes, a Police van came hurtling into the cemetery gates, careering across the grass in a desperate rush to save the life of the long gone William Dante.

At WILLARD'S PARLOUR FOR THE DEAR DEPARTED, the blissfully unaware Mr Willard was pleased beyond belief that he had seen the last of William Dante. So pleased, in fact, that he took the extraordinary step of buying two bottles of champagne from the off-licence across the road so that he and his employees could celebrate the occasion in his office.

"Here's to a job well done," he was saying. Brimming with bonhomie, he lifted his second fluteful in salute. The first had already loosened his tongue.

"I am really quite proud of you all. As a result of your resourcefulness and enterprise, we at WILLARD'S have yet again provided our customary memorable occasion …as is our promise."

He rambled on a while longer then lifted his glass again.

"Here's a toast to Mr William Dante. As difficult as the old sod tried to be, we triumphed in the end. Now we're shot of him …and good riddance."

No one moved or reflected his beaming smile. All eyes were fixed at a point above his right shoulder, where Sergeant Willis of the Nailby Constabulary was standing, cap under arm.

"Ahem… Mr Willard?"

Willard spun round, his jaw sagging at the sight of the Sergeant.

"I'm afraid there's been a bit of a cock-up down at the cemetery, Mr Willard," announced the Sergeant, barely concealing his mirth. "Nobody's fault really, but we've ended up with something of yours in the back of the van. A rather upstanding Mr Dante …a corpse of no fixed abode."

He chuckled a little then took on a stern expression.

"Half naked he is, with certain parts of his anatomy garishly decorated with sticky tape. A disgusting exhibition, if you ask me. Not at all properly dressed as befitting a memorable occasion. Having resurrected himself, as you might say, he is, I'm afraid, breaking the law. Exposing himself like that in public is gross indecency. However, seeing as how he is no longer with us, in a manner of speaking, he cannot be held accountable for his own actions. That responsibility now falls to his accomplices – those who aided and abetted him – namely, your good selves."

Willard became apoplectic. Swaying on his feet and ready to faint, he would have done so had they not planted him in his chair. George started to titter like a schoolgirl again. Charlie quickly joined in, then Cedric followed, and finally the Sergeant. Soon, to Willard's extreme embarrassment and mortification, WILLARD'S PARLOUR FOR THE DEAR DEPARTED again rocked to the music of raucous belly-laughter.

To all present but the hapless Willard, this was the unmistakable sound of Dante's revenge.

The Ugly Boy - Jennifer Nesteroff

Once upon a time, in a village far, far away from everywhere, a baby boy was born. He was ugly, so ugly in fact, that the midwife who delivered him thought he was a monkey and, assuming she had 'lost it', immediately retired and went to live a wild life in the Big Apple among way out people who never had babies.

When the baby boy's father first saw him, he exclaimed, "He's so ugly! He can't be mine!" Glaring at his wife he shouted, "I know what you've been doing!"

"No I haven't and keep your voice down. I don't want my reputation ruined," she snapped. Still, from then on the father would eye all the ugly men in the village suspiciously.

Sometimes, as the boy grew older, he would tell him to go and stand near to one or other of them to see if he could detect a likeness. Actually, the father was none too good-looking himself but, being a man, he had never noticed this. Only his wife was kind to their son, as mothers usually are. Seeing that he had no friends to play with, she gave him a kitten, but the kitten, when it saw him, let out a shriek and flew up the nearest tree where it sat, refusing to come down, so that the Fire Brigade had to be called. The firemen took it away and re-housed it on the other side of the village.

So the boy led a lonely, unhappy life being teased by all the other children at school. As time went on he developed into a tall, lanky teenager with bad skin and none of the local girls would have anything to do with him. He spent a great deal of time reading, especially about ugly characters with whom he felt an affinity. Then, one Christmas he won the village lottery. Some people thought the lottery was rigged by overworked firemen, but the general consensus was that he should take the money and go on a long trip to a faraway place. The boy thought about this and it suddenly occurred to him. Los Angeles! He would go to Hollywood and look for work at the film studios. Surely someone there would be casting a werewolf or a Quasimodo or even a Frankenstein.

On the 'plane to Los Angeles he found himself sitting next to a dark-eyed man who began a pleasant conversation with him. This was very unusual, but the boy liked it and was soon telling the man all about himself and his lonely, sad life. The man smiled and told him that he need not be lonely. He said that if he came to a country that lay in a desert he would have many friends and, with training, would become part of a great brotherhood. Then, one day, after he had done a little job for all his friends, he could have a wonderful time with seventy virgins. The boy didn't quite understand all this and the thought of those seventy virgins made him afraid. However, when the 'plane landed, some men came and took his companion away, so there was no need to worry any more about that and he decided to go on to Hollywood.

Arriving in Hollywood, the boy went into a café to have a nice cup of tea and to think about how he would go about approaching one of the studios. He noticed a man sitting nearby who seemed to be staring at him. The man got up and came over to him. "I don't mean to be rude, but aren't you an ugly one"!

"Tell me about it," replied the boy. The man smiled.

"Mind if I sit down, son?"

"As long as you don't talk about virgins."

"Eh? No, I just want to discuss your ugliness. You see, I'm a doctor, a plastic surgeon."

"You operate on plastic?" asked the boy in surprise. I've got a right one here, thought the doctor.

"No, son, I operate on ugly people like you and make them

beautiful, but it does cost a lot of money."

"Oh, I have lots of money! I won our village lottery," exclaimed the boy, proudly.

"Good, good, then you would like me to make you beautiful?"

"I certainly would, but are you sure you can do it? I am so ugly."

"Sure I can. I'm one of the best. Many of the beautiful people in Hollywood owe their good looks to me. I have golden hands."

The boy stared at the doctor. "No you haven't!"

I can charge this one double, thought the doctor, happily.

The boy was so pleased with his new face! Now he could walk tall and be accepted by everyone in the world. What would he do? Where would he go? He suddenly thought that the only place he really wanted to be was back home in his far away from everywhere village with his loving mother and his father, who would be secretly jealous and all his friends who were not his friends.

Everyone was amazed to see the boy with his new handsome face and everyone wanted to be his friend. All the girls followed him wherever he went and fought over him. Then, one day a particular girl caught his eye. She was ugly and was being teased by the others around her. She looked so sad and lonely. He walked over and introduced himself and then he asked her for a date.

"Why would you want to go out with an ugly girl like me when all the pretty girls would ladder their tights to go out with you?" she asked in astonishment.

"Well, I just know that you are beautiful on the inside, far more so than all those pretty little vixens. Besides, I know a way to make you look just like me... er, well, not exactly like me!"

So he took her away to Hollywood where the good doctor made her beautiful and himself another small fortune. Of course, our attractive couple got married and had a tribe of ugly children who needed plastic surgery and that made our doctor the happiest man in the world.

Little Windows - William Daysh

So it's Christmas again. Merry Christmas! A time for rejoicing ...but not for me, I'm afraid. The card that fell so innocently onto the doormat this morning has ruined it for me.

The card was innocuous enough. It was the photograph inside that got me going. It immediately had my mind fleeing back to something I have been desperate to forget. Please don't misunderstand, I'm no Scrooge and I'm very fond of my friends in Australia. Their cards are always welcome. It was just this particular, wretched photograph that suddenly filled me with the chill of darker memories and an anger that, finally, I had almost succeeded in burying.

I tried hard not to get dragged backwards in time by the photo but morbid curiosity finally drove me to search for that old shoe box proudly marked 'Memorabilia'. I found it eventually – tucked away under the stairs like so many other things we can't find a place for since we 'downscaled'. The old school photos immediately take me back to better times. The memory flashes that come from peering through those little windows into my black and white past show me only the innocence in the faces of the people who inhabit this world. No hint of what was to come can be seen there but, with hindsight, some clues are more recognisable now.

This first photo was taken around 1964, when we were about seven. That's Lucy Jones in the middle, beside Rex Chambers. If you look closely you'll see he has one hand making bunny ears behind her head. That was Rex – always the joker. He couldn't resist doing things like that and, typically, he just had to leave behind at least one indelible reference to Lucy's buck teeth.

That chubby little chap standing next to him is Johnny Walters – or Jonathan, as he's known now that he's a famous writer – my best friend. He still is really, even though he lives abroad now. He was an altogether different boy from Rex: considerate and gentle, the sort who would share his last sweets with you. He used to stand up for Lucy when anyone ribbed her about her teeth and got many a beating from Rex for that, but we couldn't do anything. Rex was big and strong and as tough as old boots, yet you couldn't help liking Rex and those big, penetrating pale blue eyes of his, always full of mischief.

Holding these photos now is like touching the past. I can already smell the school: the odours of youth, the scent of crayons, ink and chalk and varnished wooden desks. In my mind I can still hear the coughing silence of times when we were kept back to do lines and the deafening clatter of desk tops when we were eventually let out to freedom.

This photo in my hand stands as a permanent record of our innocent naivety at that time. There we are ...fourteen scruffy kids: grinning, scowling, skylarking, struggling and competing. Embryonic people with no idea of what we might turn into – like books with only the first chapters written. No one could tell from those if the stories were going to be good or bad, exciting or mundane.

If only it could have stayed like that!

Shortly after this, we broke up for the summer holidays. When we came back again, things began to change. Rex couldn't call Lucy 'Brer Rabbit' anymore; she'd lost her front teeth. Not only that, but his had come out as well and his gappy smile dented his ego a bit. At least Johnny didn't get so many beatings for sticking up for Lucy.

Then, as we all grew taller and Rex was no longer the biggest boy in school, he seemed to become nicer and more acceptable as a friend.

Like all children, we were going through that inevitable metamorphosis without even noticing and it came as a complete surprise when we discovered one day that we were teenagers, displaying clues as to the adults we were going to become – full of ideas and altered priorities.

Meanwhile, out of the gangling, buck-toothed awkwardness that was once Lucy, this very attractive, bright young woman suddenly emerged and Johnny was basking in the warmth of her affections – but not for long. By then, good looks and cocky charm had transformed Rex into the kind of rogue that girls like Lucy couldn't resist ...and Johnny was totally eclipsed.

When it was time to leave school, I remember the frantic preparations for our leap into the unknown but Rex wasn't concerned. "Aren't you worried about what you're going to do?" I asked him one day.

"Naah," he replied. His eyes always sparkled disarmingly. "Something'll come up. Life's not a dress rehearsal you know ...this is the real thing. Live it to the full ...you only get one." He could be irritating at times and so full of clichés.

So he just coasted along while the rest of us worried about jobs. My father's business was doing well then and he'd set his mind on getting me on board with him, but I was too independent. I had other ideas. I got a good job in an estate agents' office.

Lucy, Johnny, Rex and I remained firm friends. Johnny went to work in a book store. The beautiful Lucy became a dental assistant and Rex walked away from every job he got, but he laughed. It wasn't important to him.

Then in the pub one day, after work, Lucy wiped the grin off his face. She arrived white-faced and tearful, her head lowered. "I'm bloody pregnant!" she said, staring vacantly at the table.

"Christ!" we all said, in unison – stunned that we'd reached an age when things like that can happen. For once, Rex was speechless – but not for long.

"Don't worry, Luce. It'll be all right. You know I'll stick with you," he said, rekindling his flashy smile. It cheered her up a bit, but as soon as she'd gone, he was trying to borrow enough from Johnny and me for the abortion. We didn't have a clue what it would cost – a hundred pounds – one thousand pounds, five thousand? Whatever it was, we didn't have it.

When Lucy found out what he was up to, she went berserk and told him – in front of everyone – that she would never, ever do that. So that was that. Rex's face fell onto the table. Then he looked up, put his grin back on and proposed to her – just like that! It stunned her for a while. Then she looked him in the eye and said: "All right…if you're game, I accept."

We were amazed.

Anyway, he managed to mumble yes and we piled into my car and went to Brighton for the day.

That's where this next photo was taken – on Brighton beach in the summer of '78. There's Lucy, smiling gamely, but look closely and you'll see the apprehension lurking behind her smile. There's Johnny, next to her, manfully coping with a broken heart and Rex, of course, looking as if he's got life firmly by the tail – but he hasn't. He's got nothing – no job, no income – just twinkling eyes, a row of even white teeth and a stream of effortless blarney.

All the same, he's got the lovely Lucy and in two months they're married. Three months after the wedding, however, the story is very different and the strain of Rex being jobless is showing. While they were snapping and snarling at one another, Johnny – ever the peacemaker – was trying to convince me that I am the only one that can help.

"Go on, ask your dad," he kept saying. "He'll find something for Rex to do."

It was amazing! In spite of everything, the ever-faithful Johnny was still worried for Lucy. So, out of pity I asked my father. It was not easy, having scotched his plan to have me in his business, but I kept trying. Eventually he agreed, but on one condition. I would have to join his company as well – a tough decision for me, but I agreed, in spite of a sinking feeling that it was a mistake I was going to regret.

Everything seemed fine when we both started work. Dad's business was booming, our jobs were all right, and Rex and Lucy were happy at last. Rex even took to fatherhood when it came along.

Then – as always with Rex – something went wrong. Rex ran off the rails again and broke out of what he called 'domestic imprisonment'. He was out late with the boys, came to work late, and chased every girl that caught his eye. It was as if he wasn't married at all – and Lucy wished they weren't. However, she resolved the situation in her own way. "That's IT, Rex. I've had it with you," she hissed, in front of everyone at the pub. We'd never seen her so fired up. Her expression had the hard finality of granite. Then she packed her bags and left, baby and all.

The whole catastrophe lasted just two years.

What then for Rex? We asked ourselves. A plunge into the depths of despair? Quite the opposite. It was as if the shock of losing Lucy and the baby had finally brought him to his senses. He worked hard, toed the line, kept smiling and took money and presents to them every week. Lucy wanted for nothing.

Even when Lucy and Johnny started seeing each other, Rex kept smiling. That convinced me he'd finally grown up. We didn't know, of course, that all the time he was borrowing so heavily that he was about to go under. Then, around the time that Lucy and Johnny got married and announced their departure for a new life in Australia, Rex had the accident. I call it 'the', rather than 'his' accident, because of the way it affected all of us.

In the back yard of dad's factory, where Rex was shifting some big wooden packing cases with a fork-lift truck, he was found underneath one of the packing cases and was rushed off to hospital. I'll never forget the relief on my father's face when I told him that Rex was all right – fully conscious with nothing broken but, a few days later, he couldn't move. He was examined by one specialist after another, but no one knew why he was paralysed from the waist down.

"Must be a damaged nerve," they said, and treated him accordingly but it didn't work. Now we were all worried. Six weeks on and he still couldn't walk. Weeks dragged into months with treatment and physiotherapy, but Rex insisted he couldn't feel his legs, even when they stuck needles in them.

Finally, he was discharged in a wheelchair with the awful

news that he might never walk again. We couldn't believe it. Rex? It seemed impossible. My father took it really badly. He suddenly looked old and tired, strained as he was already by the recession that was eating its way through his business ...but there was more to it than that. It transpired that Rex's solicitors were now after substantial damages. The bad news was that dad's employer's liability insurance had lapsed. The company's bankers, mindful of its strained cash flow, had been stopping cheques here and there, including one destined for the business's insurance company. So the policy had been cancelled, and we were not covered.

The legal argument went on for months but finally damages of £1.5 million were awarded for Rex's pain and suffering, etc., and the bill dropped into my father's lap. The company then went bust, and everything he ever worked for was wiped away with one stroke of an accountant's pen. Rex disappeared after that, and we never saw him again.

So along with dad's two hundred other employees, I was then out of work and Mary, my wife, and I, in reduced circumstances, had to find a smaller house. Luckily we found this place. It's cramped, but we're getting used to it.

If only you could travel back in time and undo mistakes!

Getting back to this photo from Johnny and Lucy in Australia ...it's a shot of Rex. Apparently he turned up on their doorstep recently, demanding to see his daughter and now he's thinking of buying a house there to be near her. Because of that, Johnny and Lucy are already thinking of moving back here. So here's Rex with his new girlfriend outside Johnny's house, standing (yes, standing!) beside his new Jaguar, looking every inch the millionaire that he is.

He's fully recovered now.

It was one of those miracles you read about. Apparently, he simply got up one morning and found he could walk.

Mmm... How magical was that? No wonder his grin is broader than ever ...but he's quite safe where he is.

I can't afford the fare to Australia anymore.

Snip-Snap - Mai Griffin

Mary was able to speak normally when she woke …at least, she supposed she could have, had she tried but, living alone with no pets, she couldn't be absolutely sure. Only when attempting to answer the telephone did she find her lips too stiff to move. Her glottal mumbles at first alarmed her daughter, but Mary protested that it was not a medical emergency and Alison promised, "I'll come straight round after collecting Jenny from school. No problem". They'd visited Mary only yesterday to ask if she had kept any of Alison's toys that Jenny could borrow for a special lesson.

Jenny was six, a 'Mixed Infant' as she called herself, quoting the words carved over the archaic school entrance, and an imaginative teacher was trying to instil a sense of history into her pupils while they were still at an impressionable age – many couldn't imagine their parents as children at play. Alison had warned that Granny was unlikely to have anything and was intrigued when her mother admitted to possessing an even older toy – a rag doll from her own childhood. Jenny squealed with excitement and clapped her hands …"Please, please Gran let me take it?"

Mary already regretted having mentioned the doll but, unable to withstand her entreaties, she nodded quickly to quieten the child. Under Mary's direction, after climbing the pull-down loft ladder, Alison opened the creaking lid of an old trunk and lifted out a smaller box. Mary took it from her with trembling hands and together they went downstairs where Mary unwrapped Winnie.

Alison gasped. "How come I've never seen her before, Mum? She's exquisite, hardly in the 'rag doll' category!

"It was selfish of me," Mary smiled, "not handing her on to you, but the time never seemed right. She was really special, not like other toys. Then I forgot her until you were too old for dolls." Even as she made excuses Mary knew they were half-truths, but now Winnie was safe: not a plaything, an antique! Seeing how lovingly Jenny held Winnie, she was reassured and allowed the child to enfold the doll again in the yellowed tissue paper and return her to the box.

Restraining three-year-old Robin, so that his flailing arms inflicted no damage, Alison allowed an ecstatic Jenny to carry the borrowed doll to the car passenger seat then strapped the children in the rear. Jenny chattered happily throughout the drive. Other children would bring ordinary toys, "But", she added proudly, "My dolly will be best of all!"

Robin, excluded, demanded, "Dolly, Dolly me – want Dolly, me – ME," as he squirmed and wriggled to reach the box. Frustrated by his mother's refusal to comply and his sister's superior smile he wailed interminably.

When they arrived home he watched, exhausted at last, as Alison released him and carried the object of his desire inside. He followed, saw it placed out of reach, and turned away pretending he didn't care. Understanding his disappointment, his mother hugged him and switched on the television to distract him while she prepared tea.

Disinterested in cartoons, Jenny sat with eyes aglow gazing up at the box. Robin sprawled on the floor, his back to her. What harm could there be, she thought, just looking? Climbing onto a chair, she tipped the box and raised the lid, unaware that Robin was peeping under his arm.

When he leaped and tried to snatch the treasure Jenny shrieked, grabbed his wrist and twisted his hand from Winnie's delicate face. His little fingers curled and clutched as she rescued the doll – both grimly silent, knowing they'd be in trouble if their mother appeared. Jenny's superior strength prevailed eventually and when Alison returned, Winnie was safe, undamaged as far as

Jenny could see.

Earlier, watching the car drive away, Mary sighed; their visits were so soon over. She was disquieted about relinquishing the doll, even for a day. Seeing it again had evoked memories of her grandmother who had created it so lovingly during the months of waiting for Mary's arrival. Listening to her daughter giving birth, upstairs, Grandma put the final touch to the face, chain stitches delineating the mouth. As she cut the thread, the baby's first cry rang out. "Snipped it," she once told Mary, "just as the doctor snipped your little chord... your twinnie, that's what she is!" Mary eventually got her tongue round 'Winnie' and the name stuck but she never forgot its origin.

Winnie was always handled with care. Unlike other dolls, she wasn't shared, broken and eventually discarded. In infancy, Mary cuddled her under supervision. Later, she adorned Mary's bed during the day and rested nightly on her bedside table: a comforting presence in darkness: a friendly face every morning. Mary's husband teased her when he discovered the doll with them on their honeymoon but accepted that, to his bride, it was a symbol – almost a lucky charm. When baby Alison began to toddle, he advised putting Winnie away, knowing how devastated Mary would be if she were damaged. Alison was grown up and married when he died, and Mary considered retrieving Winnie from the attic but it had seemed too much trouble and rather silly.

Mary eventually emerged from her reverie with an unusual sense of freedom. For years, agoraphobia had prevented her from going out unescorted even though she sometimes longed to escape from the house. Was it possible to suffer from claustrophobia at the same time? It seemed ages since she had felt at ease either inside the house or in the garden but seeing the late afternoon sun casting lace-like patterns of leaves over the lawn, she opened the conservatory door and without hesitation stepped into the fresh cool air. Breathing deeply, strangely calm, Mary walked around the garden several times before sinking to the soft grass. She felt drugged by the scent of roses and overwhelmed by the novelty of enjoying open space. Her house had been like Winnie's box; suddenly they were both free.

When darkness fell, Mary reluctantly went inside. The nightly ritual of locking herself in seemed unimportant and she was soon in bed falling asleep, dreaming of simple pleasures long forsaken: shopping alone, walking in the park, or perhaps even taking the children to the zoo. Her sudden release from unidentified fears was miraculous... no longer would she be a burden; Alison would be overjoyed.

Alison's daily phone-calls were routine. The last thing she'd expected yesterday, having just seen Mary the day before, was to find her mother unwell. She didn't think it was serious but was anxious to make sure and relieved to see Jenny waiting inside the school gate, clutching the box; returning the doll would be a good excuse to visit again without being accused of fussing. Still bursting with excitement, Jenny ran to the car as soon as her teacher acknowledged Alison's arrival. Robin's interest in the doll seemed to have waned but it was placed well out of his reach as they drove away listening to Jenny's animated account of the wonderful toys she'd seen.

Mary's initial shock at her plight had passed. She felt fit otherwise. Her mouth would surely get better. It was fortuitous that Winnie would be returned quickly and she'd see the children again ...twice in one week! Although unexpected, the doll's imminent homecoming was welcome. Instead of being hidden away she could share her bedroom again – perhaps have a place of honour in the sitting room, to keep her company. When she heard the car arrive Mary made up the fire and settled down ...tea tray, juice and biscuits ready.

Even before Alison's key was out of the lock Jenny rushed in to describe the amazing things she'd seen: a teddy with only one leg and one eye, donkeys, monkeys, an acrobat tumbling...! Alison interrupted laughing, "Give Gran a chance to say hello". Instantly contrite she added, "Oh, mum. I'm sorry! How are you? Can you speak yet?"

"No!" Mary mumbled. "Don't worry. Fine otherwise. Numbness will go soon." She nodded towards the box, indicating where her greater interest lay.

"There," Alison said, lifting Winnie out. Suddenly confused, Alison halted and gasped, "Oh! Good heavens!" A shiny pink thread dribbled from the lips; the tiny chain stitches were unravelling. "How on earth did this happen?" She glared fiercely at Jenny who stared wide-eyed at Robin, sullenly shrinking far into the depths of the settee. He scowled at the doll – the cause of his trouble. "Never mind now. I'll fetch a needle to repair it – it'll only take a few minutes."

Leaving Winnie on the chair arm Alison withdrew, unwilling to meet her mother's eyes. Mary watched the children, perceiving the guilty aura between them. Alison was right. The damage could be fixed. Neither child should be punished for what must surely have been an accident. She wished she could speak, to comfort them.

Seeing only sympathy in her Gran's expression Jenny climbed on her lap and resumed her account, heedless of Robin's increasing resentment. Mary watched him edge towards the doll and stared anxiously as he fingered the hanging thread. Impeded by Jenny and unable to shout, she couldn't prevent him from pulling it. He grinned when, like magic, a loop in the centre of the mouth disappeared. Another popped up instantly and he gleefully jerked it again. With each tug, a stab of pain shot through Mary's lips. The coincidence was immediately unacceptable and horrific, draining her of strength! Jenny's weight seemed to have doubled, Mary could only stare helplessly, but thank God he stopped, looking towards the door.

Robin pondered, glaring at what was left of the rosebud mouth. His mother would notice if the line disappeared, but bruises wouldn't show if he punched the doll's soft, pink legs. His clenched fist crashed down. With a strangled howl, as pain seared her knees, Mary shoved Jenny to the floor and the affronted, screaming child ran for her mother. Robin, aware only of his own pleasure in revenge, laughed aloud. He had just found an even more satisfying way of inflicting untraceable damage.

Alison halted her headlong rush into the room and stared in disbelief. Her mother was slumped over, legs dangling as if disjointed, clutching her head. Blood, pouring between her fingers, had already soaked the sleeves of her blouse. Terrified, Alison ran to telephone for help. Whatever was amiss, coping with it was totally beyond her.

Robin was happy. The pen he'd found made satisfying plopping noises as he stabbed it through Winnie's thick, coiled hair. Not until his arm tired, did the fabric split. Stuffing burst out and would not go back. When he tried to push it in, more of the soft woolly Kapok spewed forth. Fibres rose in the warm air making his nose itch. He rubbed his face, scattering the white clumps, which then clung to his pullover.

Suddenly, the full magnitude of his crime dawned, driving instantly from his mind all but the inevitable consequences of his recklessness. Shaking with fear, desperately, he sought a solution. Hiding the doll was pointless, it would soon be found; complete destruction was his only way out!

Mary, now barely conscious, saw his gaze rest on the blazing fire and knew what he intended to do even before he raised his arm…

With Jenny crying, clinging to her skirt, Alison rushed back, calling Robin to come out immediately; poor child, how could she have left him alone to witness his grandmother's distress. He was sitting quietly, apparently oblivious to her condition, thank goodness, and she turned to reassure Mary that help was coming.

There would never be a satisfactory explanation of why, how, or what had happened.

A smoky haze hung over her mother's chair and a deep layer of ash covered the cushions. Clutching the children, backing slowly from the room, one thought kept hammering through her brain… However inexplicable, however bizarre, she had to accept the fact.

There was no one there.

The Rainforest - Michael A. W. Griffin

The noise of a helicopter reverberated from side to side of the river valley. Downdraught from its threshing blades ruffled the leaves, animals and insects, whose existence was separate from the forest floor, forty metres below. A dead tree moved and crashed into its fellows, spreading the grey graffiti of rotten wood onto the bark of living trees, spilling out nests of great centipedes and spewing into the air myriads of termites, like coffee beans. A tree squirrel, hearing the commotion, stretched wide skirt-like flaps of skin and floated down to a safer bough. It gazed at the carnage with bright eyes glittering, aware of change but showing little fear; trees often fell. Their fall left temporary spaces, enabling seedlings to feel the sun's rays as they struggled upwards, competing to fill the breach in the canopy.

The helicopter's passage, no longer a rare event over the rainforest of Batu Apoi, didn't deface the Jungle canopy permanently but did leave a visible trail. Following the line of flight, swathes of leaves vibrated in the northern mangrove swamps. Among the swaying treetops, metre-wide fruit bats floundered in the folds of leathery wings, their daytime sleep disturbed. Sunlight flashed on the bright plumage of a kingfisher, soaring to a new perch and butterflies rose in clouds from the water's edge. Hooting gibbons and chattering monkeys fell silent, wary of the unknown, as the machine – with its camouflaged back and yellow underside – competed with the python until passing from sight. When the noise waned, cicadas returned to their frenetic abdominal shrieking, fearful of losing contact with each other and the forest asserted its dominance over all.

The helicopter, one of His Majesty the Sultan's army fleet, carried the Flying Doctor to an otherwise inaccessible longhouse some miles deep in the forest. Below, the rippling, tawny river moved through channels carved by torrents of water cascading from surrounding tree-decked slopes. Recent storms had engorged subsidiary streams but a single boat moved purposefully, avoiding those places where submerged stones lay at crossing places or landing steps near isolated, stilted dwellings.

The young man in the boat glanced skyward at the whirring monster, more with a continuing curiosity rather than the awe he'd felt a few years ago. He'd first seen the flying machine crouching, silent, in a clearing near Koh's longhouse, after one of the lalang cutters slashed her leg. She bled so badly that the Bomoh had prepared for her death. Word of her plight spread many miles to a district often visited by the machine and it came to save the girl. He didn't understand such magic, but since then, if they weren't too sick to endure a two-day walk through miles of jungle, the machine and the white-coated people cured others too. Things were changing so swiftly, the longhouse elders were worried but as Koh said, more of them lived now to express concern.

The youth shifted his position and used his paddle to fend off broken branches, which impeded the passage of the small craft. Two river prawns in the bilges hid under a reed bag until his bare foot moved it. He was too preoccupied to notice them crawling frantically over each other, struggling for another sanctuary. Eventually they settled under a bundle wrapped with plantain leaves and tied with rattan strips. The water swirled, yellow with silt, as the current pushed the boat past the nipah palms towards the big river. The boy thanked the Gods that, although old and scarred – made by men of the village in the time of his Grandfather – it was still a strong, solid dugout.

Beyond the tree with the pendant wild-bee nest and the trailing lianas, another tributary brought down clearer water from a jungle-covered ridge. Nearby, the Longhouse of Koh stood proudly. It wasn't as large as his father's, only eleven doors in the great hall, but was well-built with new attap thatch. Strong wooden planking led to the jetty on the riverbank where the children played whilst their mothers and older sisters washed clothes. Four days ago, a crocodile had risen from the reeds and taken one of the women. Seizing her leg, in long, leering jaws, the buaya pulled her into the depths below, where silt bubbled with the gases of rotting leaves. No part of her was found but, after the second dawn, a piece of her batik sarong was seen, stained and torn, trapped among tangled roots, near the junction of the streams. That's where he would place his bait, he decided, and then he'd float down-stream to wait. When the moon had crossed the sky and dawn came, he would take the head of the buaya.

The clear notes of a bellbird's song rang out as the dugout swung on the current and the afternoon sun burned down on him. Where the two streams met, cicadas screamed in the tall meranti tree. Straddling its web-like roots, a bright green lizard eyed a brighter blue fly on the surface of recently trapped rainwater. The new pool already seethed with insect life.

The force of the main river had slackened considerably, making it easier for him to move away from the junction. He steered to a partly submerged trunk and fastened a cord to a sturdy branch, paying out slack to let the boat ride on the current until the line was taut. Yawing gently, it then stayed in the centre of the stream.

For bait, he'd taken five live fowl from the strings tied to the stilts under his father's longhouse. They'd been tethered next to a trussed deer and wild pig, his contribution to the feast at Koh's ... should he be successful. His people would still feast on them, even if it was to mourn his failure, but he wouldn't be there to join the dancers. After severing the heads, he'd folded the fowl in wide strips of banana palm. Now, he unwrapped the bait and threaded one carcass onto an iron hook to which, halfway along its length, a rope was fastened. If taken, either the hook would penetrate as it struck, or the shaft would jam across the beast's throat.

He tore the palm leaves into narrower strips, used them to tie the other dead birds separately onto small bamboo rafts and floated them into the wide space where the streams met. Each float with its feathered bundle had a line to the hook and a trailing streamer of rattan, mooring it lightly to up-stream bushes. Baits set, he slapped the water three times with the flat of his paddle and spoke quietly – first to the river spirits, then to this particular crocodile. He reminded them that this was inescapable destiny.

The young hunter didn't doubt that the beast he sought was the killer – the one that must be taken, before other women and children were seized. He completed the tribal hunting courtesies by acknowledging the forest spirits, performing with the confidence of a shadow player; he had absolute faith that the deities watched and listened. Having done all he could to solicit support, he released the dugout to float a little way downstream where he re-moored and settled to a long vigil.

The young man's name was Tedong. Unlike his brothers, his ears weren't pierced by boars' tusks and he used few ornaments although his hair, dressed with coconut oil, was long. Its black strands gleamed from much combing by Koh's daughter Tepi when preparing him for his mission. Women were not party to all the ancient rituals but she knew he must succeed. She'd lingered in the shadows below the longhouse when Koh, in his position as Pawai, their chief, asked Tedong, "How many enemy heads hast thou taken?"

The words were said jokingly, almost with embarrassment – the government had banned the Hunting many years ago – but all knew the rites performed by their forefathers before being recognised as men. Tedong understood and raised his eyes to the beams. There, the smoke of the longhouse fires continued to darken the rattan baskets in which, huddled among the roof-timbers, their stained, sightless contents grew even browner. The human skulls were like dark, grinning gourds. Tradition still required them to be brought out as gruesome ornaments for Great Feasts. Catching this killer buaya would prove to Koh that Tedong was a man and he knew, when near Tepi, that being a man, for her, was equally important.

Just before dusk, two helmeted hornbills flew over him and perched in a dead tree at the water's edge. The white spattered branches told Tedong clearly that this was a favourite place for them,. His ancestors had treated hornbills as gods and, even though the great brahminy kite had now taken over the role of avian deity, it was good luck to start a hunt with the tajai as friends. Their cackling laughter and exchange of opinion took his mind off the hunt and he lay in the gently rocking boat, half-dozing until dark.

His thoughts, mostly of Tepi – her smile and her firm body – were interrupted by visions of the spirit calendar at his father's longhouse. It was carved into the entrance post to which the notched log-ladder was fastened. Twelve months, each with the same number of days, were scratched there, providing a guide to the approved activity for every day. Some squares pictured parts of the scorpion, each warning of disaster. Nobody would undertake a new venture on a scorpion day. Today however, the calendar showed two circles – the sign of fruit. It was a good day to receive gifts, to sow rice or to marry.

Dreaming of Tepi and their marriage, Tedong lapsed into a hunter's sleep.

He awoke to hear splashing.

It was dark, with the deep, velvet darkness that descends after the moon goes. Had the crocodile taken the bait? It was impossible to find out safely, until dawn. Stretching his limbs, he waited, but every nerve was tense as he strained to listen beneath the forest noises. A distant nightjar clucked. Nearer, he heard dead branches dropping into the swamp as monkeys stirred ...a sound similar to the splash of a crocodile sliding from a bank. The plopping in the shallows was probably spear-like mangrove pods falling, to stand upright in the mud; or had a snake released its muscular grip on an overhead branch and fallen close to the dugout?

The noises changed with the coming of the dawn and in the faint light, he saw a small bird, with long, white, streaming tail-feathers, crossing above him. As the flycatcher swerved away into the green foliage Tedong knew it was time to act.

Uncoiling a length of hand-made rope, he fastened it to the head of a spear. Using his hilang, a long knife with a deer-horn handle carved in the shape of a hornbill's head, he notched the spear-shaft deeply, near its barbed metal point. He was ready.

Slipping the mooring, he paddled against the current towards the junction. Although the eastern sky was golden, the early shadows were long and the riverbank still dark below the thick undergrowth. Even drawing near, it wasn't easy to understand what had happened. He couldn't see the baits with their feather tufts. Then a shaft of sunlight suddenly revealed yellow mud, bloodstained feathers and the remnants of a raft.

Approaching the bank, he saw the tracks of a large monitor lizard, so that explained the splashing in the night! The great lizard had robbed him of his bait – just as his kind often stole from under the longhouse. He looked over the water but saw neither the other rafts nor their rattan trails. Had the interfering lizard dragged them all into the tangled roots of the swamp? Tedong was perplexed, the calendar showed only this day as good for hunting before the omens turned against him ...and even the tajai favoured his side of the river. What had gone wrong?

Paddling disconsolately away towards Koh's longhouse, believing the hunt to be over, he noticed a trail of rattan floating on the water. At first he assumed it had been released after the lizard's gorging, but it was moving slowly, against the current. It was his marker. The crocodile must have taken one of the baits. He prayed aloud to the spirits, as strong strokes of the paddle brought him alongside. Grasping the rattan strip, he pulled it hard and abruptly to strike the hook and, thirty feet away, the water boiled. He gazed in awe as a broad, pale-yellow, saurian throat twisted and threshed to the surface spilling water into the rocking boat. Then the crocodile lunged suddenly to the bottom, trying to break the line.

Tedong paid out and drew back the line and, feet braced against the dugout's side, he yanked the hook and bar, feeling it cut deeply into the monster's flesh. Now paying out slack, he went forward. Now straining every muscle, he pulled back. As it lunged away he let go and when it rested he gathered in the coils. The forward thrust and urgent dragging caused him to slither on the wet wood. Everything hindered his bare feet – spare spear, pieces of rattan, woven matting – and he'd thought he'd cleared everything for this battle, expecting it to be hard and long!

It seemed hours before he saw the lighter underside of the crocodile. It reminded him of the helicopter, looking just as large. Frenzied, it twisted and turned in the frothing, silted water, attempting to attack the thing behind, the thing holding it back. Tedong, almost in a trance, felt remote. He reacted by instinct. Aching muscles, cuts and bruises, were all acceptable trade-off for his moment of triumph. He had to win.

The distance between the adversaries grew shorter. During the struggle, Tedong slipped, slid, ached and scarcely noticed the bleeding cuts on his hands and feet. When the beast was within a boat's length, he grabbed a spear and looked for the yellow of the throat or stomach. He struck, felt the barb hold and, hauling as hard as he could, he brought the brute nearer until the fury of foam and waves rocked the dugout.

A massive scarred flat head with open jaws snapped past him. A huge meaty tail lashed at the boat and feet with outstretched claws seemed everywhere. He was straining at the line when the beast suddenly rolled. Tedong slipped again in the wet boat-bottom, losing his grip on the slackened rope. Kneeling, he recovered to see the crocodile trying to free both left legs, which had caught in the slack, and it was unbalanced; the river spirits were with him after all.

He pulled the lines tight again and although the creature continued to rake at the boat he sensed that its struggles were less; he knew the buaya was his. The fates were surely not so cruel as to deprive him of victory now.

The beast yielded slowly until it was snapping alongside and Tedong slipped a noose over the top jaw. He worked it behind the streaming blood-flecked nostrils then quickly put a loop of cord under the lower jaw. The snapping was replaced by snarls as the teeth of each jaw pressed into the sockets of the other.

Tedong grasped the nose feeling the power of the neck

muscles as he slipped another noose over the long slavering head. All the time the claws gouged the boat but this gradually became more desperate than vicious. He succeeded in binding the forelegs, looping the cord and tightening it across the broad, ridged back.

The same had to be done with the rear legs and it was hard to avoid the threshing tail, still pounding the water and the boat. The rasp-like leather of the prehistoric skin added another weapon to an already powerful armoury but the fight was ending. Although throaty bellows still escaped through its clenched jaws, the turmeric-coloured eyes glazed as Tedong paddled to the muddy bank where the lizard had eaten.

Mudskippers moved quickly out of his way, watching him with their periscopic eyes. He was ankle deep in swamp as he dragged his trussed trophy across the wet earth and finished the hunt with a single thrust from his hilang. Tedong rested on his haunches to recover from his exertions and scanned the green canopy, aware that the whole forest was silent, its occupants awaiting the outcome of the battle.

As his own heart began to beat normally, the jungle gradually came alive again. First, with distant gibbon cries then, in the meranti tree, the cicadas vibrated to a new crescendo. Butterflies appeared from nowhere to swarm on the acidic mud where the beast had died. Had they been hovering above, waiting for the fight to end? It wouldn't have mattered to them who died. If both fighters had survived, the beautiful scavengers would have floated above the river until the sharp stench of urine, from a stand of water buffalo, provided an alternative place to feed and adorn.

The excitement had made him light-headed but the slap of water on the boat's hull brought him back to reality. He dragged his trophy back and secured a towing line before the mud released the dugout to drift away. Echoes of the fight still filled his ears as he started to paddle upstream to Koh's longhouse and Tepi. Before he could be seen, he paused to cleanse himself of blood and perspiration with river water. He pulled off the leeches that had attached themselves to his feet and pressed leaves over previously unnoticed wounds. They were unimportant; the scratches would heal and the aches would soon leave his muscles.

Tonight, wearing a woven rattan war-helmet with black and white hornbill plumes, he would be transformed. How he would strut, carrying the ceremonial hilang with its silver scabbard, wearing the clouded-leopard coat and bearing a painted shield. He imagined the tense rhythms of the tribal musicians becoming more urgent until the blow that killed the great buaya was re-enacted. Everyone would clap and cheer – the old men drinking, smiling toothlessly and remembering. Later, Tepi would lead the girls to take his coat, shield and sword. They would rub oils on his body and all would be tending only him. He'd be excited, anticipating...

Tedong looked up into the branches of a flame-of-the-forest tree, where the bellbird sang again. Surely, there was no more beautiful or enduring place on earth than his rainforest.

After only a few minutes, the bird's melodious call suddenly stopped. At the same moment, the cicadas checked their strident screeching. A deep hollow gurgling sounded from the direction of the next tributary upstream. Wondering, Tedong paddled towards the noise and, rounding the river bend, he saw a powered launch with its squat nose thrust into the riverbank. Three Chinese men in vests and shorts were off-loading long wooden boxes over the bows to the bank, where two more were building a shelter using bamboo poles and blue plastic sheeting.

Tedong was fearful. The bright colours and strident voices of the people disturbed him. He was unused to seeing so many strangers. The nearest town was many hours paddling down the main river. Those who came were usually Malay youths exploring or fishing, who waved as they moved on up-stream. The few who stopped to visit were always welcomed into the longhouse – the occupants were vigilant but always hospitable, so why were these intruders building huts?

The engines of the launch kept the boat's prow close to the bank. Exhaust fumes gurgled at the waterline as the stern rose and fell while the sweating labourers unloaded boxes and large cans. Tedong lingered upstream, as near to the activity as the undergrowth would permit, without revealing his presence. The elation of the hunt had gone completely. Now he felt hunted himself and didn't know why. The launch swung away as the last box was added to the pile on shore and Tedong stared at the black-stencilled symbols on its side, not understanding them but memorising their shapes. They reminded him of a scorpion's nest and he sensed, in them, a threat that would change his life...

Again, he didn't know why. His head throbbed.

On each case was the legend, 'International Chain-saw Company'...

The Road to Auxerre - William Daysh

France, May 14, 1940

"Well, what now, Marie Caplan? You have lost your home, your possessions, everything. All you have left is what you stand up in. You're on your own now, with no future, past or hope. Your life is in ruins …yet I sense no despair. Are you sure that you are sane?"

Oh, yes. For once in my life I am sure of that; very sure.

"Just look at the other refugees that you walk with. They're all shocked to the core. They have lost everything too – their entire lives, everything. Look at their faces: that void of hopelessness in their eyes. That is the darkness of despair. That is how you look when you've been dispossessed of everything you once held dear – not the Mona Lisa smile that you're wearing. You're a refugee, woman! Hasn't it dawned on you yet?"

I know, I know. I feel it playing with my lips. I am trying to control it, but it behaves like a wilful child and I need it. Without its warmth I could go insane. It's all I have to sustain me and keep me going. What else is there? The Bosch took everything else. This they cannot, must not, take away from me. The road is long, and a teacher's feet are not meant for journeys like this. It must be at least eighty kilometres to Auxerre. It's not that I'm happy. How could I be happy? Relieved, perhaps, but not happy.

"Relieved are you? Just look around you. Do you see any relief in these people? Look how they've changed already. Farmers they were, twelve hours ago; shopkeepers, mothers and fathers – and proud to be – but that was all blown away in the flicker of an eye. They're sub-humans now, devoid of pride and status. Empty shells: they don't speak. They simply wander along, dragging their pathetic belongings behind them, talking only to their thoughts – just as you are, Marie. You won't survive this, you know."

I will. I must. There is no alternative. That old woman there, in front of me ...she can hardly put one foot in front of the other, but she does. She keeps going and so must I. If she can do it then so can I. The past is over. Everything is behind me now – my lovely home, Marigny-le-Châtel that I loved so much – everything I once knew, all gone! It's unbelievable that God could make a race as cruel as the Germans. Where is God now? Looking the other way? Can't he see what they are doing?

"Obviously not. But I did warn you about that a long time ago, didn't I? God is not quite the universal saviour you were given to believe, is he? He has certain blind spots, you know …lucky for you. If you're trying to make sense of this war, don't expect to find the answer in the hearts of German soldiers. They have no souls. They are machines. Look at how arrogantly they thunder through our countryside, leaving nothing but death and destruction in their path. There is nothing inside them but the taste of victory, and their disdain for us. Loathsome pigs! But we must put all that behind us now, and think only of the future. Do you have a destination in mind, Marie – any kind of plan?"

Auxerre and brother Antoine. They're all I can see. There will be safety there. My head is otherwise empty – just as Marigny-le-Châtel is, now that the Germans have come.

"Perhaps what you see is only a mirage."

No! Auxerre is definitely there. I see it clearly in my mind – and Antoine. He'll know what to do. He'll look after me and keep me safe, as he always has. His prissy wife will object, of course, but this is war and she'll have to get used to it. Somehow I will keep going until I reach Auxerre. From there, there should be some form of transport for getting to Sauvignon. Who knows what may happen then? Perhaps the Germans will run out of steam before they turn south. It's Paris they're after. If they follow us, we'll all have to walk south together. Imagine – the entire population of France on the move, in an endless column like this.

"Yes, and where will we end up but in the sea? Merciful Jesus! What has the world come to? Can we fight back? Will we?"

We'll find a way. Antoine will find a way. I know he is just one man, but what a man he is.

"Unlike husband Philippe, you mean?"

Totally different. Twice the man. With Antoine, anything is possible. Had Philippe been even a little bit more like Antoine, things would have been very different.

Oh my God, what's that in the ditch? Dear Mary, it's a child and its father! Both dead. I can't look. How dreadful! I must do something for them. They can't be left there to rot.

"Do nothing and walk on by. Everyone else does. Nothing can be done for them now, and there will be many more of those before Auxerre. No time to worry about the dead anymore; only the living. You should know that more than most."

Yes, yes, don't remind me. You know, this feeling I have now... I think this must be despair. It is a depressingly cold, hollow feeling, quite the opposite of relief.

"So at last you're beginning to feel like a refugee? That's good. It's a start anyway."

God, my feet hurt – and my knees. And this hat is making me hot.

"I am not surprised. Boots like those are for show, not for walking. Not many refugees take to the road in their Sunday best."

Could I help that? There was no time to change, was there? Everything happened so quickly. What do they call it? – Blitzkrieg. Yes, that's a word that definitely has the ring of death. It must be the German word for hell on earth. I will remember that until the day I die. As I walked home, I was wondering how such a hellish thunderstorm could come from a completely clear summer sky. Bolts of lightning? I wondered. There was no warning at all. Those little black specks in the sky seemed so harmless. I didn't know, did I? They looked like flies on the ceiling to me. Then the world just exploded. The whole of Marigny-le-Châtel erupted. The air was filled with debris and dust. Then it was terribly silent, apart from that awful moaning and the dogs barking. When I reached the house, I found nothing but a smouldering pile of rubble. I shall never forget the sight and smell of it. My clothes, my home, everything – gone.

"And Philippe?"

Yes, my husband too.

"You said that without a trace of regret. Have you no conscience?"

None. Not for him. And you're beginning to sound like Mamma.

"What, no remorse at all?"

None whatever. Why should I have? Are you certain that you are not Mamma?

"Believe me, if Mamma knew what I know, she would have nothing more to do with you…ever again."

I doubt that. I was always her favourite. Anyway, she's dead.

"That hardly matters."

But it does. It makes a big difference. Mamma, Papa, they're long gone. I have no one to answer to but myself. The world now is just me… and Antoine. But he will never know. No one will.

"I do."

But you are expendable. I can do away with you any time I choose.

"Can you?"

Oh, yes. It would only take a moment of concentration.

"I see. What would you do for company then? Who would you have to talk to? Are we not friends?"

Yes, but not when you misbehave. You get above yourself sometimes – like you are doing now.

"Because I make you think realistically?"

Yes. Please don't do it, or you will be punished. I will banish you once and for all.

"That may be more difficult than you think. We've been together for a very long time now. I am very necessary to you. You would not survive without me – now, more than ever."

On the contrary, I think I would be much better off without you. You bring me nothing but pain, and you cause me to question my sanity. In fact, I think this would be an appropriate time to dispense with you. So you can go now. Go away. Go on, I never want to speak to you again – ever. Be off with you.

Did you see that? A soldier in that truck just pointed his rifle at us and pretended to mow us all down. Then he roared with laughter. IGNORANT PIGS! We're just vermin to them. God I hate them.

I am so hellishly tired. It's getting darker. Where in God's name are we going to sleep tonight? I'll need a toilet soon.

Hello? Are you still there? …You are really, aren't you? …Have you really gone? I'm lonely now. I need someone to talk to. Come back…please.

"See? I told you, didn't I? No, I won't. I will not put up with your censorship. It must be all or nothing, if I return. If you want to talk to me, you have to listen to all that I have to say, not just the bits that please you. Do you agree?"

Yes. All right, then, I agree.

"Good. Now, what were the questions? – Oh yes, sleeping and toilets. Well, when you're too tired to go on, you'll have to find shelter …somewhere where it's safe from bullets and prying eyes; under a wrecked car in the ditch, or something like that. There are plenty of those along this road. You're bound to find one soon. But do it before darkness falls completely, or you won't find one at all. As for toilets, you surely don't expect to find one out here, do you? You'll just have to swallow your pride and crouch in the bushes like everyone else."

I can't do that – I'm a schoolteacher!

"I don't care if you're the Pope! When you've got to go, you've got to go, otherwise you'll disgrace yourself. You'll soon get the hang of it."

How disgusting!

"War is disgusting by its very nature, or hadn't you noticed? It will strip you of every vestige of pride, every trace of status.

Didn't you know that? Get used to it. Dignity you can no longer afford."

Dear God!

"Anyway, now that I'm back, I will look after you, but first I want to examine what happened at Marigny-le-Châtel."

Oh no, not that again. I've just been over that.

"Oh yes. You recalled the bombing very well, and the ruins of the house, but I couldn't help noticing that you chose to ignore what was beneath the rubble."

I didn't! As I said, there was all my furniture, my clothes, ornaments, Ellie the dog…

"And Philippe?"

… Oh yes, and Philippe. But why do I have to think about him?

"Because I want you to. You can't carry on with your life as if nothing has happened unless you face up to it. You need to deal with this, once and for all, right now..."

I cannot. I will not!

"Oh yes you will. If it is the last thing I do, I will make you face up to what happened. Once you've done that, you will feel better, and I might even leave you in peace. So cast your mind back and explain why Philippe was in the house when it was bombed."

He was asleep.

"At midday?"

He was ill.

"I see."

He had a stomach problem. I don't know why. He'd been weak and tired for weeks, and couldn't go out. He couldn't keep his eyes open. It was food poisoning, according to the doctor.

"So he couldn't visit anyone? Not even his lover?"

I don't want to talk about that!

"But he couldn't, could he? He was too ill even to crawl into her bed."

He was very ill. That's all I know.

"Excuse me. You know very well why he was so ill."

Please! The subject is too painful.

"I'm not surprised. I suppose the subject would be painful for any woman who had just murdered her husband!"

But he deserved to die!

"He deserved to die? – Just for loving another woman? But husbands do that every day, all over the world. Should they all be condemned to death without trial...then executed? Ladies and gentlemen of the jury, I rest my case."

That's it! You've gone too far now. I hate you. You are finished; banished forever. See, I'm really concentrating now. You'll be gone in a matter of seconds.

"I'm not going anywhere. By the way, you should learn to control your emotions. That man behind you is beginning to wonder about you. You shouldn't attract attention to yourself like that. It could lead you into far worse trouble. And weeping will not absolve you, either. Only confronting the truth will do that."

What is it you want of me?

"Only that you should face up to what you did, and experience some feeling of remorse. The rest is up to you. Philippe had a life too, you know. He was not entirely a bad man, nor was he worthless. For many years he loved you and took care of you."

Yes, yes, yes. He was good like that. I admit it.

"Wonderful. Now we're getting somewhere. So he didn't deserve to die, did he?"

Oh yes he did. He'd been carrying on with that tart for years. You know that.

"So why didn't you tell him to stop?"

I knew that he'd throw me out if I did. I swallowed my pride and ignored it because I didn't want our lives to change. It was the hardest thing a woman could do, but I did it. But then something snapped inside me when I found them in bed together – OUR bed... MY bed. It was more than I could bear, so I decided then to do something.

It wasn't difficult. Philippe had no interest whatever in our home. He was hardly there. He never once looked in the greenhouse in the past two years. He had no idea what I was growing. I really didn't think it would work. Honestly I didn't.

But when it did, it gave me an amazing feeling of power. No longer was I the helpless little wife, to be sneered at by him and his tart. Their nauseating happiness was suddenly in the palm of my hand, and I could end it whenever I wanted to. Of course, I had to be careful, but it was easy, really. A little at a time so the good doctor wouldn't know: little by little, day-by-day, that's how I brought their sneaky little affair to an end. You have no idea the strength it gave me – how powerful I felt. Me! Marie Caplan, the straight-laced village schoolteacher. No one could ever suspect so pure and chaste an individual.

But then things started to go wrong. He became so ill that he couldn't keep my little mixtures down anymore. That was a big problem. I suddenly realised that he was not actually going to die after all, and I would end up with a useless, infirm husband who had to be waited on hand and foot forever. I couldn't live my life like that! Why should I be punished for their wickedness? I had to finish it. I was so frustrated and angry that one day I took a poker to him. Poor Philippe! He never knew anything, lying there helpless in our bed... There was blood everywhere.

Then I panicked. I really didn't know what to do. He was a big man, you know. How could I drag him to the garden and bury him? So, I covered his face, got dressed, and rushed out in panic. I wanted to run away and never come back – then I suddenly found myself in church.

"So you didn't run away, did you?"

No. Something happened in the church. The mist in my head cleared, the anger went away and I felt calm again, like I used to. Everything became clear to me. I knew exactly what I had to do. I had to go home and call Georges the Gendarme. I was to wait beside Philippe's body until I could confess to everything, and face the consequences. I wasn't afraid anymore. I wasn't confused or angry …simply at peace.

"But then the Bosch came along and saved you?"

Yes. That was very strange. It was like a sign from above. Before I could do anything, Philippe was buried under tons of rubble. It will be a long time before anyone finds him, and when they do he will look like any other bomb victim.

"Saved by the hand of Fate, then?"

Yes. You could say that. Even Georges the Gendarme died in the bombing.

"Well. Who are we to argue with Fate? All is well then."

Precisely. So you can go now.

"Yes. For the moment, but I'm not entirely satisfied with this outcome. We will have to talk more."

Just go now – or I'll do away with both of us.

And this time I really mean it!

Echoes - Mai Griffin

Grey pre-dawn shadows lifted and light seeped relentlessly through his heavy eyelids. He endured the hardness of the rifle in the protective folds of his thaub, bruising his ribs; it must be clean and ready – free of the clinging dust, which he could feel in every pore. Physical discomfort could be ignored but memory and habit carried to his inner ear the call of the Imam. The swelling and fading chant echoing from the minaret in his now distant village was far beyond his hearing but awareness of the coming day forced him to consciousness and the realisation that where he lay there was no mosque ...no uplifting voice to inspire him when his need was so great.

He unwrapped the gun and rested it carefully in the dry branches of a long dead bush that had seemed to offer protection when, wearily, he huddled close to it the night before. After rubbing his feet and hands with the powdery sand to cleanse them he lifted his ghutrah from his head, spread it on the ground and knelt on it – facing Mecca, to seek and find peace in his God.

His prayer ended but still he knelt – mesmerised by the beauty of the desert. Shadowed tufts of arfaj that had escaped grazing camels were crowned with speckled halos of gold as the light strengthened.

His thoughts drifted to his childhood when he first saw this wilderness transformed after a single shower of rain. With such little encouragement delicate buds grow and burst into glorious life, blazing briefly before shrivelling in the fierce sun – few ever seen by human eyes. Like most men, they occupy a small space for a blink of eternity and pass unnoticed; fierce winds smooth the places where all live and die. Like the Bedu he understood the desert and was never lost in its shifting dunes. He loved this emptiness where his ancestors had existed for generations ...where his own family was wiped out so cruelly.

The savage horsemen who stormed in that day were Arabs like themselves. He had peeped from the bait ash sha'ar, lifting the heavy woven cloth. It was made of wool from their own goats by his mother and sisters. They had erected the tent too, hauling and securing the yards of brown striped fabric to stout poles to protect them all from the elements. The women were always working and even at four years old he was grateful to Allah for making him a man.

He had been excited when the strangers arrived – too innocent to perceive their haughty effrontery – and watched with pride as his father and older brothers greeted them ..."As salaam alaikum," God's peace be upon you. When, without warning, the horsemen drew their long swords, he was more astonished than afraid but when they lunged about with flashing blades he scrambled from hiding into the burning midday, desperate to find reassurance with his mother; safety lay in her arms. Terrified by the anguished shrieking all around, he ran back, but never reached his goal ...the entire tent crashed to the ground.

On waking he felt smothered; the pole that had struck him pinned him down. Crazed with fear he struggled from mountains of cloth to find air then, free at last and still unable to see, he screamed in terror, but the darkness was not in his eyes it belonged to the night. In anguish he wailed all his loved names into the stillness but heard no answer. Sobbing, he stumbled over familiar things out of place and, in that strangeness, fell suddenly into arms he knew. His cries became moans of joy – but why did his mother not speak? Why was she so cold? Seized by panic he ran into the black void, away from his grotesquely transformed world, into the real unknown.

The tiny child collapsed at last until the coldness of dawn stung him to wakefulness and he recognised the outline of an old fort. His father had often taken him there to seek advice from the elder who existed in the ruins. Wise Ali Ibrahim was loved by all his people ...when he told the old man about the horsemen, surely everything would be put right.

In a way they were. After listening to the boy Ali returned with him to the camp where he had known many friends and they wept in each other's arms. Then, as Khalid's tears dried, Ali told him who the evil men were and why their tribe hated his own. Forcing the stunned child to look at his mutilated family until their dreadful wounds were etched permanently into his brain, Ali explained that his enemies did this to all who dared disagree with them. The scene was unreal to Khalid; reality was the hatred which would burn inside him forever.

Until the old man took him there to start his new life he had been wary of the village and its people who lived so differently from his own. They need not wander with their goats and camels ... they had a good well, a small oasis with green bushes and dusty stone houses whose strong walls protected them from the fierce winds that raged from the north.

He soon became as much a part of his new family as the other sons and, as the years passed, his visits to Ali Ibrahim – a whole day's camel ride away – were irregular. If the sessions had not always ended with a prayer for his family and vengeance, he might have forgotten that he was born to another tribe. Although he loved Ali, on whom he relied for spiritual guidance, such words seemed empty to him; what could he, a mere boy, do against grown men, in their dozens and armed to the teeth!

As he developed into a slim, handsome youth Khalid's ardour was fired by Ali's entreaties to Allah but his feelings of impotence increased so, suppressing his guilt, his treks to the fort became fewer. Hearing one day that the old man was near death, remorse made him hurry to Ali's side. How could he have neglected his beloved teacher? What could he do for him now, unworthy being that he was?

They both knew it would be their final encounter. The ancient face was haggard with pain and in whispered gasps the dying sage reminded him of the duty he owed to his forebears. They lamented, recalling the wrecked site bereft of life, until in blind rage Khalid cried out for a just revenge. The loathed names, whispered again from those dry thin lips, would abide with him until all who bore them paid with their own blood.

"Why?" Khalid had to know. "Why, did the horsemen slaughter so wantonly? Are we not Arabs too?"

"There are Arabs and Arabs," said Ali, "not all are true believers."

"How can we be sure ours is the true path?" he had asked.

"Did they not butcher your father because his ideas were different? Is that acceptable? Their actions prove them wrong ...so it follows, we are right. Allah is with the righteous and gives us strength."

"It is said," answered Khalid – more than a little frightened by his own daring, "that vengeance belongs to Allah."

"Did not Allah also bid you leave your home to fight for true justice? Are you not willing to be his instrument?"

His promise never to forget was given with passion but he had been barely sixteen; other things – living – gradually obscured his distant past.

Many moons after Ali's death, soldiers came to the village. The stubby guns they carried seemed more menacing than Khalid's old hunting rifle but in fact the men were friendly and joked with him. At first their words perplexed him but he soon grasped that they were speaking his own tongue in a strange way. They were welcomed everywhere. They played games with children, sat smoking companionably with old men and bought from the souq. Khalid hovered on the fringe of their affairs wishing they would stay forever but after a few days they prepared to move on. Like soldiers everywhere the men were easy and secure with each other and he gazed after them enviously as they sauntered away to their more important world.

He followed, to their amusement, trailing ever farther behind, reluctant to be free of the spell they cast yet knowing he must return. Something flashed in the waning sunlight as it fell in their wake and he searched the trampled sand eagerly; returning it would be an excuse to join them again. There! He pounced, triumphant, but was stunned – dizzy with horror – when he beheld the loop of shiny beads in his palm. His father, lost in thought, had constantly played with this same chain, swinging it back and forth over his hand.

Khalid stared aghast at the glowing amber stone he had himself found in the desert and presented with pride one feast day after Ramadan. Their strident voices carried back to him over the still air – raucous – calling each other by name ...reviled names, which he suddenly remembered with sickness and revulsion.

He almost swooned, knowing that these men belonged to the tribe whose crimes he had sworn to avenge. He now perceived how they swaggered, weapons held ready, obviously feeling superior. How they must have sniggered at the simple villagers – mocking smiles covering the scorn they must have felt for the old way of life. Then icy fear gripped him ...would they return? Would they come swooping on horseback to kill and kill again, wiping out all he loved as they had done before? He had to stop them. They were on foot so their camp must be near; following would be easy with no wind to disturb their tracks. Even so, he hurried as he went back to fetch his rifle.

He wished he had used his small supply of bullets more sparingly but vowed that the last few would not be wasted. After filling his water pouch he drew a cloak over his shoulders; the desert could be cruelly cold at night and the fur lined bisht was essential, as he had no idea how long he would be away. The sun, a blood red disc, was already sliding rapidly to the dark purple horizon as he left home. There was no hope of catching up with the patrol before nightfall but it didn't matter; he guessed that the old fort with its sweet water well was their refuge. It would also be their grave. More than ever before he needed to commune with Allah and left the trail to offer his evening prayer.

After ritual cleansing he stood for a moment, head bowed in the flat, failing light before falling to his knees. Long practice enabled him to clear his mind of earthly problems until his prayer ended, leaving him calmly convinced that he was fulfilling his destiny, and images of death returned to feed his righteous anger.

As he trudged through the darkness he saw himself again as a tiny child holding his father's hand, comforted by its gentle strength. He had been a kindly man, who never spoke of war or reprisal and shielded his children from such knowledge, but Ali Ibrahim was more shrewd and worldly; he knew that learning must be passed on.

Khalid was grateful to have had such a teacher to show him right from wrong – making his enemies known to him so that his hatred was not allowed to die. Another sun came and waned before he yielded to sleep within reach of the fort.

Waking, in the grip of a nameless dread, he rose stiffly as recollection returned. Cold air had even penetrated the cloak which served as a blanket; the heavy morning mist covered it with a sparkling sheet of dew. He shook the wetness off it and spread it over the bush to dry, careful not to dislodge his gun. The sun was already warming the empty sky; it was for this coming day that he alone, of his whole family, had been preserved. He was the chosen instrument upon which Allah could play to wreak his will. The Divine plan was so clear to him now. His miraculous survival ...having a trusted friend to teach and guide him ...a new family to help him grow strong and, finally, being inspired to follow those vile creatures to hear the terrible names uttered. All the pieces had fallen into place; his people and his God would be proud of him.

Moving in the long shadows thrown by gold edged hills over pale ochre sand he was soon within sight of the ancient ruins. He knew every broken wall, inside and out, having explored not only its present but, with old Ali's help, its past. He had learned about wise men long dead and battles fought hundreds of years before they were born.

"Why did those Christians come to fight us?" he once asked.

The sage stroked his wispy beard and replied, "Far away in their own land Christians still fight Christians – why should we be surprised that they once fought Arabs?"

He waited, hidden by the gnarled, twisted branches of an athl tree, to discover how many soldiers were within the old stone walls. Just inside, he knew, was living space with a good roof where he had spent many happy hours. In his mind's eye he saw Ali Ibrahim sitting on the stone bench near the door. The bright rays of sunlight falling sharply over the folds of his robe were reflected up, to lighten the shadows in his lined face. The memory moved him almost to tears.

The sun rose fully before he could be sure that all the men were present but his ears picked up the distant drone of a motor vehicle, sometimes clear, sometimes muffled but unmistakably coming nearer – spluttering and roaring as it struggled over hostile, shifting sand. He was in a sweat of indecision. Should he wait or attack now? More soldiers were approaching: certainly too many to tackle alone. Or even worse, the truck might take away those still here to a place where he could not follow! He had to move. Whatever transpired he was still too far away to do anything.

From a better vantage point he saw them embracing each other as several prepared to leave. He was re-assured ...this too was fate. Allah in his mercy intended that only those most guilty should remain to die. The brief turmoil that ensued made it possible for him to slip quietly behind the outer wall through secret ways to the place where the guards would return. The room was smaller than he remembered – perhaps because it was now crammed with boxes, bedrolls and other comforts men always needed. A ray of sunlight slanted over the hollowed stone seat and he imagined he could still see white cloth draped over Ali's frail shoulders and his pale, steady eyes, smiling encouragement.

Shouts outside banished his vision. The jovial taunts of those departing mingled with the grumbles of the few who must tarry but they would meet again soon they said, "Inshalla."

They were calling on his God!

Now hiding among the crates, so near his quarry, tremors of self-doubt shook him. The loaded gun felt awkward and almost slipped from his grasp. To bolster his resolve he recalled the senseless carnage. His parents, brothers and sisters had not deserved death. These killers did! His eyes, growing used to the dimness, took in details previously missed.

The embers of a dung fire still glowed and the aroma of green cardamom coffee wafted from the long curved beak of a pot resting in the hot ash. Had he come in peace he would have been offered a drink in one of the tiny cups, in the same spirit of hospitality that was part of his own tradition. Seeing rolled prayer mats against the wall he was torn again...! If they lived and prayed as he did, was he after all making a terrible mistake?

The truck pulled away and three men returned. Trembling with uncertainty Khalid watched as two prepared for their afternoon rest, spreading rugs and goatskins on the hard-packed sand – their guns within reach. The third squatted in the cast shadow of the thick wall near the open door, his weapon across his knee. Khalid knew he would have time for only one shot before he was himself cut down but it was not fear of death which made him hesitate. He stared along his rifle sight, not at a brutish enemy but at the fresh young face of a brother Arab ... the one whose buttermilk and laughter he had shared in the souq. How could he, after all, bring death to one of his own?

Sand swirled in from the burning desert heralding a Shamal and the guard threw a corner of his ghutrah across his face as the horsemen had. Fine dust spiralled upwards in the sunlight and Khalid suddenly saw old Ali Ibrahim: there, where he always sat. His gnarled hands clenched as he howled encouragement. His voice, echoing from the stones, merged with the wind... "Have you forgotten the horsemen? These are their kin, our foes ...Shoot! Kill! Death to all who wrong us!"

Khalid must have fired. He saw the guard jerk forward to slump lifeless in the dust. As the others rolled towards him, guns blazing, he was deaf to their cries. He heard only sighs of pride from Ali, his friend who had not abandoned him, even in death. He was beckoning, smiling, waiting to guide him as rightly in the next life as he had in this.

The Wolf - Gaile M. Griffin Peers

They were comfortable on the open naya. The music from the kitchen, still on since supper, could barely be heard and the wine had flowed freely throughout the evening.

Cora and Sibyl sat together away from the railing; Tom had taken the cushioned lounger near the veranda steps. The moon was hidden behind low lying clouds, which were busy replenishing the snow across the Cantabrian Mountains that surrounded them.

Cora turned casually away from Sibyl, surreptitiously checking to see if Tom's glass was empty. It was, so she rose gracefully and sauntered into the house, turning to check that her husband and her friend were still engrossed in their conversation.

A few minutes later the music ceased to intrude, even slightly, on the cool silence of the crisp, winter evening.

When Cora returned, she was carrying a bowl of olives in one hand and an opened bottle of Rioja in the other. It was the very best place to be, she thought, inwardly smiling as she set the dish and the wine on the table and settled back into her seat.

Tom leaned forward and started to pour wine into his empty glass, too absorbed in what he was saying and doing to notice that the other glasses were also dry. Just as he was about to deliver his witty punch-line, the night was ripped apart by an ear-splitting, ululating cry from the trees beyond the garden's edge.

Conversation stopped.

As one, the two women turned to Tom, waiting for him to speak or react.

Tom, however, was too rigidly glued to his chair to utter a

sound. The howl had seemed so near to him that it took him several tries to move his head. His tongue seemed to be stuck to the roof of his mouth and he could feel his heart pounding. Staring in focussed concentration at the women transfixed on the sofa was unnerving, but better than turning round to see what might be behind him. Neither woman seemed to be staring beyond him though, just at him, which was reassuring.

"A wolf? It must have been a wolf."

Tom spluttered, as he thought that through. Why would a wolf come so close to the villa? Spanish wolves were only aggressive if provoked. They were shy, wild and scattered across remote areas. OK his was the last villa in the 'urbanisation' – in the wildest patch, away from the lights, cars and traffic ...and OK, their neighbours had gone south to Valencia to winter in the mild Mediterranean breezes, away from the snow, but it was still odd that a wolf would be alone, so near habitation.

"Tom, is it in the garden?" As she spoke, Cora reached out to Sibyl for support. Tom cringed, was he so ineffectual that his wife felt Sibyl was the better protector of the two?

Sibyl just held Cora's hand in support and waited for Tom to answer.

"How the hell do I know?" He snapped at them. It had been a long evening, he was tired; the last thing he wanted to do was go rousting potentially dangerous wild animals out of the garden.

Another howl...

Tom, using the adrenalin gathered from the anger spurt he had felt for his wife, jumped up from the chair and turned to face the dark garden.

Nothing: he could see nothing, but it sounded so close.

As he stared out into the dark, he could hear the women whispering behind him.

OK, he had been frightened when the wolf first howled, but the fear was gradually giving way to reasoned thought. Wolves were rarely dangerous on their own, they were pack animals, everyone knew that; or at least they did if they had read the old classics like 'Call of the Wild', like he had when he was a kid. Cora, however, had never read anything beyond fashion magazines and shopping catalogues…

This was his chance to resurrect his image in the eyes of his wife. He would be quite safe in the garden, with little more than a stick to make a noise as he poked about. Give the animal enough warning he was coming and it would slope off back into the Cantabrian country-side.

Trying not to smile as he turned back to the women, clutching each other in fright, he went for an expression that conveyed 'white knight in shining armour coming to the rescue' and, wearing it, he headed past them into the house; it took only a few minutes to pull a nine-iron from the back of the cupboard where he kept his golf bag. It was annoying that the only coat not at the dry-cleaners was his old army camouflage jacket, but it would do. He wouldn't be outside for long and it would be warm enough; he just needed something to protect him from the lightly falling snow, once he left the covered veranda.

As he stepped outside and headed for the steps to walk down into the garden, he made sure that they were both watching him. If he was going to put on a show, he wanted to make sure that he had the full attention of the audience.

Stumbling in and out of the trees that lined the property border, he walked the perimeter of the garden twice before the shot rang out.

Of course, as the Medico explained later, Tom had died so quickly it was doubtful that he had even heard it.

"Such a terrible accident", consoled the Judge, as Cora sobbed her way through the brief trial, which exonerated her dreadful mistake as an accidental death. "Of course you and your friend must have been frightened, alone in the house, while your husband went to face the wolf. How unfortunate that he wore camouflage and blended into the tree-line so well. So unfortunate that you should be such an excellent shot and sad, that the wolf you killed should turn out to be your husband…"

As they had expected, they got through it all and used very little of Cora's inheritance in legal fees; so much better than having to sell the house to pay Tom off. Inheritance taxes were a lot less than splitting everything equally for a divorce.

Cora never felt quite the same way about her iPod as she had before so, with the animal noise tracks deleted completely from her library and from the machine, the iPod went to charity, along with its neat little battery powered speaker and to delete her purchase history Sibyl closed their iTunes' account, making casual discovery of the purchase impossible.

Their 'catalogue buys' were among the best they had ever made they decided, as they sat comfortably on the naya the following summer. The music from the kitchen, still on since supper, could barely be heard and the wine flowed freely throughout the evening.

'Picked & Mixed' Authors

The authors who have kindly contributed their work to the making of this Anthology have donated their royalties from the book to Cancer Research UK – Our thanks to all. They are listed here in Alphabetical order along with the page numbers where their stories can be found. They are also featured on www.pickedandmixed.com

Mac Black

Author of the Derek Series including 'Please... Call Me Derek,' Mac has his own website www.macblack.info. In his own words – "I think of myself as one of the few authors included in this book lacking a suntan, which is only to be expected of someone still based in Bonnie Scotland. As a resident of the town of Cupar in Fife, I live with my wife who complains that I am always 'playing' on the computer: obviously untrue, I tell her – a few of my books are out there about a character called 'Derek' – but she is not convinced...

Having discovered the pleasure of writing only a few years ago, when I retired, the natural style for me has been humorous fiction. A simple fellow, writing simple stories, hopefully that bring a gentle smile, or on a very good day, a real laugh to the reader.

This tale, written specially for a worthy cause, is fiction, but based on a true moment in my own life – a vague memory from a time long, long, ago..." *p59*

Margaret Cornwell

Margaret was born in India and started writing as the bombs rained down on Calcutta, "Mainly plays, to keep us kids occupied," she says.

Later, in England, she had articles published in 'She', 'Parents', and twice in the Bristol Evening Post.

When living five thousand feet up on Kilimanjaro, Margaret started writing her autobiography and also a biography of the famous Margarete Trappe. She now lives in Spain and concentrates on short stories. *p32, 51, 63*

Andy Crabb

Andy won the 2006 International Story Writing Competition in English and subsequently appeared in the 'Anthology of Short Stories – Torrevieja, Another Look 2006'. In fact, two of his stories were included!

Andy was the winner of the Bay Radio Competition.

One of his favourite pastimes has always been walking. He has walked along beaches, through African National Parks and rambled around mountains. He says it is an inexpensive pursuit and allows him time to get his thoughts into perspective.

"Poisoned Petals" is the title of Andy's first anthology of Short Stories with a Spanish Flavour. The second is "Blood Blossoms" His website is www.andycrabb.info *p42*

William Daysh MBE

In William's working life there were two distinct phases – Royal Navy and post-Royal Navy – both roughly equal in time terms at around twenty-two years each. The stories that stick in William's mind come from several different areas of his RN service – flying, diving and the events leading up to his M.B.E. However, the most relevant one to William's first book *Over By Christmas* came from diving.

When William was the Diving Officer of the shore base HMS CONDOR in Scotland, he also founded and led the ship's Sub Aqua Club. They dived on a number of wrecks in Scottish waters. On one such expedition, they found the two huge propellers (each weighing 14.5 tons) of HMS ARGYLL, a battle-cruiser that ran aground on the Bell Rock during WW1.

Many years later, while carrying out research for *Over By Christmas*, William unearthed the true story of how ARGYLL mysteriously came to be on the rock, and the drama that unfolded inside the lighthouse that night. He published a short story about this little piece of history on the highly recommended web site at www.bellrock.org.uk.

William's story, *The Death of HMS ARGYLL,* is on the site. The dramatic demise of the ship is also featured in *Over By Christmas.*

William's website is www.williamdaysh.com *p110, 157, 181, 194, 216*

Sue Frost

Miss Winifred Robins was Sue's inspiration. Slightly eccentric, with her wild white hair and ballet pumps, Sue says her 'ancient' English teacher bewitched her with mythical Greek Gods and enchanting poetry and urged her to write herself.

Life-events interrupted Sue's flow for the next 40 years but she wrote when she could. Being an archetypal Scorpio, a perfectionist and horribly critical, it was not easy!

In her own words, Sue reports: "My little story, written especially for the competition, came very easily to me: partly because I believe I have lived the life of a vagrant in another karma."

Sue plans to use it as an outline for a novel and added, "I absolutely know that Miss Robins will be at my side, her usual encouraging and enthusiastic self. Watch this space!" *p16*

Vonnie Giles

Vonnie was born in Tewkesbury, Gloucestershire. A graduate of Cardiff University, she is an opera fan and a lover of Baroque music and has been a resident of Spain for twenty-five years. *p28, 54, 67, 71, 83, 91, 102, 121*

Gaile M. Griffin Peers

As the editor, knowing that the authors' royalties are being donated to Cancer Research UK (with U P Publications matching that donation) I couldn't resist adding one of my own stories to the mix. I have written, edited and contributed to various magazines and publications under a variety of names since my first foray into publishing in 1975 as the Art Editor of RAF Brize Norton's Gateway Magazine. As a teenager, I helped my mother in the production of a variety of fund-raising publications for local associations. Not only have I worked with U P Publications since 2003, but I also manage and edit 5Ws Magazine. www.5Ws.biz *p233*

Mai Griffin

Alongside a successful painting career spanning sixty years (including Portraits of foreign royalty and HM Queen Elizabeth for the British Embassy, Qatar) Mai has been writing and contributing articles to various publications since the early fifties. Ghost-writing and supporting others became a quiet passion and apart from a publication in 1977, Mai's name rarely appeared as the author. 'Echoes' was a winning entry in an international short story competition, so she finished writing the first of her 'Grey Series' of paranormal mystery thrillers, finally writing under her own name. Mai is writing her fifth, now. www.maiwriting.com and www.maigriffin.com. *p168, 200, 225*

Michael A.W. Griffin (1928-2005)

In 1949, as a young army Captain, Michael was fighting in Malaya, during the Emergency. He knew and loved the jungle and, in his late sixties, he wrote the story in this collection. It is the only one he ever wrote.

Successive postings took him to Hong Kong, Germany and again to Singapore from 1962 to 1965 during Confrontation.

After the Army, Michael became a senior executive in the NHS and subsequently (with Crown Agents) took his expertise to both Brunei and Qatar to commission prestigious modern hospitals for both governments.

He retired to Spain in 1989 and joined the Jávea Computer Club which, under his Presidency, grew from 40 to over 500 members.

He was also Chairman of the local Conservative Association for several years. www.mawgriffin.com *p206*

Tony Henderson

Tony was born near London and since leaving home as a teenager has lived half his life overseas. Starting work as a reluctant accountant, he became a successful designer and implementer of computer systems.

He now lives with his wife Jo in a 150-year-old finca in Jesus Pobre, a small 'pueblo' in Valencia, that most of Spain has never heard of, he says.

Finding a love of researching and writing, and using his experience of living in Hong Kong for 10 years, he wrote his first novel A Circle Has No End. Having despaired of reducing his golf handicap, he is now writing a sequel The Hong Kong Circle.

See 'The Circle Trilogy': www.tony-henderson.com *p25, 78*

Irene Hogg

A graduate of the Royal Academy of Music and Drama, Irene was employed full-time in Secondary Education. In addition to senior school, she taught children and adults of all abilities, including physically and mentally-challenged groups. During this time she wrote mainly for school projects. As secretary of an Arts group in her local community Irene directed new groups subsequently created.

As a result of her sitting on the Clydebank Centenary committee in 1986, Irene had lunch with the Queen, whom she met again at a Holyrood Garden Party in appreciation of her work within the community. She wrote and directed a three-hour production for Glasgow City of Culture 1990. Excerpts were performed in the New Athenaeum Theatre.

Now retired, living with her husband in Spain, Irene puts her energies into writing and painting. *p19, 88, 99, 119, 126, 131, 145, 159*

Linda McGillycuddy

Linda is a writer who lives in Spain. Twelve years ago, both statements would have amazed her, and they still cause her some surprise. Being Irish, she says that if talking was an Olympic sport, she would be in the medals, her husband concurs.

Like most women, Linda has to find time between various jobs as Mom, partner, driver, cook, femme fatale (but that's mainly on weekends) to write anything longer than a shopping list but, now that the genie is out of the bottle, she does not intend putting it back. *p22, 39, 96, 106, 128, 137*

Jennifer Nesteroff

Jennifer Nesteroff-Gilmour of Scottish/ English descent, was born in 1942 in inland Queensland, Australia (where her family had a sheep property).

She met her Dutch-born husband, who was on his way to study at University in London, on the ship to England. They married in London and lived there for seven years before settling in Holland, where they lived for thirty years. After all their world travels, Jennifer and her husband settled in Moraira, Spain, in 2005. They have a daughter living in Holland and a son in Australia. *p15, 36, 141, 152, 161, 164, 173, 191*

Sheila Skinner

Sheila settled in Spain twenty-four year ago, is married with no children. She worked latterly in London as PA to a Managing Director of sales and marketing. She loves reading, but says she is quite picky, not the bodice ripper and chicklit variety.

She writes with the Jalon Valley Writers' Group and is encouraged by the variety of styles and the support of other members. In Sheila's own words, "I am happy with my small Spanish village life here in this beautiful Valley."

Her outgoing Leo personality qualifies her well for the work she does with Jalon Valley HELP Charity, to benefit local people and village projects. *P11, 177*

Gail Tucker

Gail has been an English teacher, shopkeeper, sometime cook and a guide at Roman ruins; now retired with her husband and his camper van, she continues to be fascinated by people, whoever and wherever they are. She invites the reader to explore beyond the narrative to share private moments with her characters. Life is rarely what it at first seems. *p47, 166*

Acknowledgements

This collection of short stories was tremendous fun to put together. I am so grateful to all our authors for the high standard of their contributions and for allowing us to donate their hard-earned royalties to Cancer Research UK. As publishers we are matching their donation. If you are inspired join in, we have a page that we have started on the Cancer Research Website so that all funds collected go directly to the Charity and not to us.

www.justgiving.com/uppublications

Our thanks go to Bay Radio for granting us permission to contact their authors and for making the initial approach on our behalf. We were hugely inspired by their competition and the high standard of the entries.

'**The Rebel**' by Gail Tucker (originally released as "Rose") and '**Remember Me**' by Linda McGillycuddy first appeared on a writers blog hosted by Lesley Ann Sharrock.

By Mai Griffin – '**Snip-Snap**' was short-listed in Writers' News (The last line 'There was no one there.' was dictated by competition rules) '**Echoes**' was published in Writers' magazine in 1997. '**Checking The Facts**' was written in 1985 but never previously submitted to a publisher – for reasons that may become apparent on reading it!